CHERRY

CHERRY

Lindsey
Rosin

First published in Great Britain in 2016 by
HOT KEY BOOKS
80–81 Wimpole St, London W1G 9RE
www.hotkeybooks.com

A CIP catalogue record for this book is available from the British Library.

ISBN: 978-1-4714-0576-1
also available as an ebook

1

This book is typeset using Atomik ePublisher
Printed and bound by Clays Ltd, St Ives Plc

Hot Key Books is an imprint of Bonnier Zaffre Ltd,
a Bonnier Publishing company
www.bonnierpublishing.com

For JSP

The Beginning . . .

To be honest, the sex pact wasn't always part of the plan.

Layla Baxter started it.

She announced it super casually to the rest of the girls – Alex, Zoe and Emma – between bites of froyo, as if it were simply another addition to her massive, ever-evolving to-do list.

"I added a new bullet point today," Layla said as she mixed a fresh spoonful of snow caps into her frozen yogurt.

Every Sunday afternoon, at exactly 4 p.m., the Crew (as the girls were commonly known) would meet at their favorite froyo spot, the Bigg Chill, and huddle around their regular table for an important hour of sugar and gossip.

"Oh, yeah?" Zoe asked, humoring Layla.

"Yeah. Well. Actually . . ." Layla smiled. "I added *three* new bullet points. Three felt like the right number." Layla swept her long blonde hair up into her signature bun, which was always equal parts messy and adorable. With Layla, *everything* was an "always". Everything had an order or a pattern or some sort of special meaning. True to form, she always – *always* – ordered the same frozen yogurt combination: a chocolate, peanut-butter swirl with snow caps on the side.

1

Zoe Reed also always ordered the same flavor: classic, plain vanilla. Vanilla really was Zoe's favorite flavor, but the truth was that she also made most of her life choices with the hope of drawing as little attention to herself as possible. She blamed the habit on her bright red, almost orange-ish hair. It was frizzy, dry, and almost entirely unmanageable, but unless Zoe wanted to rock some sort of buzz cut – which was obviously out of the question – there wasn't much she could do to improve the situation. She was stuck with it. With the hair. And the red. And the frizz. Which meant that everything else about Zoe had to be toned down accordingly. Even her frozen yogurt flavor: always vanilla.

"Lay, you gonna actually tell us about your new bullet points," Alex prodded, "or are you just gonna be a cock-tease about it?"

"Alex. I am not being a tease—" Layla fought back playfully.

"All right. Except you totally are . . ." Alex said, smirking.

Unlike Layla or Zoe, Alex Campbell wasn't into the "always". She preferred randomness. Chaos, even. Alex was always looking for something new and exciting. Case in point: she had never (*ever*) ordered the same flavor twice. The Bigg Chill changed its flavors every week, so every week Alex would make a big deal about trying all of them and then inevitably end up with the most eccentric option of the bunch, something like Chocolate Pistachio or Oreo Cheesecake. Today, it was Caramel Custard.

When you looked as naturally good as Alex, it was easy to pull off the boldest choices. Alex had soul-piercing blue eyes, light chocolate skin, and endlessly long legs. The overall combination was, in a word, stunning.

"Okay, okay . . ." Layla said. "At some point between this very moment, right now, and approximately six months from now, on Graduation Day—"

"Really? Hi," Emma interrupted, "I thought we weren't talking about that."

"About what – graduation?"

"La, la, la," Emma sung, sticking her fingers in her ears.

"Oh, come on," Layla said. "Our high-school graduation—" More la, la, las from Emma. "—is happening whether we talk about it or not."

"I know it's happening, but that doesn't mean we need to dwell—"

"I'm not *dwelling*, I'm just saying it's the due date for my new bullets."

"Okay, but I'm just asking why it has to be the end of the school year?"

"It seems fitting and thematic. One door closing, another door opening." Layla had clearly given it a great deal of thought already. Of course, Layla didn't do much of anything without giving it a great deal of thought.

"Don't worry, Em," Alex chimed in. "I'm sure Layla will just add more bullet points to her list soon. Then there'll be a new due date anyway."

"You know, some people say that success means never getting to the bottom of your to-do list," Layla retorted.

"Because those people never actually finish anything?" Alex laughed.

"No, because they're always busy adding more things to do."

"That makes no sense."

"It actually makes so much sense. And I'd very much appreciate if you could please stop hating on my life system?"

"Only if you stop saying super cool things like 'life system'?"

"Oh, you love it—"

"Layla, I love *you*, but that's not the same thing—"

"Yes, okay," Emma said, interrupting Layla and Alex's familiar back-and-forth, "that's great and all, but can we please just stop talking about it?"

Emma O'Malley plunged her plastic spoon into her Cookies 'n' Cream froyo, piling on an oversized bite. Emma's weekly order was typically somewhere right between Alex's peculiar and Zoe's plain. In other words, she liked to keep things interesting, but she didn't feel the need to stray too far from the status quo. Emma's "always" was an order of extra rainbow sprinkles, which she got on the side for everyone to share. Emma was thoughtful like that. However, at the moment, all Emma could think about was trying *not* to think about graduation . . . but she was failing.

Under normal circumstances, Emma was the most laid-back member of the Crew, the girl most likely to go with the flow, but senior year was throwing her off her game. Emma liked the way things were right now – her friends, her parents, her classes, and her job as senior photo editor of the school yearbook – and she didn't really understand why any of it had to change.

"Ooooo-kay," Layla said, starting her announcement over again, "before the-day-that-Emma-will-not-let-us-name, I am going to, in no particular order: get an A in Mr. Moore's Advanced Placement Lit class . . ."

"Yes. Super doable," Zoe interjected.

4

"Put blonde highlights in my hair . . ."

"Ugh, *finally*," Alex approved. Layla had been talking about getting highlights almost literally for ever.

"Aaaaand," Layla said, pausing slightly for dramatic effect, "I am going to have sex with Logan."

Layla's sexclamation made Zoe spit rainbow sprinkles across the table.

A saliva-covered red sprinkle landed on Alex's hand. "Ew. Zoe, c'mon."

"Sorry, sorry," Zoe said as she scrambled to pass Alex a napkin. "I was very much not expecting that."

"The highlights?" Layla asked playfully.

"The Logan."

Layla and Logan had been together for more than two years, so it wasn't entirely surprising that Layla was ready to do it . . . but actually hearing the words *I'm going to have sex* come out of her mouth was a whole new sensation. All of a sudden, sex was something the Crew actually did. Or at least it was something Layla did. Or was going to do. Or something.

"I'm ready," Layla added definitively.

"Wow," Zoe said. Or maybe she only thought it. She wasn't sure if the "wow" had actually managed to come out of her lips or if it was still stuck, rattling around inside her head.

"I like this," Alex said. "But why not just go for it?"

"I *am* gonna 'go for it'. That's exactly what I'm saying."

"No, I know, but then why do you need to do it with a due date?"

"Oh. Have you met me?"

"Yes. You plan everything—"

"*Ev-er-y-thing.*"

"Right, but what if this time you were just, like, 'Hey, Logan. I want you inside me.'"

"Ohmigod, Alex." Zoe blushed.

"What? I have a feeling he'd be down with that."

"Yes, I feel that too," Layla laughed, "but I can't just say that—"

"You *could*, actually—"

"You know spontaneity makes me nauseous. Besides, a due date is an essential element of any well-plotted plan. Otherwise it's just, like, what's the point of having a plan in the first place?"

"That's basically my entire question," Alex agreed. "I'm trying to say that maybe you don't need a plan."

"Again: have you met me?!" Layla countered as one of the cell phones vibrated in the phone stack on the table. "I think that's mine. Probably Logan." The Crew had decided – well, Layla decided and everyone else agreed – that froyo Sunday would be a phone-free zone. The girls would always stack their phones in the middle of the table when they first sat down, and the only way they were allowed to check a text message before they got up was if someone else in the Crew read it first.

"You want me to check?" Emma offered.

"No, all good," Layla said. "I think his flight just landed. I'm sure he's fine."

"More than fine. He's about to have sex."

"Not, like, immediately about to."

"Right, 'cause spontaneity makes us nauseous," Alex teased.

"Exactly." Layla winked, knowing full well that Alex was making fun of her.

"But for real, Lay," Alex said, trying again. "The first time you try and have sex you can't just, like . . . force it. I mean, there are moving parts involved. Body parts." Alex was the only member of the Crew who wasn't a virgin. She'd only done it one time, but that was still one more time than anyone else at the table.

"I know it's gonna take time to figure it all out," Layla insisted. "That's why the due date is six months away – plenty of time to work out the kinks."

"Ultimately, you're saying you want to have a lot of sex." Alex grinned.

"A lot of *good* sex," Layla clarified.

"I think it's supposed to be good even when it's bad," Emma chimed in.

"No-o, it can definitely be bad," Alex maintained.

"Right, but I think it's also like pizza: like, when it's good, it's really good, and then when it's bad, it's still pretty good," Emma said with a laugh, which made Alex and Layla laugh too. Zoe joined in half-heartedly, but the entire conversation was making her anxious.

"I'm gluten-free," Zoe managed to add.

"What does that have to do with anything?"

"It makes it harder to find good pizza."

"Zoe, it's a metaphor."

"I know . . ." Zoe stuck some more vanilla froyo in her mouth.

"I'm thinking Logan and I will do it for the first time on Valentine's Day," Layla said proudly, as if she were the first person in the history of premeditated sex dates to select the national holiday of flowers and candy and Hallmark cards. "It's gonna be perfect."

"Were you always this corny?" Alex laughed.

"I am not corny—"

"I bet you want rose petals and candles, too."

"Who *doesn't* want rose petals and candles?"

"Me, for starters," Emma said.

"Me, for seconds," Alex agreed.

"Okay, okay," Layla said, turning towards Alex. "We can't all be lucky enough to lose it on make-out rock behind the boathouse at Camp Waziyatah."

"It was make-out *ledge*, thank-you-very-much."

The girls knew that Alex's camp boy was named Cameron, and that he was "tall" and "hot" and "lived in Massachusetts", but that was pretty much it. Alex wasn't really a big talker whatever the subject, but she definitely didn't like to kiss and tell. Probably because then she'd have to be talking all the time. More often than not, she was tired of her boy-of-the-moment before the end of their first make-out session.

"Okay, fine. Make-out *ledge*," Layla corrected. "I'm sure it was magical."

"Yeah, well . . ." Alex paused, searching for the right words to explain what had happened. She knew "magical" certainly wasn't going to be one of them. "I think the first time's gonna be awkward no matter what you do."

"So you're saying I should plan for awkward," Layla said, translating Alex's advice into a language she could understand.

"If you must . . ." Alex grinned, knowing full well that Layla *obviously* must. "All I'm trying to say is that it's probably smart not to expect . . ."

"An orgasm?" Layla offered.

"Ohmigod," Zoe said, squirming in her chair.

"Oh my god, *yes*, Zoe, we're talking about *orgasms*," Alex teased.

"I realize that, but . . ." Zoe's face turned red, and she couldn't finish the rest of her thought. She was still wrapping her head around Layla's sex date, and the thought of Alex's orgasms, or anyone's orgasms, or really just the entire *concept* of an orgasm.

"Just think of them like . . . fireworks," Layla said.

"Fireworks . . ." Alex repeated, trying the word on for size.

"I actually love fireworks," Emma laughed.

"Who doesn't?"

"Okay, *okay*. Thank you, but now I hear you saying fireworks and it all just sounds like 'orgasm' anyway, so . . ."

"Zoe, if it *really* sounded like an orgasm—"

"Ohmigod, Alex, I swear, if you start moaning right now—"

Alex, Layla and Emma exploded into another fit of giggles. Zoe heaped another spoonful of rainbow sprinkles onto her vanilla frozen yogurt.

"I'm excited for you, Lay," Emma said once all the laughter had died down again. "You're lucky you have Logan."

"I am lucky, but . . ." Layla trailed off, getting lost in her racing thoughts.

"But?" Emma asked.

"Do *you* want to have sex?"

"Me? Like, ever?"

"Like . . . *now*?"

Emma considered Layla's question for a moment. "Yeah. I do," she said. "I mean, if I had a boyfriend. Or someone who knew what they were doing."

"I like that we're talking about this," Layla said.

"Me too," Emma agreed.

"Me three," Alex piled on.

Layla, Emma and Alex all turned towards Zoe.

She shook her head. "We've already established that I'm bright red, and I'm pretty positive I have massive armpit stains and a rash on my chest . . ."

"*That*'s your answer?"

"I don't know . . ."

"Oh, c'mon, Zoe," Layla pushed. "We're having a bonding moment like we've never had before and all you're gonna give us is an 'I don't know'?"

"I love/hate this conversation. Is that a possible correct answer?"

"Zo, it's not a test," Emma said through more giggles.

"Okay, well, whatever it is, my final answer is that I'm one hundred percent having a love/hate relationship with it," Zoe declared before getting swept up into Emma's giggles.

Alex and Layla were already there too, laughing so hard they couldn't breathe, and it was simply impossible to tell whose laughter was whose. It all just mixed together perfectly.

That's how it worked. Layla, Zoe, Alex and Emma had been an inseparable foursome ever since the fateful day they were all randomly assigned to the same desk cluster in Miss Morgan's first-grade class. All these years later, they were still just as close as ever.

"Most people aren't this lucky," Layla said, as always.

"Not even close," Alex, Emma and Zoe answered.

Then, Layla got lost in her racing thoughts. She swirled another spoonful of snow caps into her frozen yogurt and a brand new thought bubbled up into her brain.

Zoe was the first to see Layla's face light up. "Oh no," she said.

"'Oh no' what?" Layla laughed.

"I see you, Layla," Zoe said. "I can see all the gears in your pretty little head spinning like crazy. It's like that time you decided we should toilet-paper Xander Murphy's house. Or the night you made us go skinny-dipping at Zuma—"

"Hey, I did not *make* you do anything—"

"Layla," Zoe said, wiping her clammy hands onto her jeans, "I know what this face means . . ."

"That I often have good ideas?" Layla asked, loving this moment.

"Wait, *what* is a good idea?" Emma asked.

"Yeah, what are you talking about?" Alex asked. "Unlike Zoe, I don't have psychic powers."

"Layla thinks *all of us* should have sex," Zoe blurted.

"Together?" Alex asked.

"Ohmigod, no," Zoe squeaked, too nervous and awkward and rash-y to even entertain that kind of joke.

"Wait, but what if we really did?" Layla asked, getting all sorts of excited. "I swear that wasn't my first thought when we sat down this afternoon, but now that I hear Zoe say it out loud—"

"Please don't blame me—"

"Zoe. There's no *blame*. This is brilliant."

"You're really saying you think we should all have sex?" Emma asked.

"Yes," Layla said definitively. "Before graduation."

Emma shook her head at Layla's use of the G-word.

"I think we're forgetting that Alex has already *had* sex," Zoe said, as if that somehow made it impossible or unnecessary for the other girls to do it too.

"Yeah, but she still hasn't had good sex—"

"Okay, but *no*," Zoe said, still fighting the idea. "Layla has a boyfriend. Alex always has a million options. Emma's adorable. And then there's me over here with my frizzy hair and freckles and permanently red cheeks. I just got my braces off two weeks ago!"

"Luckily 'braces off' exponentially increases your sex appeal," Alex teased.

"No. No one looks at me and thinks about wanting to have sex."

"That's not true," Alex insisted. "I could be thinking about it right now . . ."

"Yeah, yeah . . ."

"Zoe," Layla pushed, "you could totally have sex if you want to."

"I do want to have sex!"

It took Zoe a moment to realize that those six little words had actually come out of her mouth and were now hanging in the sugar-coated air of the Bigg Chill, echoing off the froyo machines and the wall of glass windows and all the tables and toppings and people in between. "Ohmigod . . ."

"Ohhhh my god, *yes*," Layla replied, all sing-songy.

"No. Stop. No more smiling . . ." Zoe said. "My point is that—"

"Your *point* is that you want to have sex," Alex pressed on.

"No—"

"Don't you mean *yes*?" Emma joined in. "I'm positive I already heard you say yes."

"No, still *no*. My point is that I don't exactly have a lot of options."

"That is false," Emma said.

"If you want to have sex, you can find a way to have sex," Layla insisted.

"The last thing I wanna do is just 'find a way'. I'm not gonna sleep with a random guy or lower my standards because Layla had a stupid idea—"

"It's not a stupid idea. In fact, I think the sex pact might be the single greatest idea I've ever had."

"Sex pact? Since when is there a sex pact?" Zoe was now officially freaking out.

"Well, now that we've established we all *want* to have sex—"

"Good sex," Alex interjected.

"Right. Duh. Now that we've established we all want to have good sex, I think we all should."

"I'm down," Emma laughed.

"Totally," Alex agreed.

"Ohmigod . . ." Zoe blushed.

"Is that a yes?" Layla asked.

Zoe couldn't quite believe it, but the truth was that "yes" it was.

"It's *hap-pen-ing*," Layla declared triumphantly. "Now I think step one is to put the positive intention out into the universe." Layla loved step-by-step instructions almost as much as she loved her lists and due dates. "Before high school ends, we are going to do this last, big thing together."

"But not *together* together," Alex teased.

"Right. We'll do it concurrently. With the right person in the right place at the right time . . ."

Alex and Emma nodded firmly in agreement.

Zoe managed to tip her head forward slightly, which was more than good enough for Layla. "We're having *sex*!" she exclaimed.

And that was it.

One serving of frozen yogurt later, sex was no longer simply a daydream or a wet dream or a piece of juicy gossip that happened to somebody else. All of a sudden, it was something the girls all wanted to do – and were going to do, *together* – before high-school graduation . . .

169 Days Until Graduation . . .

Layla almost couldn't believe it.

The Crew had a sex pact.

And the sex pact had a due date.

And the whole thing was happening.

In Layla's head, plans and dreams were basically the same thing, but suddenly this one felt like it was actually gonna come true. Obviously there were still variables to consider and the need for contingencies and everything, but Layla loved that sort of thing: the planning and the over-planning. She realized it might even be thematically appropriate to say she got off on it, which made her grin, equally embarrassed and excited at the same time.

ALL THE FEELS, Layla texted Alex, Emma and Zoe in the Chat, which is what the Crew called their ongoing text-message conversation. *I am having all of the feelings at the very same time.*

RELAX, Alex texted back. "Relax" was a pretty standard Alex response, but Layla could not relax. She tried not to get too far ahead of herself, she really did, but her mind was always racing away from her – past the pact and the due date – and before she knew it, she was thinking about the next year and then the next decade and suddenly all she could think about was the firepit where the Crew would spend all their nights together. Of course the firepit would be located in the backyard of the property that the girls would all purchase together, where they would build four separate but architecturally cohesive houses, one for each girl, and they'd all live happily ever after with their husbands and their children – and each other, obviously. The compound, as Layla called it in her dreams-slash-plans, would materialize sometime shortly after the girls all wore the same blush-colored bridesmaid dresses to each other's weddings, but sometime before they all took a coordinated sabbatical from their successful and well-established careers to travel through Europe.

But that was the future.

Right now, Layla was lying on her bed, holding her cell phone and watching a string of texts pour in from her best friends, who all seemed to be just as *everything* as she was. Layla already knew that she was ready to have sex with Logan, but the fact that her best friends had just piled onto the plan with her was the icing on the cake.

Or, no, not the icing . . .

The cherry on top.

It was Sunday, January 4th. High school graduation was Monday, June 22nd. Therefore, according to Layla's precise calculations, there were exactly 169 days until graduation and the official "doing it" due date.

How thematically appropriate, Layla thought.

The sixty-nine of it felt like a giant wink from the universe; like a sexy, numerological all systems go.

As Layla double-checked her math, recounting the days from January to June, she could feel that same splendid smile, the one Zoe had caught onto at the yogurt place, creeping back across her face. She realized that the smile had most likely been stuck there ever since she got home from froyo. Probably all the way through dinner, too. Thankfully, no one else in the Baxter family seemed to notice. Layla's younger sister, Maxine, had spent the whole meal lobbying their mom for permission to go on the upcoming middle-school ski trip, while her dad and little brother, Avery, were engaged in a heated discussion about their fantasy basketball league. Luckily, all of this mundane commotion let Layla off the hook. She didn't have to explain why she was unusually quiet. Or why her toe wouldn't stop tapping under the table. Or account for the fact that she had somehow eaten all the lima beans off of her plate even though she absolutely *hated* lima beans.

The only real explanation for all of that was that Layla was too busy thinking. She was always thinking, but if her parents or siblings had asked her what she was "too busy thinking" about tonight, she would've turned as bright and red as Zoe's hair. Behind Layla's calm face and that plastered smile, there were approximately a million thoughts running through her head; almost all of them were X-rated, and every single one was moving at a mile a minute.

After dinner, Layla *re*-recounted the days a third time, just so she could be entirely, one hundred percent sure that she was planning accordingly. As expected, she was right the first two times: 169 days.

She glanced at the clock on her phone. It was almost 9 p.m. She had one more winter-break homework assignment to finish. There was a huge stack of laundry to fold. Her nails desperately needed a fresh coat of paint. But all she'd managed to accomplish since she came home from the Bigg Chill almost four hours ago was to count the days in her calendar three times and survive dinner.

Finally, the doorbell rang.

"Lay-la!" her mom called from downstairs. "Guess who's here?!"

Layla didn't have to guess.

She fixed her bun and reached for her lip gloss, semi-stalling. She couldn't just go barreling down the stairs, even though she wanted to. It took every ounce of self-control she had to hold back her response until after her mom yelled for her a second time.

"Coming!" she yelled back, trying to make it seem like she'd been in the middle of something super important. She waited one more moment, and then walked slowly to the top of the staircase.

The second she saw Logan, a knot in her stomach she hadn't even realized was there loosened. He'd only been on vacation for a week and a half, but it had felt like for ever. Logan grinned at her as she made her way down the stairs, his one perfect dimple on full display. That dimple was so small, and seemingly insignificant, and yet it made Layla melt every single time.

"Layla, you never told me that Logan's grandparents live in Miami," her mom scolded, as if that was a very important detail about her boyfriend that she absolutely needed to know. (It

18

wasn't.) Or as if their family had some sort of close connection to Miami. (They didn't.)

"Sorry," Layla said, as much to Logan as to her mom.

She must've been grilling him. *What did you do for the holidays? Is Florida nice this time of year? Are you glad to be home?*

"We're gonna go outside," Layla said, grabbing Logan's hand and pulling him gently but quickly towards the back door.

"Nice to see you, Mrs. Baxter! And Happy New Year!" Logan called back over his shoulder as they made their way outside. He was the kind of teenage boy who knew how to talk to parents: he looked them in the eye, he answered their questions, he remembered to wish them a Happy New Year. Layla's mom and dad bragged about Logan as if he were one of their own kids. Layla found it mildly embarrassing, but she couldn't exactly blame them. There was a lot to brag about. Logan was president of the senior class, which meant he was also president of the entire student body. He had gotten an early acceptance to his first-choice college, the University of Pennsylvania, and in his spare time Logan was organizing a school-wide fundraiser to help fight pediatric cancer.

He was also a phenomenal kisser. Layla was obviously the only one who bragged about that last part, but it really was the best.

As soon as they made it outside – and out of her mom's sight line – Logan pulled Layla in close, kissing her hard, just like she could tell he'd been wanting to since he saw her at the top of the stairs.

Logan's kisses were fast at first, then slow, and then somehow both at the very same time. He slid his hands up Layla's back to grip her neck, pulling her in even closer, pressing his lips even harder, and pushing his hips up against hers.

"Come here," she said, pulling Logan further across the grass and up onto the trampoline in the corner of her yard to continue the make-out session.

Layla's parents had what they called an "open-door policy". Logan was pretty much always invited to come over to the house, but the door to any room he and Layla were in had to stay open at all times, which meant that the backyard was actually their most private hangout option.

After a few more minutes of kissing, Layla pulled back to ask, "Do you remember what you asked the night before you left for Florida?"

"Is that a trick question?"

Layla knew he would remember.

They'd been making out on this very trampoline, and he stopped to ask if she wanted to have sex. His voice had cracked as the words came out of his mouth, which made Layla laugh. She really was laughing at his voice cracking and not the actual question, but Logan assumed that her laughter simply meant no, so he backed off the question as quickly as he'd brought it up in the first place. They hadn't talked or texted about it since . . . until now.

"The answer is yes."

"*Yes?*" Logan's voice cracked even more than it had before. "As in: yes, you want to have sex with me?"

Layla nodded.

"*Now?*"

"Not now." She smiled.

"Okay. But . . . soon?" Logan flashed that perfect dimple again. As always, it drove Layla absolutely crazy. "I know you've probably got a whole plan worked out already," Logan added, "but, um . . . I just want to let you know that I have a condom in my glove compartment."

"Oh. Okay. For emergencies?" Layla teased.

"For realistic situations," Logan teased back. "At least I know better than to keep it in my wallet."

"Thanks for that."

"You sure you don't just wanna go upstairs?"

"I'm super sure that my parents aren't going to let us into my bedroom without the open-door policy in full effect, so unless you want to do it for the first time with the door wide open . . ."

"How about my car?"

"Your car is at the top of my list of places we are not going to have sex."

"You would have a list like that," Logan laughed.

"I don't actually have anything written down, but I can tell you right now there is no possible way I am going to lose my virginity in your car."

"Right. Right. *Your* car would be a much better option—"

"Logan," Layla said, loving him even more than she did a moment before.

"What? Your back seat is far more spacious, and you have leather seats, so . . ."

"I can't deal with you." Layla grinned before rolling up on top of him and pressing her lips to his.

"I can't with *you*!" Logan teased through kisses. "You can't just stick your tongue into my mouth and expect this conversation to be over . . ."

Layla knew that their conversation was just getting started, but as far as tonight was concerned, there wasn't going to be any more talking, only kissing.

Layla reached for Logan's right hand and slipped it under her shirt. He unhooked her bra clasp and then slid both of his hands onto her boobs. Her nipples were already hard, mostly because it was cold outside, but also because Logan's lips were warm and his fingertips were everywhere and his hips were pushing up against hers along with the rise and fall of the trampoline.

Zoe's chest had grown an entire cup size since the beginning of winter break.

She hadn't measured them exactly or anything, but now, basically without any proper warning, her boobs were popping out of all of her bras. Zoe considered the alternate possibility that maybe every single one of her bras had simultaneously shrunk in the laundry at the exact same time, but she had to admit that seemed rather unlikely.

Zoe stood in her bathroom, wrapped in a towel, having just gotten out of the shower. Normally, she didn't spend much time staring in the mirror – that was really more of a Layla or Alex thing to do – but she couldn't stop admiring her new brace-less teeth. Maybe it was the fact that Alex said the lack of braces increased her sex appeal exponentially, but even Zoe had to admit that her smile looked good. Honestly, she knew her newly upgraded boobs looked good too, but that felt weird to think about. Then she felt weird for feeling weird about thinking about it and then all of the weirdness quickly amplified in her head until there was nothing left to do but unwrap her towel and force herself to take a look.

When Zoe saw her naked reflection, the first word that came to mind was "pale". The second word was "red", for her hair. The third word was "freckles" because they were basically everywhere. But then the next word was "nipple" followed closely by the word "boob" and then, undeniably, "big". It had become simply impossible to deny the fact that her boobs were decidedly larger than they'd been even a few weeks before. Still, Zoe could only look at them for so long before achieving maximum weirdness levels, so she reached for her towel again.

Just as she rewrapped herself, one of the bathroom doors began to swing open, which caused Zoe to shriek, which then caused her older brother to slam the door shut again. Zoe's brother, Joey – or J, as Zoe called him so as not to acknowledge the embarrassing fact that their first names rhymed – was two years older than Zoe. He was a sophomore at University of California in Berkeley but still home from school on winter break. Zoe and Joey's bedrooms were connected by the shared bathroom. The layout wasn't such a big deal when they were younger, but now it was clearly causing some growing pains.

"I'm sorry!" Joey yelled through the closed door.

"What happened to knocking?" Zoe yelled back.

Joey knocked softly, making a joke out of it.

"Great, thanks . . ." Zoe scoffed, pulling her towel more firmly around her.

"Zoe Reed," Joey teased with a loud, booming voice. "It's your brother. I am moments away from opening the door to the bathroom. Brace yourself."

"Yeah, okay. Got it," Zoe said, as Joey opened the door again. "I know you're all used to coed showers at the dorms or whatever, but come on."

"Come on yourself," Joey laughed. "You could also try locking the door. Or, you know, maybe don't just stand naked in front of the mirror."

"J," Zoe said sternly, not even sort of ready to laugh about such a close call. "Tell me right now you didn't see anything. If you did, I think I'll die."

"Zo, please don't die. I saw nothing."

"Thank god. But also, I wasn't just, like, standing naked. I took a shower."

"All right, all right," Joey said, backing off quickly. "I'm truly sorry for cramping your style. I'll be back at school soon enough, and then you'll miss me and these awkward encounters."

As anxious as Zoe was, Joey was just the opposite: calm and collected, always unfazed. Zoe envied that about him. He turned his attention towards the mirror, running his fingers through his hair, spiking it up on top. Although Joey's reddish highlights clearly identified him as a member of the Reed family, he didn't have the full-on red color that Zoe did. Not even close. Zoe and Joey had the same deep brown eyes, but beyond that, they barely looked related. Zoe joked that Joey had taken all the attractive qualities out of the Reed family gene pool and left her with nothing but frizz and freckles.

"Going somewhere?" Zoe asked.

"Yeah. Shawn is having a party. Track people." Joey had been on the track team in high school. He was a pole-vaulter, and he wasn't half bad, but Zoe knew he had mostly joined the team to hang out with his friends. "You wanna come?"

"It's a school night."

"Right. High school . . ."

"Oh, whatever. Have fun."

"I will, but I actually need your tree first." Zoe's bedroom was in the front of the house, and there was a giant sycamore tree right outside her window. Zoe was too anxious and awkward to try and use it, but it gave her brother the pole-vaulter a perfect escape route into the front yard.

"Really? You're sneaking out? I thought you were a big college guy now?"

"Ye-ah. You've met our parents . . ." Joey exhaled, running his fingers through his hair again. "Their house, their rules . . . Mom turned the alarm on, like, an hour ago."

"Lame," Zoe commiserated.

"Totally. But here's the beginning and end of tonight's unsolicited brotherly advice: pick your battles. Always. But especially with Mom and Dad. "

Zoe nodded. She and Joey had fought like crazy when they were younger, but for the past few years, ever since Zoe had started high school, they'd come to understand each other in a way they never had before.

Zoe's cell phone vibrated even louder than usual as it rattled on top of the tiles next to the bathroom sink. And then it buzzed three more times as a new flood of texts poured into the Chat.

"Say hi to the Crew for me."

"The Crew doesn't care about you . . ."

"Cool, cool. Appreciate that."

"Love you, bro."

"Love you too, sis. Just leave your window open for me, please? Thanks."

Joey slid out the window without waiting for a response, climbed onto the nearest tree branch, and swung down to the front lawn in one fluid, seemingly effortless movement. He'd perfected the art of sneaking out of the Reed house.

Zoe refocused her attention on her phone, scrolling through all the new texts in the Chat. Layla was providing a detailed recap of her and Logan's latest epic trampoline make-out session. Zoe put on her pajamas – comfy flannel pants, and an oversized T-shirt – as Layla's texts continued to pour into the Chat. Zoe loved reading all the texts, but she never really had much to contribute to the conversation. Besides, at this moment, her hair required all of her immediate attention. She had a whole hair routine. First, Dream Curls spray. Second, Daily Moisturizer mousse. Then, Frizz Ease serum, which she referred to as her secret weapon. And then finally Dep Gel. She crunched the thick gel into her red locks as hard as she could. Barring any natural, sleep-induced hair disasters, Zoe would wake up with dry, moderately acceptable curls.

Then her phone buzzed again. Another text.

This one was from Dylan: *Ready?*

Zoe noticed that the clock on her phone read 11:11. She kissed her hand, touched the phone, and then kissed her hand again. Layla wasn't the only one who believed in little signs from the universe. Zoe had no clue what this particular sign meant, but she always seemed to catch the clock at 11:11, and after today's sex pact conversation, she felt like it must be at least marginally important.

Normally, Dylan didn't text her until closer to midnight, but Caroline, Dylan's girlfriend, must've been going to bed early. Caroline was the captain of the varsity cheerleading squad. Zoe would have to sprout two more cup sizes in order to catch up with her. Not that Zoe was trying to catch anyone. She actually liked Caroline. She was a big upgrade from Dylan's last blonde, skinny girlfriend. And the one before that, too. Dylan Riley was a serial monogamist. He was tall, almost six foot four, and thin. He'd probably describe himself using the word "lanky". He kept his blond hair short, usually in a buzz cut. And he had an eight-pack. *Eight.* As in, two more abs than the already impressive six-pack. Not that Zoe went out of her way to notice his abs, but Dylan was co-captain of the varsity water polo team, and their uniform Speedos didn't exactly leave much of anything to the imagination.

Zoe closed her bedroom door, turned off the lights, and then jumped into bed. She quickly dialed Dylan's cell phone. He picked up on the first ring.

"Hey, hey," he said, as always.

"Am-I-sexy?" she asked, the question tumbling out of her mouth, all quick and jumbled, as if it were a secret.

"What?" Dylan asked, his voice getting squeaky for a moment.

"Okay, fine," Zoe said with an exhale. "I'm not gonna make you say no."

"Last time I checked, 'what' and 'no' aren't even sort of the same thing."

"Then you already heard my question."

"I didn't. Swear."

"You just want to make me say 'sexy' again."

"I promise I didn't hear you before, but now that you said 'sexy' I want to hear it for real – and I'm positive that your face is matching your hair."

"My face matching my hair is the story of at least fifty percent of my life."

"Nah. Only, like, forty percent," Dylan teased. "And now you've got this giant, brace-free smile on your face and you're probably blinding the bedbugs with your ridiculously bright white teeth."

"Yeah, yeah . . . Thanks."

"I'm sure it's all matching your pasty skin."

"Pasty? You really want to talk about who is more pasty? Last time I checked, we were both painfully pale." Zoe fought back, making Dylan laugh.

Point for Zoe.

Then the conversation got quiet for a moment. It wasn't an uncomfortable kind of quiet. Zoe appreciated that Dylan knew the importance of a good pause. Knowing when to stop talking was almost as important as knowing what to say in the first place, and Zoe and Dylan had spent enough hours on the phone to perfect both. Almost every night they would talk for an hour or two or sometimes three if there was something particularly exciting to talk about. The tradition had started back in ninth grade when they were lab partners in freshman chem class. Their last names, Reed and Riley, were next to each other alphabetically, so they'd been paired up. Most lab partners split up the assignments and then copied each other's work during passing period on the way to class, but Zoe felt like she needed to do the whole assignment in order to understand it, and Dylan wasn't going to let her do all of his work for him, so they got in the habit of doing their homework together on the phone every night.

In the beginning, their conversations were quick and entirely academic. They didn't have much in common. Zoe was in the theater crowd. She liked show tunes and jazz hands. Dylan liked contact sports and video games. The truth was, they still didn't have much in common, but something about their friendship just seemed to work. And it worked best on the phone.

So, every night, Dylan would text Zoe when he was ready to talk. And then Zoe would call him. And he would pick up on the first ring. And they'd spend the next hour or two or three talking and trying not to fall asleep. The funny part about these nightly falling-asleep phone calls, "phonefalls" as Dylan and Zoe called them, was that they were entirely platonic. Even though Zoe and Dylan agreed that it was more or less impossible for boys and girls to simply be friends – the "sex thing" really did always seem to get in the way – they also believed they were the exception to the rule.

After the comfortable pause had passed, Dylan returned his attention to Zoe's initial phonefall question. "But really," he persisted. "What were you trying to ask me? Something about something sexy?"

"It was nothing. I didn't say anything."

"Z, you are the Worst. Liar. Ever. We've been through this . . ."

"D," she said sternly, teasing him back, "I'm not lying—"

"It's okay. You're a pasty, freckled, red-haired liar . . ."

"Ohmigod . . ." Zoe giggled.

And Zoe and Dylan went on like that for an hour or two, laughing and teasing and talking and pausing, appreciating their conversation and the quiet spaces inside it, until finally, somehow, drifting off to sleep together.

168 Days Until Graduation . . .

Alex was pressed up against the largest rock on make-out ledge.

Cameron was leaning up against her, his tongue in her mouth, his hands everywhere. And it was all happening so fast. Cameron paused just long enough to pull his jeans down to his ankles. The air was cold against her cheeks and her chest, and her black Converse high-tops sunk down below her into the soft summer grass. Of all the things Alex had thought about when she imagined having sex for the first time, the location of her shoes was not one of them.

If she had thought about it at all, Alex probably would've assumed that her shoes would just simply be off, lying on the floor next to the bed. Of course that assumption would also require that there be a bed in the first place. Alex had never thought that her first time might happen outside. On a cluster of rocks. As her Converse sneakers sank down into the grass. But that's what it was.

Cameron's breath was soft and warm as he moved his kisses from her lips to her neck and then up onto her earlobe. Whatever he was doing with his lips and his tongue sent a tingle all the way down to her toes and then back up into her arms, which were entirely covered in goosebumps.

Cameron met her gaze, his green eyes bright and wide and alive, and this feeling of incredible closeness washed over Alex, making her feel as if she and Cameron were the only people who could possibly exist in this moment. Alex leaned in for one last kiss . . .

But before she could find Cameron's lips, Alex's cell phone rumbled on the top of her wooden nightstand, jerking her awake. It took her a moment to confirm that she was only dreaming about that night at sleep-away camp, but she somehow managed to wake up with real goosebumps on her arms, as if they'd morphed from her dreamland into the real world. But there wasn't any actual morphing involved. The goosebumps were as real as the car horn coming from her neighbor's driveway.

Shit.

Alex's one and only New Year's resolution had been to not be late for carpool anymore. She wasn't big on unnecessary commitments, and resolutions certainly fell into that category, but she also wasn't above self-improvement. Lately, even she had to admit that punctuality was her weakest link. Now it was only the first day of the new semester and she was mucking it up already.

She glanced at her phone. It was already a quarter till eight. She could've sworn she had set her alarm before falling asleep last night, but it seemed to have betrayed her. The honking continued as Oliver Miller, the literal boy next door and Alex's carpool driver, waited impatiently in his car.

Alex jumped out of bed, ripped off her pajama pants and bee-lined for the bathroom. Toothpaste, hairbrush, clean underwear, fresh socks – it more or less happened all at once. Her dad was out of town on business, per usual, and her mom had left early with her twin brother, Max, who went to a specialty school on the other side of town. She grabbed her cell phone and a banana and her shoes and her backpack and her wallet and tore out the front door – still barefoot.

Alex was a sprinter on the track team, so she certainly knew how to move quickly, but normally when she ran she would have a chance to stretch first, she wouldn't have just woken up, and she wouldn't be trying to balance all her possessions in her arms at the same time. Her super speed commonly led to stupid jokes about how she liked to move fast in other places as well – like between the sheets, for example. One time she even showed up to school and found the word "slut" spray-painted on her locker. That was a particularly shitty day.

The upside was that Alex was fast enough to leave most of her haters in the dust. She was also fast enough to be recruited by Stanford University, which gratefully took all of the academic pressure off her upcoming second semester. Her main concern these days – besides pledging to not always be late for carpool – had to do with the 100-meter dash. The Southern California high-school record hadn't been touched in nearly a decade, but Alex had a real chance to break it, and she was determined to make it happen. If she were to make her own Layla-like to-do list, "break the state record" would be the one and only thing on it.

"I'm sorry, I'm sorry," Alex said as she jumped into the passenger seat of Oliver's black Jeep Grand Cherokee.

"What happened?" Oliver asked as he peeled out of the driveway.

"My alarm clock didn't go off. I swear I set it for five past seven, but I think it must've been p.m. instead of a.m., 'cause I was using it to sleep late over winter break."

"That is far too much information."

"You asked what happened."

"Yeah, but I don't really care," Oliver said, which was the type of statement that contributed to his reputation for being an asshole. "I swear, I'm just going to start leaving without you."

Even when Oliver said ugly things like that, he was still really nice to look at. Today, he wore his red-and-black varsity basketball jersey over a white T-shirt. He was the starting shooting guard and the top scorer on the team, and yet somehow he managed to be even cockier off the court than he was on it.

"You're not gonna leave me. You've been saying that all year."

"'Cause you've been *late* all year," Oliver said, rolling his eyes.

"We both know this ten-minute drive is the best part of your entire day."

"Please, don't flatter yourself," Oliver jabbed back. "Aren't there enough boys at school who'll do that for you?"

Now it was Alex's turn to roll her eyes. She was used to getting compliments, but she didn't care too much about them. They were mostly about the way she looked, and the infuriating truth was that she didn't actually do anything to look this way. She woke up like this. Literally. Four and a half minutes ago, she had still been in bed. Alex wasn't complaining – she liked the way she looked – but she cared way more about what her track performance looked like than what *she* looked like. Sometimes she felt as if she was the only one who felt that way. When Alex ran, she was responsible for the outcome. She worked hard, and the hard work is what made her worthy of the praise.

Alex put her foot up on the glove compartment so she could pull on her sneaker, a black New Balance running shoe. Then she reached for the second one and realized it wasn't a match but a bright pink Nike cross-trainer instead.

"Oh, damn."

"We don't have time to go back," Oliver said, noticing the mismatch.

"Ugh. I know," Alex said as she pulled on the pink shoe. "Whatever. I'll make it work."

"Knowing you," Oliver smirked, "you'll probably start a new school-wide fashion trend."

"I don't think anyone's paying much attention to my shoes."

"I'm paying attention," Oliver said without missing a beat. "To everything."

It was statements like that one that managed to counterbalance Oliver's reputation for being an asshole – and made him so crushable. If Oliver thought *Alex* got a lot of compliments, he should hear the way girls talked about him in the locker room. But Alex wasn't going to tell him any of that. Oliver had more than enough of an ego already, which was a shame because if it weren't for that, Alex might have had an actual crush on him. She would've been lying if she said she wasn't attracted to him, but that was more or less unavoidable, considering the way he looked and carried himself, all confidence and charm. All year, their morning car rides had been overflowing with sexual tension.

Alex glanced up at the rear-view mirror and caught him staring at her. Most boys would've been flustered and looked away quickly, but not Oliver. He kept staring, owning the moment. He had no fear.

Alex didn't have any fear either, but she wasn't interested in being pulled in any further. Oliver had already succeeded in providing her with a fresh set of goosebumps. Like it or not, they were completely out of her control.

Emma could not stop taking pictures of Nick . . . and his lips.

She'd taken about five dozen pictures, but none of them was quite right. To make matters worse, Emma had no clue what would actually make them "right" or what she wanted them to be "right" for, but there was only so much she could worry about all at once.

Nick had been talking to the yearbook staff for the past seven minutes, ever since the first bell rang, signaling the start of homeroom. He was the editor-in-chief, so he had a lot of ground to cover, but Nick barely even paused to breathe as he laid out the schedule for the rest of the year, breaking down the delivery calendar and explaining when they would need to lock in the layout, text, and candid photographs. It was all super nerdy, but Emma thought it was fun too, and so did Nick, which might be why they got along so well.

When Nick first started talking, he had run his fingers through his hair, leaving himself with an accidental Mohawk. Emma was sitting in her usual spot in the back corner of the room, and even though she was only half awake – and definitely not a morning person – something about Nick's hair had compelled her to look alive and take a picture.

Emma didn't know why she was suddenly so obsessed with taking his picture. To be fair, she didn't know why she wanted to do almost anything ever, but at least she knew when she had to do something. She had started by framing his whole head, including the accidental Mohawk, but then she zeroed in on his face, and now, finally, on just his lips.

Emma always noticed people's lips.

It was the first thing she was drawn to whenever she looked at someone – boys, girls, adults, whoever – but especially when it was someone she had never seen before. Mostly, she'd just stare, taking in their size and shape and shade. Then she would inevitably wonder what it would be like to kiss those lips. And it didn't just happen with the kids at school either. It was teachers, too. Like Mr. Moore in English. Or even fully fledged adults like Dr. Saperstein, her dentist. She knew it was a weird habit, but like so much of the weirdness in her life, it was completely involuntary.

With Nick, she didn't have to wonder what it might be like to kiss him since it had already happened on at least three or maybe four different occasions. It always seemed to happen at a party, usually while one (or both) of them was slightly (or even very) drunk. But their kisses were mostly just casual and never got in the way of their ability to work on the yearbook together.

After eleven solid minutes, Nick finally stopped talking and took his first extended breath of the second semester of senior year. Emma seized the quiet moment and snapped yet another picture of him. This time his lips were closed. Finally, that felt right. As always, Emma was thankful to her camera for giving her purpose. Without it, she knew she probably would've been stuck awkwardly staring at Nick's lips for ever.

When Emma was about nine years old, her staring became so prolonged and intense that her teacher recommended she go see a therapist. Even her parents had to admit she was a bona-fide creeper, which was not an official diagnosis but still totally accurate. It turned out that Emma was totally fine. She just had an uber-long attention span, which was rare. Most of Emma's friends could get bored watching a six-second video, but Emma could sit and stare at people for hours. It didn't even matter what they were doing exactly; she just had this overwhelming urge to look. If Emma did the looking all by herself, it was weird and felt invasive. If she did it with a camera in her hands, she could call it art, and it felt important.

She snapped a few more quick pictures of Nick's lips. They were full and pink. A solid, masculine sort of pink. And they always tasted like Chap Stick.

Now that she thought about it, Emma's lips were actually pretty chapped. Maybe she should just walk right up to the front of the room and kiss Nick. Of course, the more practical thing to do would've been to just borrow his actual Chap Stick and use it herself, but at this moment, all she wanted to do was walk across the classroom and plant a wet, slippery kiss on his Chap Sticky lips.

Emma was really glad that no one could get inside her head. More than half of her thoughts were incredibly embarrassing, even though she was the only one who knew about them. Emma exhaled, trying to clear her mind. She ran her fingers through her straight black hair, pushing it into place behind her ears. As features went, Emma liked her ears. They were symmetrical and round and not too big. In fact, Emma really liked the way she looked in general. She felt like it all just kind of worked. She had olive skin and deep, dark brown eyes that slanted ever so slightly, commonly prompting people to ask her where she was from. Born and raised in Southern California was her first answer, but when people grew more persistent and/or rude, she'd go on to explain that her dad was Irish–American and her mom was Japanese–American, which made her one fourth Asian and three fourths Cauc*asian*, which also has the word "Asian" in it and always made Emma crack a smile. Not because she thought it was funny, but because it was a strange quirk of words and spelling.

It was weird, just like Emma.

"Em, can you do me a favor?" Nick asked from across the room. Everyone else had already begun working on their assignments. "Can you show the newbie how to use the page layout software?"

Emma nodded, glad to have something productive to do instead of staring at Nick's lips any longer. She walked over to the bank of computers where Savannah, "the newbie" girl, was sitting.

Savannah was petite, rocking a pixie cut and thick glasses. Emma couldn't help but notice that her thin lips were a light, bright, grapefruit shade of pink. Emma had the feeling that their lips might be the exact same color, but she couldn't be entirely sure until the next time she looked in a mirror.

Emma slid down into the empty chair next to Savannah and immediately got a weird sensation of déjà vu. Her forehead crinkled.

"Everything chill up there?" Savannah asked, gesturing towards her head.

"Oh, yeah . . . Sorry . . . Just too many thoughts all at once."

"Tell me about it," Savannah said, seemingly unfazed. Emma knew that was a common expression, but something about Savannah's tone made it sound like she might actually want to hear a real answer, so Emma responded honestly, opening the door to her weirdness ever so slightly.

"I'm having déjà vu all of a sudden," she said.

"*Tell me about it*," Savannah said again, with newly added emphasis.

Emma thought she just had.

"Sorry," Savannah added quickly. "You said 'déjà vu', and apparently I thought that meant it was okay for me to act like a total weirdo." Emma was glad she wasn't the only person in the room who was capable of such weirdness. "Okay, *anyway*," she said. "I'm Savannah."

"Hi. Emma."

"Hi."

166 Days Until Graduation . . .

Layla couldn't stop smiling.

"Uh oh," Zoe said warily as Layla joined the rest of the Crew at their usual lunch table in the middle of campus. "The last time your face looked like that, you convinced everyone at this table that we should all have sex together."

"But not *together* together," Emma teased.

"Don't worry. This is still that same face." It had been about sixty-five hours since the girls agreed on the sex pact, and Layla was pretty sure she'd been grinning continuously ever since. "Guys. It's happening. All of it. First, I bought a box of blonde highlights on the way to school this morning. Then, I asked Mr. Moore for an extra credit assignment in AP English and informed him – and also the universe – that I will be getting my grade up to an A by the end of the semester."

"What did the universe have to say about that?" Zoe asked.

"*Ob-vi-ous-ly* the universe is thrilled. Thanks for asking. And so is Logan. I'm sorry you didn't get to see the look on his face last night."

"Before or after you were sucking on it on the trampoline?" Alex asked.

41

"When I told him we were gonna have sex."

"Wait, wait: you told *Logan*?" Zoe squirmed. "I thought we weren't telling anyone about the pact." To be fair, the Crew hadn't officially decided whether they were telling anyone, but as an ongoing rule, whatever happened at the froyo table stayed at the froyo table.

"I didn't tell him about the sex pact. But I *did* tell him that we're gonna have sex. As in, him and me. I figured he should know that much." Layla winked and then instantly regretted it. She was not a winker.

"You told us before you told Logan?" Emma laughed.

"Well, yeah." Layla didn't even think that was strange. *Of course* she'd tell the girls first. "But he wouldn't care. He's just so excited. It's gonna be his first time too, so . . ."

"Sometimes I forget he's a virgin," Emma said.

"I know, right? He's good at sex *stuff,* but he hasn't actually . . ."

"What do you mean by *stuff* exactly?" Zoe asked before Layla could finish her sentence.

"She means he gives good head," Alex offered.

"Ohmigod . . ."

"Well, no," Layla said, correcting Alex. "I mean he's a good kisser – *phenomenal* actually – and he knows—"

"Hell. No." Alex interrupted. "Don't tell me he's never gone down on you."

He hadn't. He'd never even really tried. And Layla had never thought to ask him. "I don't think I'd like it," she said.

"How do you know if he hasn't done it?"

"I don't know . . . I just . . . I mean . . . have you thought about where his head would have to be in order to do that?"

42

"Um, yes. Yes, I have." Alex grinned.

"I'm pretty sure he'd do it if I asked. I think he's done it before 'cause he mentioned that it tastes like fish . . ."

"Layla. It does not taste like fish," Alex insisted.

"How do you know?" Emma laughed.

"I don't *personally*, but I know that fish crap is some super silly boy bullshit Logan's trying to pull."

"Yep. Total bullshit," Emma agreed. "And it's not like *dick* tastes all that great or whatever."

"Right. Boys want head, but then they don't want to give it back. Not only is that lame, but it also sucks because it's the best way to orgasm—"

"Ohmigod, ohmigod . . ."

"Or firework or whatever we're calling it for Zoe," Alex added.

"I can think of a few other *best* ways," Emma laughed.

Emma didn't realize that was such a bold statement . . .

. . . but it made Alex smirk and Zoe squirm and Layla's mouth drop open.

"Emma. O'Malley," Layla said after a moment. "Tell. Me. Everything."

"There's not really a whole lot to tell," Emma said, suddenly feeling shy.

The truth was they'd never really talked about this before.

It was hard to believe that after more than ten years of friendship and thousands of school lunches and hundreds of helpings of frozen yogurt there could still be new topics for the Crew to discuss, but orgasms were uncharted territory. They'd talked about kissing almost endlessly. About tongues and teeth and saliva. They'd talked about breasts and nipples and the appropriate amount of squeezage. About which boob moves turned them on and which ones made them feel like a cow being milked. They swapped stories about hickeys and dick pics and which boys knew how to unhook a bra with only one hand. They'd talked about what to do with their lips or tongues or teeth or hands whenever they were in close proximity to a boy's lips or tongue or neck or penis. They'd talked about penis size and shape and width and color. About shaving and waxing and even what made them wet . . .

. . . but they'd never really talked about *this*.

Until now.

"But you've . . . fireworked?" Layla asked.

"Yep," Emma giggled.

"With who?"

"Oh. Mostly it's just . . . well, *me*. I have a vibrator."

"Whoa," Zoe said.

"Well. It's not, like, a *vibrator* vibrator," Emma clarified. "I think it's supposed to be, like, a back massager or something, but it vibrates, so . . ."

"How often do you use it?" Layla asked.

"Um . . ." Emma thought for a minute. "Not, like, a lot . . . but sometimes."

"Same," Alex added. "I don't have a vibrator, though."

"I've never tried . . ." Layla admitted.

"Ever?" Alex asked, sounding genuinely surprised.

"Yeah, no . . ." Layla said, making a mental note to at least consider adding "masturbate" to her to-do list. "But I put a couple links about it in the Sex Doc."

"I haven't either," Zoe offered. "But you guys obviously knew that already."

"The Sex Doc? Is that what we're calling that *textbook* you sent us?" Alex grinned.

"You're welcome. Did you read it?"

Zoe shook her head.

"There's, like, a thousand articles . . ." Zoe said, as if that was the only reason she hadn't read Layla's extensive Google Doc of sex-centric information yet. Unsurprisingly, the whole thing made Zoe nervous, but from what she'd skimmed last night, the whole doc was basically a data dump alphabetized and color-coded by subject matter: what to do, how to do it, where to do it, when to do it, how to be safe about it. There was a whole section on birth control and condoms and morning-after pills. There were links to first-person articles about losing your virginity and an extensive collection of YouTube videos. It was basically the most Layla thing ever, Zoe thought as she unzipped her hoodie.

"Whoa," Emma said.

"Whoa, what?" Zoe looked down at her tank top. "Did I spill something?"

"It's . . . *your boobs*."

"Ohmigod, stop."

"They're hot, Zo," Alex added. "Just use them wisely . . ."

"Ha. Right." Zoe blushed. "I don't know the first *thing* about using them." She was still getting used to having them attached to her, let alone trying to figure out what to actually do with them. Zoe turned to Alex, hoping to change the subject. "I have an important question for the sexpert."

* * *

Alex was definitely *not* a sexpert.

"Okay, in comparison to the rest of the table you are," Zoe pushed.

"Maybe your answer is somewhere in the Sex Doc," Alex said, trying to avoid the question, but Zoe was already forging ahead.

"So, last night, when I was talking to Dylan—"

"You two are *still* doing that?"

"Oh. Yeah. We fall asleep on the phone almost every night."

"Forget the sleeping part," Alex said. "Who *talks* on the phone?"

"Me! My fingers are too fat for texting."

"Zoe."

"What? They are. And autocorrect hates me. I'm completely un-keyboard-inated and can't type without making every mistake possible. I also never know what to type in the first place."

"But you somehow know what to say for hours every single night?"

"Yes. It's really so much better. You should try it sometime."

"I can't imagine having that much to say to the same person, even Logan."

"Yeah, I don't know." Zoe smiled. "It's really just the easiest . . ." Then she ran her fingers through her hair again and launched back into her question for Alex, the sexpert, which basically boiled down to: does the G-spot actually exist?

The truth was, Alex had absolutely no clue what a G-spot was, let alone whether it existed. But what she did know was that there was only so much longer she could go without setting the record straight about what actually happened with Cameron at sleep-away camp. Or, more accurately, what didn't happen. There was a good reason why Alex's sex dreams always ended in exactly the same place, right before the actual sex part.

It was because she'd never made it to the actual sex part.

165 Days Until Graduation . . .

Alex never meant to lie about it.

Technically, she didn't *actually* lie about what had happened, but she also didn't have sex with Cameron that night at camp.

It was an honest misunderstanding, she thought as she laced up her shoes in the locker room before track practice. Surely the girls would get that. Still, the thought wasn't doing much to quell the growing dread in the pit of Alex's stomach. She knew she would have to set things straight with the Crew as soon as possible, but getting up the nerve to do it was the hard part.

As Alex walked out of the locker room, she heard a chorus of laughter coming from Coach Kolbert's office at the end of the hallway. Coach K, as everybody called him, had been coaching track for almost twenty years. They all teased him about being an old man; he had no problem teasing all the "young kids" right back. Alex watched him for a moment through his office window as he talked and laughed with a few older boys she recognized as former members of the track team, all recent graduates. They must've still been home from college for winter break.

One of the boys in particular caught her eye.

It was Joey Reed.

Alex always found it rather funny that his name rhymed with Zoe's, but apparently that was a total accident. Mr. and Mrs. Reed were formal people and only called him by his full name, Joseph, for the first six years of his life. It wasn't until he got to elementary school that people started to call him Joey. By that point, Zoe was already four, and they certainly weren't going to change *her* name, so there was nothing anyone could do to stop the rhyming. Joey and Zoe for ever.

Alex had known Joey ever since she and Zoe met in first grade, but they became friends in their own right more recently through their time on the track team. Joey hung out with the kind of stupid boys that liked to play pranks or make lame jokes, but he wasn't like that. Joey was a sweetheart, and he'd go out of his way to apologize for his friends. Alex watched Joey and the other boys for another minute. College life seemed to be agreeing with them. They were only a year or two older than she was, but they looked so much more mature and comfortable in their own skin. And their bodies, too. Especially Joey. Especially *his* body. Alex didn't want to walk over and interrupt the reunion, but she hoped he would look out in her direction so she could wave hello.

He didn't.

Things didn't always work out the way she wanted them to.

An hour later, in the midst of track practice, Alex hadn't been able to stop thinking about him. She should've just gotten over herself and said hello. It was stupid she hadn't, but it was too late to do anything about it now. Especially right now, at this moment, as she sprinted around the track, pushing herself as hard as she could. She could feel the blood pulsing from her fingertips down to the tips of her toes. She could feel her knees buckling beneath her. But mostly she could feel every single second of time as it slid away from her. She knew too much time had slipped off the clock before she even crossed the finish line.

"Almost," Coach K said, looking at his stopwatch.

Alex let out an exasperated groan. She had been stuck at "almost" for months – and she hated it. "Almost" doing something meant that you almost *didn't* do it as much as you almost did. "Almost" certainly wasn't going to help her break the state record.

"You're so close," Coach K said, trying to find the bright side.

But Alex didn't want "close" and she didn't want "almost" either. She wanted *actually*. It didn't matter that she was close to breaking the record, just like it didn't matter that she was close to having sex with Cameron.

She still wasn't the record holder, and she was still technically a virgin.

And at this moment, Alex wasn't sure which "still" was worse.

"You're just getting in your own way," Coach K said, sensing Alex needed more of a pep talk. He was talking about breaking the state record, but he might as well have been talking about everything else in her life too. "I can see you're all up in your head right now, overthinking yourself, second-guessing every choice you've ever made, revisiting all your old mistakes . . ."

Alex nodded, mildly worried that he might be reading her mind.

"But you know that's not going to get you where you want to go. That's only going to send you backwards. And you don't need to go back. You've already been there, right?"

Alex nodded again, but more subtly this time.

"Yeah?" Coach K asked, pushing for an actual response.

"Yeah," she grunted back, frustrated.

"Good. Get angry," he pushed, "because, as far as I'm concerned, this record is already yours. But that's not how winning works. It's not a decision."

He wasn't wrong. She felt like the record was hers too, but her feelings were pretty unreliable sometimes. There were still six track meets left on the calendar, but she already felt like a failure.

"Things don't just happen. They have to be achieved," Coach K said, choosing his words carefully and making Alex even more certain that he could read her mind. "Alex Campbell, I know – no, *I believe* – that you can do this."

Alex finally cracked a smile.

"Yeah, there we go. I can see that you believe too. But if you beat yourself up in the process? Well, then it's never gonna happen, right?"

Alex nodded one more time, more firmly now.

"I need your faith to be bigger than your fear, Ms. Campbell."

Alex needed that too.

"Let's do one last lap and then call it a day," he said.

She walked back to the starting line with her hands clasped on top of her ponytail, trying to clear both her lungs and her thoughts at the same time. She did her best to push unhelpful words like "failure" and "Cameron" and "lie" and "virgin" to the edge of her mind, but as she worked to clear space in her head, she couldn't help but think about how hard she was trying to clear that space, which made her think about her twin brother, Max, and about how hard he had to work to do just about anything. Even though she was never entirely sure what was going on inside his head, she and Max had a special twin bond. She felt like she understood him even when she didn't. They truly connected over their shared loved of *Star Wars*. Really, Max adored *Star Wars*, and Alex loved how much he loved it, but that just made her actually love it too. Max could quote every word any character said in any of the movies, but he liked Yoda's words best – never in quite the right order, but somehow always making sense anyway.

One of Max's favorite Yoda sayings was: "Do or do not. There is no try". Alex liked that too, because it didn't pretend that "almost" was acceptable. You either succeeded or you failed – there was no in between. There was no "close". There was no "almost". There were no points for trying or planning or expecting.

Max was only two minutes and thirty-five seconds younger than Alex, but that time – that "only" – was everything. Alex, always the fast one, came out first, while Max got stuck backwards or upside down or something. The doctors went in and grabbed him, but those two minutes and thirty-five seconds had already changed everything.

Immediately, expectations were recalibrated. Bars were lowered. Dreams were reimagined. Alex knew her parents loved her and Max equally, but they all knew that she could do so much more than he could, so they expected more too.

To put it simply, Alex had to be both the good daughter *and* the good son. Maybe that's why she was such a tomboy. Maybe that's why she liked to play sports. Maybe that's why she approached making out with more of a "boy mentality" – or whatever that meant.

The irony was that if she actually was a son, no one would ever have written "slut" on her locker. She probably would've been called a "stud" or "pimp", like Oliver. He hooked up with everyone all the time, and he was "the man". She made out with guys semi frequently – admittedly more often than most girls but not *all* the time – and she was called a "ho". And, ironically, everyone thought she was even more of a slut because she'd had sex before, which she actually hadn't, so it was all just a jumbled mess. And it was all still swirling around in Alex's head even as Coach K blew the whistle to start the last lap of the day.

Alex sprinted hard off the starting line, running fast as she could, but it wasn't enough. This time was even less "almost" than the lap before.

"It's okay. We'll pick it up again tomorrow," Coach K said.

It actually *wasn't* okay, but arguing just felt like another lost cause.

A few minutes later, Alex walked toward the parking lot, carrying her backpack and gym bag and all of her thoughts and fears and expectations. It was more than she knew what to do with. Mostly she was just sweaty and frustrated and tired, and her mom wouldn't be able to pick her up for at least another hour, and that's when she saw Oliver, sitting on the front hood of his car, texting. His hair was still wet from a recent shower.

"Hey, you," he called as she approached.

"Hey, *me*?"

"Yes, you. Who else would I be waiting for?"

Alex smiled.

"Maybe don't answer that . . ." Oliver smiled back. "Do you want me to give you a ride?" he asked, his innocent tone not exactly matching the gleam in his eyes.

Alex raised her eyebrows, a new, bold smirk stretching across her face.

"A ride in my *car*," he clarified, as Alex added Oliver to the list of people she suspected might be able to read her thoughts. "You coming?" he asked one more time. "I'm not gonna beg."

Oliver didn't have to beg. Alex was in. Literally. Figuratively. *Actually*.

She climbed into the front seat of his SUV, flashing him her trademarked "Mona Lisa smile".

"You gonna tell me what that smile means?"

But Alex couldn't, because she rarely knew what it meant herself.

It was the kind of smile that says yes as much as it says no. It was the kind of smile that had gotten Alex into trouble before, and probably would again.

"Whatever it means," Oliver said after a moment, "it's driving me crazy."

The look on Oliver's face was driving Alex crazy, too. She didn't tell Oliver, but she was totally positive he already knew.

158 Days Until Graduation . . .

Layla felt like Vanessa was doing it on purpose.

And by "it" she meant *everything*.

Vanessa Martin was the most popular/unpopular girl in the sophomore class. Opinions were evenly drawn down gender lines. The boys all loved her low-cut tank tops and her push-up bras and her super-short shorts. They loved her flirty laugh and the way she was always sucking on something, be it a lollipop or a strand of her hair. Meanwhile, the girls generally hated all the things the boys loved about her. The part that annoyed Layla the most was that everything about Vanessa felt so calculated. It wasn't just that she knew what she was doing; she also seemed to know the kind of reaction it would illicit. Case in point: she had been sucking on the cap of her pen since the student council meeting started almost forty minutes ago. Not just sucking, but *sucking*.

And it didn't look like she was going to let up any time soon.

Layla didn't blame Vanessa for wanting a reaction; she just wished she would own up to it a little more. If you're in a meeting sucking on a pen cap for forty minutes, you're going to give all the student council boys hard-ons and you're going to piss off all the girls. So don't act all shocked when your guy "friends" want to hook up and your girl "friends" don't actually like you.

"Does anybody have any new business?" Logan asked from the front of the classroom.

"Oh, his *voice*," Vanessa whispered to Layla as if it were part of some inside joke between them. It wasn't. "Don't you, like, *die* every time he talks to you?"

No. She didn't, like, die.

At all.

Somehow, Layla managed a fake smile in Vanessa's direction, but her beady, calculated eyes were already locked back on Logan. Layla could practically see her mentally undressing him . . .

There was no new business, so Logan wrapped up the meeting, telling everyone to have a good week and that he'd see them next Thursday.

"Sucks there's so much time between meetings, huh?" Vanessa whispered to Layla. "It's, like, literally the worst."

Layla couldn't help but notice Vanessa's use of the word "suck". How appropriate.

A few minutes later, as Layla and Logan walked towards the senior parking lot, Layla was still stewing about Vanessa. "I just don't like her."

"Yes, it's very Captain Obvious of you—"

"But it's like she has no idea. She thinks we're best friends. And she is completely, shamelessly in love with you."

"Lay, she flirts with *everyone*."

"So then you admit she's flirting with you?" Layla teased.

"I think I've always admitted that."

"Oh no. You usually try to say she's just being nice."

"She *is* being nice."

"Nice is not even sort of a strong enough word. It feels like all she wants in life is just to get inside your pants."

"That is not what it feels like. And whatever. Everything in my pants is already entirely occupied by you." Logan flashed that dimple and then pulled Layla in close, pressing his waist up against hers.

"Oh, hi," Layla said, teasing him – and his hard-on. "You sure that's for me, though? Not just left over from Vanessa's extended pen-sucking exhibition?"

"Pen sucking? I hadn't noticed," Logan tried to say with a straight face, but Layla knew he'd noticed. All the boys always did. There was no point in trying to deny it. "Hey, so is it annoying or still sort of cute to remind you that I have a condom in my glove compartment?"

"It was never cute."

"A little bit cute? No?"

"Nope." Layla let the dust settle for a moment as they reached the car before telling Logan that she wanted to have sex for the first time on Valentine's Day.

"All right," he said with a nod. It looked like he was doing the mental math in his head. It was twenty-nine days away, just over four weeks. Layla had obviously already counted. "That'll be cool. Losing the V-cards on V-Day."

"A little less cool when you make it sound all corny like that."

"*The day* is corny; there's not much I can do about that."

"Actually, I think there's a lot you can do . . ."

"Oh. Is this your way of telling me that you want a whole production?"

"Not, like, a *production* . . ."

"But a scavenger hunt or something like that?"

Layla smiled. Yes, something *exactly* like that.

Logan pulled her hand up to his lips and kissed her fingers.

"For a second I thought you were going to do your best Vanessa impression," she laughed.

"Oh, you mean like this?" Logan playfully slipped Layla's pointer finger into his mouth and sucked hard. She yanked her hand back.

"Ew, Logan. Slobber."

"You wanna try me?" Logan held out his hand, wiggling his fingers.

"No thank you . . ."

"Fine. Whatever. I'm sure I could get Vanessa to do it," Logan said as he finally pulled his car out of the parking lot.

He was joking.

And Layla knew he was joking.

But there was something about the way he said it, or maybe something about the fullness of his smile *as* he said it, or maybe even just something about the twinkle in his eye as the words came out of his mouth . . . Whatever it was, *something* about the moment didn't sit right with Layla. She simply couldn't shake it.

Zoe couldn't quite reach the tallest leaves.

She was standing on her toes on the highest rung of the ladder, trying to paint the top of the wooden trees green, but so far she was failing miserably. She could feel the ladder wobbling.

"Please don't fall!" Austin shouted from the back of the theater.

Zoe was startled by the sound of his voice and it made her sway on her heels. She had to crouch down on the top step to steady herself. She hadn't realized anyone else was around, but apparently Austin had been watching from the tech booth.

"Sorry for the scare," he said. "I'd just be super sad and embarrassed for you if you fell. But then I'd also have to laugh at you."

"I'd also be sad and embarrassed too," Zoe said, already laughing. She realized she probably looked pretty ridiculous up there, covered in green paint. This year's spring musical was *Into the Woods*, and, as the stage manager, a big part of Zoe's job was to make sure that the woods on the stage looked like actual woods. So far this involved a lot of brown and green paint and was only turning out to be a mildly successful endeavor.

"You need a hand?" Austin asked, walking toward the stage.

"Yes. And longer legs and arms," Zoe said, instantly feeling lame about it.

"What?" Austin asked before realizing it was a bad joke. "Oh, ha, right, yes," he added quickly. Austin was a nice guy like that.

He held the ladder as Zoe climbed down and even offered Zoe his hand as she jumped off the bottom step. Zoe's hand was sweaty and covered in paint, but she reached for Austin's anyway. She wanted to know what his fingers felt like.

"You greened me," he said, looking at his hand after Zoe let go.

"Oh no! Here." Zoe held out the bottom of her already paint-covered tank top so he could wipe his hand on it. Austin looked at Zoe for an extra beat, catching her eyes as if to confirm that she wouldn't mind. And really, she wouldn't. "It's all good," she said. "I'm a mess already."

"You're not at all," Austin said sincerely as he wiped his hand. Then, Austin shifted his weight in his shoes, seemingly nervous. Zoe wasn't exactly sure why he was nervous, but she was nervous too, so it sort of made sense. Austin ran his hand over his short hair and then looked down at his shifting feet. Zoe followed his gaze, down his body, and it suddenly occurred to her that she'd never really noticed his body before. She'd noticed his dark skin and his deep brown eyes and the shape of his hands and maybe even his neck and the curve of his ears, which were slightly larger than average and maybe even a little bit pointed in an adorable sort of way, but she'd never really noticed his body. Maybe it was because he was usually sitting in the tech booth designing lighting cues. Or maybe it was because he and Zoe hadn't actually spent that much time together. Yes, they'd been in the same place, at rehearsal, for hours and hours, but they weren't really *together*.

Not like this, anyway.

Not this close.

Even though they weren't even touching, Zoe could feel him. His presence. His body. And the way it was right next to hers.

"You have some, um, some more green," Austin managed to say, getting bashful as he pointed in the general vicinity of Zoe's chest.

Zoe looked down. Yep. There was a big glob of green on her chest, right between her boobs. Not only had Austin noticed her boobs, but he'd basically just told her that he noticed – and that made Zoe smile. And then blush, too. She hoped her face was only a little red and didn't look like a full-on fire engine, which is what it felt like. All the red and green was probably making her look like a giant Christmas elf. She wiped the paint off her chest as slickly as she could, which wasn't very.

After some mildly awkward silence, Austin asked Zoe if she liked the Other Team. "It's this band," he explained. "My buddy's the drummer. They play at house parties sometimes."

"Oh yeah," Zoe said, pretending like maybe she had heard of them. She didn't go to all that many house parties, but when she did, they certainly weren't cool enough to have live bands.

"Yeah. They're pretty great, actually," Austin continued. "And they have a show coming up at the Roxy this Saturday. A bunch of the tech guys are gonna go, so if you want to come too, that would be . . ."

"Cool," Zoe said, completing Austin's sentence for him.

"Cool," Austin agreed. And then they just stood there on the empty stage, grinning at each other, until Austin finally regained his ability to speak. "Um . . ." he started timidly, ". . . can you do me a favor and stand in my spotlight for a minute?"

"Oh, sure, but I bet you say that to all the girls," Zoe said, trying to maybe sort of flirt with him. In her head it had sounded like something an actress would say in a movie. In reality, Austin looked pretty confused, and the whole exchange just made her feel self-conscious. "Where do you need me?" she asked.

Austin pointed to a mark in the center of the stage and then scampered back to the light booth. He turned on the spotlight and worked to focus it, and now it was Austin's turn to make Zoe nervous. It was mostly his spotlight's fault. At least all she had to do was stand still.

"Got it!" he said after what seemed like an eternity. "Looks good!"

"Thanks," Zoe said as a new feeling of excitement washed over her. It was the kind of feeling that made her want to break into song. She wasn't really going to start singing, mostly because she couldn't carry a tune to save her life, but she really did feel like a character in one of the musicals she loved so much. Like a character who lived in a magical, musical world where it was normal and acceptable and maybe even encouraged to break out into song at any given moment. Zoe could hear a whole orchestra in her head, and the instruments were playing the opening notes from the song "I Know Things Now", which was Zoe's favorite song from *Into the Woods*, and might also be her favorite Stephen Sondheim song, which was a very big deal considering how many incredible Sondheim songs existed in the universe.

"I Know Things Now" is the song Little Red Riding Hood sings about her journey into the woods and her first meeting with the wolf. At first, Little Red describes the meeting as being exciting, but then she clarifies that it's actually both exciting and scary, which was exactly how Zoe felt at this very moment. She was both at the same time.

Austin and his spotlight and his voice and his smile and the way his body felt next to hers was the most thrilling *and* terrifying thing that had happened to Zoe in a very long time. Quite possibly, ever.

157 Days Until Graduation . . .

Emma had been tossing and turning for what felt like for ever.

She rolled over and glanced at her digital alarm clock.

12:02.

It was already tomorrow and she was still awake, so clearly *something* was bothering her.

She'd been in an epically bad mood for the past few weeks or maybe even the past few months, since the very beginning of the school year. She could pretty confidently surmise that it all had something to do with the calendar and the finality of G-Day approaching, but she didn't know what to do about it.

All she wanted to do was go to sleep, but she couldn't manage to turn off her brain. She was having too many thoughts and feelings – and overthinking and over-feeling all of them. Sometimes, when Emma really couldn't sleep and she just needed to take a break from herself, from all her thoughts and her brain and everything, she would masturbate.

But right now even *that* didn't sound like fun.

Even if Emma somehow managed to get up enough excitement to actually go for it, she didn't feel like she was going to be able to finish it . . . and the thought of ending up without any fireworks made her more frustrated than anything else. Still, she took her vibrator out of the bottom drawer of her nightstand and turned it on, hoping maybe the sound would un-frustrate her or at least get her in the mood. Sometimes that worked.

This time it didn't.

Zoe wanted to go to sleep, but she couldn't stop staring at her phone.

It was almost 12:15 in the morning, and Zoe's phone had been buzzing for the last few minutes as Layla sent a string of motivational quotes to the Chat. Layla loved quotes. And she seemed to love them even more when they were displayed on abstract pictures or on top of sunsets or on seascapes or color backgrounds. Zoe liked Layla's quotes, but she was much more partial to song lyrics. Something about the music made the words feel more important, Zoe thought. She was almost always listening to music.

Tonight, she'd made it all the way through her Songs Of The Moment playlist *twice*. Zoe was constantly updating her SOTM mix, but it always consisted of about two hours of pop songs, classic favorites and show tunes. She could happily listen to her mix almost endlessly, but at this point, she was just stalling and waiting for Dylan's nightly *Ready?* text message. It was Dylan's job to text first, but it was already much later than usual, so Zoe figured if there was gonna be a phonefall, she'd have to break tradition.

Ready? she texted him.

Ten minutes passed. No response.

Just as she was about to give up and go to sleep, her phone rang. She picked up on the first ring.

"Sorry," Dylan said before Zoe even had a chance to say hello. "I just got off the phone with Caroline, I swear."

"Everything okay?"

"She was being dramatic." Dylan was clearly in a mood.

"Sorry. But I'm glad you're all right. I was starting to think you might be lying in a ditch somewhere."

"No ditch, just my bed," he said, softening ever so slightly.

"Oh, okay, so then you basically forgot about me. That's cool, too," Zoe teased, still trying to pull him out of his bad mood.

"Z. Puh-lease. I could never forget about you," Dylan replied, finally sounding like his goofy self again. "I'm sorry. It was just stupid Caroline bullshit that went on for way too long. Whatever. What's up with you?"

"So much," Zoe said excitedly, thrilled to finally have Dylan's attention. "At rehearsal this afternoon, the lighting designer, Austin – do you know him?"

"Do I?"

"I don't know. Austin Jones. He's tallish. Cute. Black. He's a theater kid."

"Oh yeah, one of those losers . . ." Dylan chuckled.

Zoe knew Dylan was just teasing, but she'd been waiting so patiently to tell him about the paint and the concert and the spotlight and the way everything with Austin was both exciting and scary, so Dylan's jab seemed rather insensitive.

"We're going to see the Other Team on Saturday," she replied.

"Which team?"

"The Other Team. It's a band, not an actual team. Some of the other tech people are coming to the concert too, so it's like a group thing, but still . . ."

Zoe waited, hoping for even just a mild amount of excitement from Dylan, but all she got was a little bit of a grunt. It might even have been just a cough.

"Well. It was cute," she said.

"I'm sure."

"And then he asked me to stand in his spotlight," Zoe added as if that might mean something to him.

It didn't.

And, for the first time, Zoe couldn't figure out how to explain something to Dylan.

155 Days Until Graduation . . .

Emma still had no idea what was bothering her.

The girls were seated at their usual froyo table, phones stacked in the middle as always, listening to Zoe recount all the adorable details of her first date with Austin. Like the way she'd done her hair – half up, half down – and how he'd nervously rung her doorbell and then had been forced to talk to Zoe's dad, who wasn't *really* intimidating, but his broad shoulders and full beard seemed to make teenage boys rather anxious. But then it turned out Austin's dad was driving them to the concert, so that made Zoe's dad like the situation a whole lot more.

Emma wanted to get excited about Zoe's date night, like Layla and Alex seemed to be, but she was mostly just distracted and frustrated. It wasn't Zoe's fault. Emma had been in a mood lately. At this point she was even annoying herself. After Zoe finished her story, Layla turned her attention to Emma and asked her for a "progress report" on the sex pact.

Layla meant well enough, but it was exactly the opposite of what Emma needed right now. Layla had asked Zoe the same question, but the difference was that Zoe had some actual progress – an entire date night – to report.

Right now, Emma had nothing. She could barely even figure out how to complete a sentence. "I don't . . . I just . . ."

Okay, forget *finishing* – apparently Emma couldn't even figure out how to *start* a sentence. All she knew for sure was that Layla wasn't helping.

"I just . . . I think you're making this whole thing very stressful," Emma finally managed to "report", between bites of caramel frozen yogurt.

"What whole thing?"

"The pact. Obviously."

"Not *obviously*. Em, lately you think everything is stressful."

"Yes, but . . ." Emma said, attempting to start another sentence but she trailed off, deciding to focus on her rainbow sprinkles instead.

"Maybe there's a better phrase we could be using instead of 'progress report,'" Zoe chimed in, trying to help.

"The problem isn't what we're *calling* it." Emma could feel a sharpness in her voice and she didn't like it at all.

"Then what *is* the problem?" Layla pushed back.

"I don't know . . ." Emma exhaled. "It's only been two weeks since you first said the words 'sex pact' and it's like you're already expecting us to have it all figured out. You're the only one who has a boyfriend."

"Aw. No, I don't mean it like that," Layla said sweetly. "I just want to know where your head's at."

Yeah. That was pretty much the only thing anybody – her parents, her friends, her teachers – wanted to know these days.

Where *was* Emma's head?

Literally: it was sitting on top of her shoulders.

Beyond that . . . she had no clue.

The clock was ticking and time was flying, and there was nothing Emma could do to stop it. She wanted to enjoy the second semester of her senior year and have fun with her best friends and laugh about boys and penises and sex pacts, but she just . . . couldn't.

"Everything's feeling like a lot right now."

"All the feels?" Layla asked with a smile.

"Something like that . . ." Emma said, forcing a smile in return. Layla's heart was in the right place, but Emma's heart and head, and whatever else was involved in her decision-making process, had already reached peak emotional capacity. There simply wasn't room for anything else. Not a Sex Doc. Or weekly progress reports. And especially not all the feels.

Honestly, Emma didn't have room for *any* of the feels.

She would've been perfectly happy to give them all back, but that didn't seem to be an option.

Zoe had spent hours waiting for Dylan's *You ready?* text message.

Again, he was running late.

And *again*, she felt like an idiot.

All she wanted to do was tell him about her date with Austin, but he wasn't responding to any of her text messages. It wasn't their usual phonefall time, but still, it sucked. She sent a text to the Chat – *Dylan's avoiding me* – just to make sure her cell phone worked and it had service and the ability to deliver messages to other cell phones.

He's jealous, Alex texted back immediately.

Then Layla texted a picture of a typewriter with the quote "Love means never having to ask 'Did you get my text message?'" written on it. Zoe wanted to text back that Dylan clearly didn't love her, non-mystery solved, but that seemed like too much effort.

Mostly she wished she could forget about Dylan entirely. He'd been so distracted by Caroline recently that she couldn't remember the last time they had had a satisfying conversation, and now that she had something worthwhile to tell him she didn't want to miss her chance.

She tried sending Dylan one more text: *Are you okay?*

Still nothing.

She put her phone down on her desk, willing it to buzz. And then all of a sudden, it did.

Hey.

That was it. The incoming text was one word, three letters, one period. Zoe had to recheck the text and then *re*-recheck it, three times altogether, before realizing that the incoming message wasn't from Dylan.

It was from Austin.

Ohmigod.

Hi, she texted back, laughing at herself for how much time and energy it took her to settle on that one word, two letter, no punctuation reply.

Thanks for last night!!!!! he responded almost immediately.

Zoe noticed the exclamation points. She started to type back "you're welcome" but erased it before she even had time to consider using exclamation points of her own.

Before she could come up with a better, flirtier response, she got another text from Austin: *We should do it again sometime . . .*

Zoe noticed the dot dot dot. She loved all three of them. And then she promptly freaked out, running around her bedroom, doing a full-on happy dance, until she realized Austin had no clue how happy she actually was because he couldn't see her victory dance and she hadn't managed to respond to either of his last two text messages.

So far all she'd *actually* said was *Hi*. One word, two letters, no punctuation. That was it. Zoe really was just horrible at texting.

Yes! she typed as quickly as possible, pressing send before she could overanalyze it.

Then, even more quickly, she added a bunch more exclamation points – *!!!!* – as their own separate text message.

Then she wished there was a "text recall" button so she could get rid of all her extra exclamation points, but it was too late. She'd already sent them.

But when she thought about it, she realized she didn't even care.

Alex would've said she was disrupting the delicate "flirting power balance" between them or something, which might even have been accurate, but Zoe didn't want to play games right now.

Luckily, Austin didn't, either. He quickly sent back a smiley face.

Zoe very much appreciated that Austin was also a beginner-level flirt and added her own smiley face to the conversation.

Then she added: *But only if your dad doesn't drive this time.*

Deal, Austin texted back.

She took a screenshot of their conversation, mildly embarrassed by all the exclamation points and smiley faces, but mostly too proud to care. Before she could send her screenshot to the Chat, there was another incoming text.

This one was from Dylan: *Caroline and I broke up.*

At least that explained why he hadn't responded to her sooner.

Wanna talk? she texted back, but Dylan didn't reply again.

She'd seen Dylan go through enough break-ups to know that he was hurting right now, but in a couple of days, or maybe weeks, he'd wonder how he ever let himself get so consumed by Insert-Ex-Girlfriend's-Name-Here and all of her stupid bullshit. And then, maybe a couple of days or weeks after that, he'd be back to his cheerful self – and ready to move onto the next skinny blonde girl.

At least once all that happened, Zoe and Dylan could go back to their regular phonefall schedule.

153 Days Until Graduation . . .

Emma was only really happy in the yearbook room.

Lately, it was the only activity that managed to distract her from herself, so she'd been spending almost all of her free time there. She might not be able to give Layla a progress report on the sex pact, but at least she could make progress on something worthwhile. Today she was working on the layout for the Senior Superlative page. They hadn't even voted on the Superlatives yet, but Emma knew they would soon. Someone would be voted Most Likely to Succeed. Someone would have the Best Eyes and the Cutest Smile. Emma thought she should nominate herself for Most Likely to Have a Nervous Breakdown Slash Panic Attack before Graduation.

"Your photo layout looks good," Savannah said as she sat down at the computer next to Emma.

"My photo layout looks *excellent*, thank-you-very-much," Emma confirmed playfully. "It's just the rest of everything that's all over the place."

"I swear you don't look like you're all over the place."

"Yeah, well, you can't see or hear any of the thoughts inside my head."

"Yeah, *well*, I think if I *could* really see or hear them, we'd have some sort of intense medical emergency on our hands," Savannah said with a laugh.

Emma loved Savannah's laugh. It was substantial and unapologetic and always the perfect pitch. As Savannah flipped open her notebook, Emma couldn't help but notice an impressive collection of doodles and scribbles interspersed with a smattering of notes about the boys' soccer game.

"I'm sports news editor," Savannah explained.

"Really? Sports?"

"Yes. Really."

"I mean. You just *look* like such a huge sports fan . . ."

"Little known fact: the sports section is the busiest beat on the paper. There are dozens of sports teams, and they all have dozens of games. There's always something to write about."

Emma nodded, sensing there was something more to the story.

"Anddddd, yeah. I didn't get my shit together fast enough at the start of the school year and all the other editorial beats were already taken."

"So we're saying my judgments are right?"

"If we must."

"Oh, we must." Emma laughed again. Savannah laughed again, too. Emma appreciated her laugh more and more each time.

"What's so funny?" Nick asked on his way into the room.

"Sports," Savannah said in a deep voice that made Emma laugh harder.

"All right," Nick said, clearly missing the inside joke. He grabbed his binder off the counter and then noticed the Senior

Superlative layout on Emma's screen. "Oh, woah . . ." he said as he leaned down, right over Emma's left shoulder, to get a better look. He didn't need to be quite so close to see it, but Emma would've been lying if she'd said she didn't like that he was there. "It's *brilliant*," he concluded after another long look. "Em, your layouts are *always* worth geeking out about. Every single time . . ."

Emma smiled, trying not to blush. Nick squeezed her shoulder and then hustled out the door. The girls watched him leave.

"I officially nominate him for Best Butt," Savannah announced.

"Unfortunately juniors don't get to vote for Superlatives."

"What. Ever. You should add his butt to your layout. It's that good."

Emma hadn't really noticed his butt before . . . His lips? All the time. But never his butt.

Then, Savannah's lips cracked into an embarrassed smirk. "I'm actually the weirdest," she blurted out as if she simply couldn't keep the words inside for a moment longer. "Butts aren't even my thing, like, sexually speaking or whatever. It's not like the thought of them turns me on or anything, but I always feel like I want to put my hand inside the back pocket of people's pants. It's not even that I really want to *touch* their butts or anything, but I just, like, need to know what my hand will feel like inside their pocket. Don't worry, I'm super normal . . ."

"'The only normal people are the ones we don't know very well,'" Emma replied. Layla had sent that quote to the Chat one time, and Emma loved it so much, she wrote it down on a Post-it note and stuck it on her bathroom mirror.

"So then you agree that I'm weird?"

"Oh, totally. But I am, too."

"You keep it together pretty well."

"God, no. I told you," Emma insisted. "*My thoughts* . . ." She tried to decide just how much crazy she was willing to unleash into Savannah's world. "Okay, so you want to put your hands in people's pockets? Fine. That's weird. But my weirdness is that I literally want to kiss everyone I meet."

"Everyone?"

"Yup. Everyone."

"By 'kiss' you mean, like, a peck on the cheek or like you actually want to stick your tongue inside their mouth?"

"Tongue in mouth," Emma said with a giggle, but she was entirely serious. "It's not really even sexual, either. I just have this urge to know what it would be like."

Emma had never said that out loud before. She didn't know what it was exactly, but something about Savannah made her want to say it.

150 Days Until Graduation . . .

Alex still wasn't quite sure how she felt about Oliver.

"It's complicated," she explained between bites of her chopped salad.

"Obviously. It *has* to be complicated or you would've gotten bored so long ago," Layla said without judgment.

"True," Alex agreed. "Sometimes I think he's a misunderstood nice guy. Other times I think he's the asshole everyone thinks he is. I can't tell. This morning he finally asked if he could see me somewhere besides his car."

"Wait, w*hat*?!" Layla asked excitedly.

"Yeah," Alex said as if it wasn't a big deal. "He said he wants to take me out somewhere. He actually said he wants to go somewhere sexy, which was ridiculous, but I swear it came out of his mouth."

"It's only 'ridiculous' if you actually mean hot," Layla said.

"Yeah, it was hot too, but who just *says* that?" Alex asked.

"A guy with a lot of confidence in the size of his penis," Emma offered.

"You know," Layla said seriously, "penis size is actually *not* the most important factor in determining the amount of pleasure

78

a woman has in any given sexual experience."

"I'm not having sex with Oliver. At least not on our first date."

Emma thought it was weird that Alex was even *having* a first date.

But then again, Zoe had a second date coming up with Austin and Layla had a *sex* date planned with Logan, so maybe Emma was the weird one. As always.

"It's cool," she said, tucking her hair behind her ears, "you guys go ahead with all that . . . I'll just be here, hanging out by myself . . . It's fine. I'm totally fine."

"You *sound* totally fine with it," Alex teased.

"Let's find you someone to date," Layla said excitedly. "Or maybe someone you might want to hang out with. Like, for the pact . . ."

"I don't want to 'hang out' with someone just because of the stupid pact."

"Emma. The pact is not *stupid*," Layla defended.

"You're obsessing about it. It's all you want to talk about anymore." Emma directed that statement mostly to Layla, but she meant it for the other girls too.

"Em, it's just supposed to be fun," Layla said, trying to calm Emma down.

"I think it'll be a lot more fun if we stop making such a big deal about it."

"I swear I'm not trying to stress you out," Layla insisted, "but I *am* trying to say that I think it matters. Or that I think it *should* matter. But it's obviously not something you *have* to do, so if you don't want to do that pact—"

"No, I do," Emma insisted. "I'm not saying that, but school ending is already stressful, and now you've decided that this has to have the same due date . . ."

"You're the one who's mushing it together with graduation." Emma flinched at Layla's use of the G-word. "If you don't want to do the pact . . ."

"I'm not saying that . . ." Emma said, trying her best to open up to her best friends. "There's nothing more frustrating than a feeling you can't explain."

"I always want to know what's going on with you. Even if it's confusing."

"I know," Emma said, taking a deep breath. "I'm starting to think something is seriously wrong with me."

"Nothing is wrong with you," Layla insisted.

"I'm just . . . frustrated. All the time. And I don't know why . . ." Layla and Zoe nodded in support.

"Sounds like you need to get laid," Alex teased like only she could.

"Ha. Thanks," Emma said, finally cracking a real smile.

"Oh, look, there she is," Layla said, noticing Emma's grin.

And Emma felt more like herself, at least for a moment. And she *did* want to get laid. Or at least she still liked the idea of the pact.

Mostly, she liked that the girls were all in it together.

A few hours later, after Emma's last class ended, she walked into the yearbook room and found Nick working on the copy for the Senior Superlative page.

"Lookin' good," she said as she slid a chair up next to his computer.

"Just trying to keep up with you . . .

"So, what's up?" Nick finally asked after Emma had watched him work for a while. It was an innocent question, but Emma couldn't help but hear the weight of all her frustrations in it.

"Ohhhh . . ." Emma started, but before she could finish, she heard Alex's words from the lunch table echoing in her head: *sounds like you need to get laid.*

"*Ohhhh,*" Nick repeated back to her when she failed to say anything else. "I know you, Em, and I know *something*'s up, so tell me what's bothering you."

Emma shuffled through her thoughts and ultimately decided to play it safe: college applications and grades and the end of high school and all that.

"Yeah, it blows." Nick nodded as she explained. "Especially when you don't know what you're doing next."

Yep, Emma thought.

"My early application got rejected from New York University," he added after another moment.

"Oh, that sucks," Emma said before she could filter herself.

"Thanks," Nick chuckled.

"Sorry, I mean—"

"No, you're right. It does suck. And basically everyone I've told so far just wants to say sorry and talk to me about things happening for a reason and finding a bright side and all that. But what if I don't want a bright side? Maybe I just need to sit in the rain cloud for a little while, you know?"

"I do," Emma said, appreciating Nick's honesty.

"And what if things don't actually happen for a reason?" Nick asked, picking up steam. "What if all the time we spend trying

81

to make sense of the meaning behind things is actually just time that we're stupidly wasting because there is no meaning?"

Nick looked up from the screen, catching Emma's eyes. She couldn't seem to take them off him.

"I'm glad you get it," he said.

Emma nodded. She did get it. She totally, *totally* got it . . .

. . . just as long as she didn't have to define what "it" actually was.

"I feel like there's something more you're not telling me," Nick said intuitively. "I can practically *see* the thought bubbles floating up out of your hair. They're a little blurry, but . . ."

Emma shook her head.

"Really? I put all my lameness out on the table and you still don't want to share?"

Nick licked his lips.

They looked particularly kissable.

"It's not that I don't *want* to share . . . it's just . . ." Emma could hear Alex's words echoing in her head again: *sounds like you need to get laid*.

"Come. On," Nick pushed one more time. "What's on your mind?"

"Sex."

"Ha. Right." Emma had answered so quickly and without hesitation, it took Nick an extended moment to realize she wasn't kidding. "Wait, *actually*?" he asked, his eyes popping a little.

Emma focused her attention on her fingernails.

"Oh, all right. Well, I didn't mean . . ." Nick bumbled, still surprised by Emma's boldness. "You know, sex is just, like,

82

basically in the back of my head one hundred percent of the time while all my other thoughts attempt to exist in front of it."

Emma nodded, finally looking up long enough to make eye contact.

"Can you keep a secret?" she asked after an awkward pause. Emma knew it was against protocol to talk about the pact with anyone outside of the Crew, but telling Nick felt right. It was the only thing she'd been sure of in weeks. She knew he'd think it sounded cool. He'd probably say it was "awesome sauce" or something nerdy cute like that.

"Wow," Nick said after she brought him up to speed. "That's amazeballs."

"It is," Emma said, smiling at his nerdy cute word choice (and impressed with herself for calling it). "But now the girls are making a big deal about it."

"Your girls make a big deal about everything. No offense."

"None taken." That was Emma's point exactly. "But it's not, like, *binding* or anything," she clarified, "there's 'no pressure' in the pact, or whatever, but I don't want to get left behind . . . I'm sure I'll figure it out."

Nick nodded, maybe a little too enthusiastically. "Well. Hey . . ." he said with a little chuckle, ". . . if you end up needing any help with that . . ."

"Help with what?"

"The . . . the pact," Nick said, suddenly turning into a jumble of nerves. "You know, I've . . . I've had sex before. Not, um, a lot. But a few times. Probably a decent amount. And we've . . . you know, I think we kiss well, and, so, I just want you to know that I'm . . . I'm *here*. And if you ever need, like, a hand . . .

or . . . a penis . . ." Nick laughed before the word "penis" even came out of his mouth. ". . . I'm happy to help."

"Aw," Emma said, "no one's ever offered me their penis before."

"Ha. Yeah. So. That's all I'm saying: I'm here, and I *have* a penis . . . and that's, like, half of the sex thing right there, so . . ."

"Nick."

"Yeah?"

"Are you saying you want to have sex with me?"

"Mostly I'm saying, um, no pressure, but if . . . you know, if *you* wanted to have sex with *me* . . . then . . . Yes, Emma, that is totally what I'm saying. I would very much like to have sex with you." Nick finally cut the bullshit. "But now, looking at your face . . ."

"Yeah."

"Yeah, okay, so we can just forget I said that . . ."

"No," Emma said, feeling as calm and confident as she had in a very long time. "I mean *yeah* as in *yes*. I would very much like to have sex with you too."

149 Days Until Graduation . . .

Emma didn't believe it was actually going to happen . . .

. . . until she heard the doorbell ring.

Her parents had a date night every Saturday. They were always out of the house and on their way to the movies or some charity function or something by 7 p.m. at the latest. Nick had been over to her house at least a dozen times before, mostly to work on the yearbook or other assignments for class, and had met her parents quite a few times. But this time, since he was coming over for a very specific and completely non-school related purpose, Emma felt like it made sense to avoid any unnecessary or potentially awkward parental interaction by telling Nick to come over at 7.15 p.m.

The doorbell rang *exactly* on time.

She opened it. And he was standing there.

And that was it. It was going to happen.

Yesterday, before Emma had left the yearbook room, she'd told Nick that she would have the house to herself all night, and that he could come over and they could watch a movie or whatever. They both knew that the "or whatever" clearly meant "have sex", but it was just *a little bit* too awkward for

Emma to say out loud. It occurred to Emma that if it was too awkward to say out loud, then maybe it would also be too awkward to do in real life, but she decided not to dwell on that thought.

Especially since there were so many other more important questions to take its place, like: 1) Would it hurt? 2) Did she have a condom? And 3) When was the last time she'd shaved her legs?

The answers were: 1) Hopefully not. 2) Nick would bring one. And 3) Absolutely no clue.

Emma made sure to shower that afternoon and shave her legs, armpits and bikini line. Then she tried to figure out what to wear. Normally, she was a jeans and hoodie kind of girl, but that outfit seemed rather casual for the occasion. Emma reminded herself that one of the upsides of sleeping with Nick was that it *would* be casual.

But still.

There was a fine line between being laid-back and being lazy, and even though she definitely didn't want to obsess about this moment or stress about it . . . she still wanted it to be significant. Ultimately, Emma decided to just be herself and wear her favorite dark blue jeans and her softest, most perfectly worn-in purple hoodie. Something about it felt right, so Emma went with it.

Nick had apparently also showered and shaved since the last time Emma had seen him. She appreciated the effort, as well as the fact that he also seemed to be hanging out in the space between "casual" and "significant". He showed up wearing too much aftershave on his baby face and too much gel in his hair, but he had the perfect mixture of sweetness and nervous excitement in his smile.

"Are you hungry?" Emma asked as she led him inside her house. Mostly the question was just a way to fill the silence.

"I ate dinner at home, but if you're . . ."

"No, I ate too."

"Okay. Cool."

And then there was more silence.

"I was thinking I'd make some popcorn," Emma said after a moment.

"Yes!" Nick said a little more enthusiastically than he intended. Making popcorn seemed like a safe warm-up activity, and, since they'd technically talked about watching a movie, it made sense.

When the microwave beeped, Nick asked, "Beer?", interrupting another moment of silence. He didn't wait for an answer before pulling three Sam Adams Christmas Edition beer bottles out of his backpack. He explained that was all he could take from his dad's refrigerator in the garage without getting caught. "Hopefully they're still good or whatever."

Emma took a sip, realizing that she wouldn't be able to tell if they were good or not. Beer always just tasted like beer, and she didn't particularly like the taste, but the bubbles felt good on her tongue.

Emma and Nick took the popcorn and went into the den, where there was a big flat-screen TV. Apparently continuing the "we're here to watch a movie" narrative felt good for both of them. To that end, Emma's parents had a very extensive DVD collection. Her mom had taken all the discs out of their cases and arranged them alphabetically in oversized, three-ring binders. Nick started flipping through the first book, which contained all the A–G movies.

"What do you want to watch?" he asked before looking up and catching Emma's eyes. He paused. "You don't actually want to watch anything, do you?"

"No."

All Emma wanted to do was kiss him.

She wasn't sure exactly how many times they'd kissed before, but she knew they'd made out on three or maybe four different occasions, which made her wonder how many kisses there were in a make-out session: 100? 1,000? She had no clue. Emma realized that they'd never really planned any of their kisses before. They were always drunken or spontaneous, usually at a party in an upstairs bedroom or a guest bathroom or something. One time they made out for an hour on the trampoline in Layla's backyard. Emma couldn't help but think that out of all the hundreds (thousands?) of kisses they'd shared, this very next one would be the most important one of all . . .

And now, thinking about all that, all Emma really wanted to do was put her lips on Nick's lips and stick her tongue in his mouth.

That was it.

That was literally all she could think about, as if that one thought was filling her entire head and pushing everything else, all of her other thoughts, to the edges of her skull. The one thought was so strong and overwhelming that she was worried it might ultimately pop all the bubbles and somehow smush her brain up against her skull and flatten out her entire capacity to function.

"Do *you* actually want to watch something?" Emma asked back.

Nick shook his head no.

Clearly, Nick had come over (with beer and lube), planning to have sex. But judging by his quickening breath and the sweat on his forehead, he was still nervous about it . . . Weirdly, Emma *wasn't* nervous.

Excited? *Sure.*

Awkward as hell? *Always.*

But not *nervous.*

Emma tried to tell herself that was a good thing, and she almost managed to believe herself too. Then she looked at Nick again and absentmindedly licked her bottom lip. Suddenly, she was extremely aware of all the blood flowing through her body, especially the part that was pulsing past her hips and up between her legs like a not-so-subtle reminder that she had hormones and hands and boobs and a vagina, and they were all demanding attention, all at once.

Emma's lack of nervousness, combined with the foam at the bottom of her beer bottle and all the buzzing in her body, pushed her head forward until her lips slipped onto Nick's lips and her tongue pushed into his mouth, and finally all of the thinking stopped and the bubbles and biology just took over.

That first kiss, the newly crowned most "important one", was the perfect combination of sloppy and sweet. It was casual but also special at the same time . . .

. . . And the next ten, twenty, one-hundred-something kisses that followed soon after were similarly enjoyable. And the best past wasn't *just* that Nick knew exactly what to do with his tongue, which he did, or that he knew *exactly* how hard to press his lips against hers, which he also did, but that Nick's kisses seemed to have the ability to listen to her kisses. They knew when to speed up or slow down, pushing harder or softer, always perfectly in rhythm.

He pulled back, catching her eyes, as if to ask: *are we really doing this?*

Emma smiled back at him. *Yes, we are.*

The next two, five, ten-ish minutes felt like they happened all at once.

They moved off the floor and up onto the couch.

Nick's kisses moved to Emma's neck and then onto her chest.

Emma's bra came off.

Nick's pants slid down.

Her hands moved to his waist and then between his legs.

She thought she got up to turn off the lights, but, then again, Emma might've done that before any of the kissing even started . . .

Even as it was all happening, she couldn't quite remember the order. It all felt like a series of jump cuts, moving from one moment to the next. From fumbling to closeness to nakedness. It was all cold and hot and the whole thing made her want to giggle and cry at the same time, not because she was happy or sad, but because she was entirely, completely, one hundred percent in the moment. She was so *in* her body and *out* of her head – a rare feeling for a champion overthinker like Emma – that she did everything she could to embrace it. And she could tell that Nick was appreciating it as much as she was, in the same way she was, and that it was actually way more special than casual. And then Nick pulled away for a minute to put on a condom. He opened the packet with his teeth, rolled it on rather quickly, and then squeezed some lube on top of it. As Emma watched him from the couch, feeling naked and exposed, she was suddenly able to recognize the fact that he'd done this before.

Then he climbed back on top of her with a big, boyish grin on his face.

Emma made sure to take a mental picture of him, and the muddy-green glint in his eyes, his accidental half Mohawk, and the palpable glow that seemed to wrap around his entire face and his entire him . . .

And then, finally, without much fanfare, he slid inside her.

Pushed was actually probably a more accurate word.

It didn't hurt.

Not really.

Or exactly.

But it wasn't all that comfortable either.

"Are you okay?" he asked softly.

She nodded. She was.

Nick pulled out a little and then slid back in, slowly at first and then faster, finding a rhythm . . .

It was all sort of fast and mostly clumsy.

As it was happening, Emma kept having the urge to remind herself that it was, in fact, happening. *This*, she kept thinking. *This is sex, and this is real, and it's really happening.* She was losing her virginity right now, at this very moment. And then the moment ended, just as quickly and awkwardly and sincerely as it had begun. And that was it.

148 Days Until Graduation . . .

Layla did not expect it to happen quite so fast.

Obviously the whole point of the sex pact was to actually have sex, but Emma's sexie more or less came out of nowhere.

"What's a sexie?" Zoe asked as they waited in line at the Bigg Chill.

"An after-sex selfie," Layla explained.

"Oh, is that what we're calling it?" Alex asked.

Yes it was. Layla was very proud of her new word.

After Nick left Emma's house last night, not too long after they'd had sex, Emma snapped a picture of herself with all her postcoital afterglow and sent it to the Chat. She added a text message saying that she "nailed it".

The (not-yet-named) sexie, as well as Emma's text, came as a complete surprise to Alex and Layla and Zoe, who didn't even know Emma was *hanging out* with Nick, let alone sleeping with him. Once the girls realized that Emma wasn't joking, and that she had, in fact, just had sex with Nick – and therefore *lost her virginity* to Nick – they sent an avalanche of texts, full of expletives and exclamation marks and emojis. Layla was pretty sure they'd sent more texts per minute than ever before in the history of the Chat.

"I haven't even managed to *kiss* a boy since we started the pact, and Emma's already done." Zoe laughed.

"She's not done," Layla corrected.

"True," Emma admitted. "Still waiting on the fireworks . . ."

"Shhh," Zoe said as they reached the front of the line, where Bigg Chill Aaron was waiting to take their order.

"Why are we shhh-ing?" he whispered.

Surprising no one, his question made Zoe blush – and that was even before Layla honestly answered, "Fireworks."

Of course Bigg Chill Aaron didn't really know what that meant, but it made his lips curl up into a sideways smile. There was always something memorable about his smile, Layla thought. His bottom teeth were slightly crooked, not in a bad way, but just enough to be interesting, and he had a little scar right below his bottom lip. The girls had only known him since September, when he started his freshman year at UCLA, but they'd seen him every single Sunday since, and now he was by far their favorite Bigg Chill employee. They always made small talk as they placed their order, but the truth was, they didn't know all that much about him other than the fact that he grew up in Philadelphia, and he was always incredibly generous with his frozen yogurt and topping portions.

Today, everyone collectively decided to order large-sized cups instead of their usual small servings because Emma lost her virginity last night, and it was just that kind of day.

"Tell. Me. Everything," Layla insisted once the girls had settled at their usual table. "Like, did you like it?"

"I texted you most of it," Emma added more seriously.

"Yeah but I still have so many questions," Layla said. "Like, did you *like* it?"

"The sex?"

"Yes, duh, the sex."

"Yeah. It was good. I told you it was good. Why do you keep asking like you don't believe me?"

"Maybe it's the tone of your voice. It keeps creeping up at the end of your sentences."

"I don't know what to say about the 'creeping' but as far as the sex goes—"

"Ohmigod-I-still-can't-believe-you-had-sex," Zoe blurted out all at once, causing the whole table to erupt into another round of giggles. "I'm sorry," she said as soon as she could manage words again. "I'm just . . . it's, like . . . *wow.*"

"Yes, it's wow . . ." Layla confirmed playfully for Zoe, "but we're still trying to get the full mental picture of whether it was good or not."

"I swear it was good," Emma said, still laughing. "But I guess if you really want the full mental picture, maybe we should define what 'good' actually means. And possibly also 'it' too."

"Okay, so *it* would be sex," Layla offered.

"Yep. Nick put his penis inside my vagina."

"Ohmigod . . ." Zoe managed to put a napkin in front of her mouth so as not to spit rainbow sprinkles across the table. Her squirmy, sex-pact-related reflexes already seemed to be improving.

"And *good* means you liked it," Layla said in a way that made it sound more like a question than a statement.

"I *did* like it," Emma insisted, "but it wasn't . . ." She paused, as if she were trying to listen to her own thoughts. "I think the truth is that it didn't last very long. Like, it was happening, and I knew it was, but then it just sorta *ended*."

"Right. No fireworks," Layla said definitively.

"Guys, you can just say the word *or . . . org . . .*" Zoe melted into a puddle of giggles before she could get the entire word out of her mouth.

"Zoe, can *you* say the word *orgasm*?" Alex teased.

Zoe apparently could not.

She also felt red and rash-y and ridiculous, but even she had to admit that this was fun. The conversation made her feel mature even though she was still anxious and sweating in strange locations, like the back of her knees.

"Was Nick on top of you?" Layla said.

"As opposed to . . .?" Emma asked.

"I don't know. Like, some other position . . .?"

"Ha. No," Emma said quickly. "We barely got through *one* position . . . I mean, we got *through* it, but then he finished and that was basically it."

"Hmmm," Layla said, looking a little bit like an inflated balloon.

"Also, it got a little messy, so I had to deal with that afterwards," Emma explained. "We probably should've just put a towel down on the couch. I had to put one of the cushion slipcovers in the washing machine. It got wet . . ."

"Oh, from the . . .?" Zoe started to ask before realizing she had no clue how to even finish the question.

"Didn't you use a condom?" Layla asked.

"We did, but there's, like, fluid," Emma tried to explain. "*You* get wet and so that's . . . it gets all over. And there was a little blood, too," she added. "Not a lot, but . . ."

"So it *did* hurt?" Layla asked.

"Not really. 'Hurt' isn't the right word . . . it's hard to explain. Sorry, I keep saying that, but maybe it's just something you have to do to totally understand."

Zoe wished she understood a little bit better, but the only way to do that really did seem to be to do it – and that definitely wasn't happening yet.

Wow.

Did Zoe really just think about herself and also about sex and *also* about all of it actually happening, but just not "yet"?

She did. She was making more progress than she thought.

Emma began to notice there was something distant about Alex.

As the other girls chatted and laughed, Alex seemed more focused on how many chocolate-covered gummy bears she could pile on her spoon at once. Emma frowned but decided not to say anything.

"So then what happened afterwards?" Layla asked, still curious.

"First I cleaned up, and then we thought about watching a movie, but we never really picked one, so Nick went home. I called my sister, Heather, 'cause she's the oldest, and I knew she'd be all excited, which she was . . . but then she got a little too sentimental, and then she told me that I had to pee *immediately* and then shower, so I did both things . . ." And then Emma explained that she had been left alone with all of her thoughts and feelings, but they were all jumbled and cluttered with hormones and questions that she wasn't sure she would ever be able to recall in the future. She felt a thousand feelings she just couldn't define, which is what led her to snap the first sexie. "Also, I wanted to share the moment with all of you."

"I can't wait to see the next three sexies," Layla said.

"The next two, technically," Zoe clarified. "Alex would've had to have taken hers already. At camp."

"You didn't, did you?" Layla asked, only half-joking.

"No," Alex said quickly. "No cell phones . . ."

"Right, duh. Well, that's too bad. But you can take one this time."

"Sure . . ." Alex said.

Now that they'd both had sex, Emma thought she understood Alex a little better than before. But even though Alex forced a smile back at her, Emma got the sense that something wasn't right, though she didn't press her. She wasn't going to make Alex explain herself, but Emma was pretty certain there was something more Alex wanted – or even needed – to say.

Alex was "technically, actually, completely" still a virgin.

She said it to Layla as plainly as she possibly could, but Layla seemed to be having trouble wrapping her head around this new information.

"Wait, wait, wait," Layla said, rubbing her forehead. "You're saying you did *not* actually have sex with Cameron at sleep-away camp last summer?"

"Correct. I did not," Alex confirmed. She rolled over onto her stomach, propping herself up on her elbows, so she could get a better look at Layla. The two girls were lying side by side on Layla's trampoline, and Alex felt like she needed to see Layla's face in order to finish the conversation. She wanted to make sure that Layla understood.

"Okay," Layla said. "But here's the bump for me . . ."

"Bump away," Alex said, bracing herself.

"If you didn't do it at sleep-away camp, then why did you come home and tell us that you did?"

"I didn't. I mean, *technically* I didn't."

"Why do you keep saying *technically*?"

"Because . . . well . . ." Alex couldn't seem to find the right words to explain. Maybe the problem was that she wasn't even sure she had the right answer.

"Hey, if it makes you feel better . . ." Layla started.

"Nothing is making me feel better," Alex said sharply.

"Don't get pissy. You're the one who's been lying to all of us."

Ugghhhh.

The last thing Alex wanted to do was lie, but the truth felt complicated.

Most simply, she was trying to protect Cameron.

And maybe she was trying to protect herself, too.

At the very least she wanted to save them from the embarrassment of failure, but now, looking at Layla and seeing the hurt in her eyes, it just felt like Alex's best intentions had backfired.

"Can we maybe pretend I didn't say anything?" Alex asked.

"Nope."

Alex could see that Layla and her half smile were doing the best they could not to get mad. Alex smiled back at Layla, but she still didn't know quite what to say, so she just kept on smiling. And then she remembered that this whole mess had started with that little Mona Lisa smile in the first place. It's what made the girls in her cabin jump to conclusions. They all knew that she had snuck out in the middle of the night to meet Cameron at make-out ledge. And, because there is no such thing as a secret at sleep-away camp, they knew she was planning to have sex with him. But, as Alex's mom liked to say, "Man plans and god laughs". It was her way of explaining that expectations can often lead to disappointments. Alex had heard her mom use the expression hundreds of times before, but she hadn't really understood what it meant until that night with Cameron on make-out ledge.

They had planned to have sex.

They didn't.

But then, the next morning, Alex had just simply smiled. Understandably, all the girls in her cabin had just assumed that meant she'd sealed the deal.

Alex should've spoken up right there and then. She should've just said, "No, we did not have sex. Not technically. Not actually. Not completely. Not at all."

But she didn't.

Alex knew that if she did, the girls would inevitably have asked why. And then she would've had to tell them that even though she wanted to do it and Cameron wanted to do it, and even though they tried – and tried and tried – to make it work, they simply *couldn't*.

Now, all these months – and many other make-out sessions – later, Alex understood that there simply hadn't been enough foreplay. Now she knew that attempting to go from zero to "doing it" in almost no time for the very first time on a chilly summer night was a recipe for disaster, but in the moment the whole thing had just made Alex feel like a failure. And there was nothing – *nothing* – Alex hated more than failing, especially when it was her fault.

And that's exactly what the whole thing felt like: her fault.

Like she wasn't attractive enough or desirable enough or good enough. Cameron tried so hard to reassure her that wasn't the case – she was perfect, he told her, everything about her was perfect – but Alex didn't believe him. She could still feel the tears from that night welling up in her eyes, and her Converse high-tops sinking into the grass, and the goosebumps on her arms, and the lump in her throat. She could still feel the sharp rocks against her back, and the lump in her throat, and Cameron pushing up against her with his pants and boxers hanging down around his ankles. And when their best-laid "get laid" plan fell apart, it really did feel like the kind of thing that god or mean girls or just about anyone might laugh at. It was awful.

"What happened, Al?" Layla asked softly, pulling Alex out of her head.

"You want the full mental picture?" Alex managed to ask.

Of course Layla *always* wanted the full mental picture.

And so Alex told her.

Everything.

She told her about that cold night and Cameron's warm breath, about the sharp rocks and the soft grass and her sinking sneakers and the way Cameron's eyes glowed in the dark.

"And then, after all of that . . . he couldn't get it in."

"Is it really that hard?" Layla asked.

"Well, it is if he can't *stay* hard . . ." Alex explained, using her right pointer finger to demonstrate the problem.

"Ohhhhh, okay," Layla said, finally wrapping her head around the mechanics. She let out a big laugh.

Alex laughed too.

It felt good.

And then it got quiet again.

"But that's camp," Layla said softly. "What about us?"

Alex had known that question was coming.

"I guess . . ." Alex said, trying to explain it to Layla and maybe also to herself at the same time, ". . . by the time I got home, Emma had already seen some stupid posts online from the camp girls, and then you and Zoe just couldn't stop giggling. And you were all asking what it felt like to do it, and the thing was . . . it basically felt like we *had* done it. We decided to. And I *wanted* to. And . . . I let him try. So. If he *could've*, we would've. And the more I thought about it, the more it felt like saying we didn't do it was just as much of a lie as saying that we did."

"So *technically* you're a virgin, but it feels like there's a 'but' at the end of that sentence," Layla said, still wrapping her head around it.

"Yeah. I know it sounds strange, but I had a feeling you'd understand."

"It's different, obviously, but I feel like that with Logan sometimes too," Layla said after a bit of a moment. "Like, we've thought about having sex so much and talked about it so many times that it almost feels like we've done it already. Not *actually*, of course, but . . . sometimes I find myself wondering, what's the real difference, you know?"

"I do know. But I think the 'real difference' might actually be everything."

147 Days Until Graduation . . .

Emma always saw things more clearly in the darkroom.

The irony wasn't lost on her.

The whole point of a darkroom was to give pictures the time and space to develop. It occurred to Emma that high school, in theory, was sort of like a darkroom for teenagers, a time to find out who you really were, and a space to turn into the kind of adult you were supposed to be. Or something.

The problem, Emma realized, was that in order to turn into the person you wanted to be, you had to know who that person was. And how could you know without getting there? It was a vicious circle of epic proportions. It was impossible to know what had to come first. All Emma knew was that there were only about five months left of senior year, and she felt further away from figuring herself out now than she did on the first day of high school.

Everyone in Emma's life was expecting her to be fully developed already. They wanted superlatives. They wanted answers. They wanted college acceptances. Basically, everyone wanted fireworks. But the process of getting there, of lighting the fuse or whatever it was that made the fire actually work, seemed to be undervalued or maybe even lost completely.

Emma was so deep in her own thoughts that it took her a second to realize that someone was knocking on the darkroom door.

"Em?" Nick called from outside. "You still here?"

"I'm here, yeah," Emma responded. "One sec!"

Emma finished developing her last photo, hanging it on the line to dry, and then told Nick it was safe to come in. Maybe it was because (almost literally) the last time she'd been alone with him he'd (*actually* literally) been inside of her, but when he walked in, there seemed to be something even more adorable than usual about Nick's lips and his bed-head hair and his sweet, open expression.

The truth was that Emma didn't need any more words.

She could feel Nick's attraction from across the room, and all she wanted to do was feel all of him again. She stepped forward, pulling him close and pushing her lips onto his. The kiss was a big, sloppy kiss, all hormones and anticipation. Nick kissed Emma back with just as much intensity and suddenly his hands were everywhere. On her chest. And then unbuttoning her shirt. Her hands rushed to keep up, moving to his zipper and then into his boxers.

Emma didn't know how long they'd been kissing before Nick suddenly pulled back just long enough to say the word "yes".

It was a statement kind of question.

Emma nodded *definitely* yes.

And so Nick pulled her back in closer, grabbing her thighs and lifting her up to sit on the counter. He pulled his jeans and boxers down to the floor as Emma slid her own cords and underwear off, too. She was thankful she was wearing a simple black thong and not a pair of grannie panties or something with polka dots or the days of the week or any of the other equally embarrassing options that were currently sitting in her underwear drawer.

"You good?" Nick asked as he pulled a condom out of his pocket and started to roll it on.

"Yeah," Emma said, her whole body tingling. "You?"

"Yeahhhh," Nick said like an exhale.

"You're adorable," she said.

"And you're sexy as hell."

No one had ever said that to Emma before. She mostly thought of herself as weird. Or smart. Or maybe pretty if she was in a particularly good mood. But sexy? That was new.

"Thank you," she said.

"No, thank *you*," Nick chuckled and then took a step towards Emma.

With Emma sitting on the edge of the counter, and Nick standing in front of her, their hips were at exactly the same height. Nick pushed inside of her with far more confidence than he had before. Everything seemed to fit better the second time around . . . It maybe even felt good, Emma thought. But the fact that she had to *think* about the way it felt and also that her thoughts still included the word "maybe" made her wonder if she had no clue what "good" actually felt like . . .

When it was over, Nick slid down onto the floor. He was close enough that she could see the little beads of sweat on his forehead, his chest rising and falling with each heavy breath. Close enough that she could tell he was still processing what had just happened. She liked everything about the way he looked right now, all honest and vulnerable. All she wanted to do was take a picture of him. She probably would've, too, if her camera weren't so far out of reach and his pants weren't still down around his ankles.

She didn't want to take *that* kind of picture.

"You still good?" Nick asked again, looking up at her.

Emma nodded, noting his use of the word *good*. "You?"

"Ye-ah," Nick said quickly.

Emma could hear the implied "duh" in his voice. He took off the condom, concealing it inside of a paper towel before dropping it into the nearby trash can. Nick leaned forward, just enough to pull his boxers back on and his pants, too. But then it seemed to occur to him that he may have forgotten something.

"Ohhh," he said, with another implied "duh" afterwards.

He slid over to the counter where Emma was still sitting and rocked up onto his knees. His head was now exactly the same height as Emma's waist.

"What are you doing?" Emma asked, even though she was *pretty* sure she already knew the answer.

"I want you to . . . finish." For a brief moment, as the "f" of the word "finish" started to come out of his mouth, Emma thought he might be saying the word "firework", and she had to bite down on her lip to keep from laughing. "Unless you don't, um, want to?" Nick asked, misreading her lip-biting for hesitation.

"No. I . . . I do," Emma said softly but quickly, as if she were trying to take up as little space as possible with her words.

And she really did want to, but she must've looked nervous because Nick asked if she trusted him. And she did. And she told him that she did. And then he looked up at her with his big brown eyes, holding her gaze as he pulled her underwear back down to her ankles.

"I'm gonna . . . kiss you," he added, as if to make sure there wouldn't be any confusion.

Emma nodded again, this time with a smile.

Maybe that's what Nick had been waiting for.

He smiled back and then leaned forward into Emma's legs. *Between* her legs. And she felt his tongue against her body. *Inside* her body. And that definitely felt good – no question. Just like there was no question that her entire face was turning bright red, Zoe style. And she was sure her whole face got even redder as she thought about where *Nick*'s face was and exactly what he was doing with it – and also with his lips and his tongue and then also his fingers . . . And all of it together, all of it at the same time, felt so good that Emma would not have been surprised if her entire body somehow suddenly turned red.

After a minute or two, Nick pulled back. His face was flushed and his lips were slightly wet. "You okay?"

"Yeah. Why? Do I not *seem* okay?"

"No, no, you do," Nick assured her.

What Emma really wanted to ask was if she looked weird or smelled weird or tasted weird or anything. She wanted to ask if any of her *parts* measured up to any other parts that Nick might have seen or smelled or tasted before. But that would've been far too much talking and way too many questions for this moment.

Still, Emma couldn't keep the words "No one's ever . . ." from escaping from her lips.

Nick raised an eyebrow as he waited for Emma to finish her sentence.

"This is my . . . I mean, no one's ever done what you're doing before. I just . . . I want you to know that . . ."

"That's cool," Nick said sweetly. "I sorta figured."

Emma wanted to ask him *why* he "sorta figured" and also a dozen other anxious questions, but before she could, Nick found her eyes again and simply said, "Thanks."

"For telling you?" she asked.

"For letting me."

Then he leaned into her again . . .

. . . and she leaned back against the wall, totally in the moment with Nick and his tongue and all of her feelings . . .

. . . and it was *good*.

And then pretty soon it was even better than that.

And then . . . it was everything.

So.

Many.

Fireworks.

Layla had never blushed at a text message before.

She'd laughed at them.

She'd cried at them.

She'd gotten nervous and excited and maybe even turned on by them.

But she'd never actually *blushed* . . . until she saw Emma's texts about Nick's tongue and the massive fireworks display they'd set off in the darkroom this afternoon.

Layla was already sitting at the dinner table when Emma texted the Chat. Her little sister, Maxine, was lobbying their mom for a spring-break trip to the beach. Her little brother, Avery, was discussing the incredibly important and rapidly approaching fantasy basketball trade deadline with their father. And Layla did everything she possibly could not to choke on the piece of mustard chicken that was already in her mouth. She coughed and coughed, causing enough mild alarm to be excused from the table.

She ran upstairs and closed her bedroom door, scrolling back through the Chat as quickly as she could. There were already dozens of old texts to read, but new texts from Emma and Alex and even Zoe kept pouring in too.

WAIT, Layla texted. *I want to hear all of this . . .*

SCROLL UP, Alex texted.

No, no, I want to HEAR it. Trampoline in ten?!?

Layla knew it was a long shot to get the whole crew together in person after dinner on a school night – they all had rules and curfews and all that – but she figured it was worth asking.

Zoe said her parents had already turned on their alarm, which meant that unless she wanted to pull a Joey and climb out her window and down the tree, she was stuck inside for the night. Alex said her parents were still out to dinner, which meant she was hanging with Max. Emma texted that she *totally woulddddddd* come over, but she was about to put on her pajamas.

110

Okayyyyyyy, Layla texted. *Do I have to mention that there are only so many more times we're actually going to be ABLE to all meet in person before the-day-that-hurts-Emma's-heart?*

NOT UNLESS YOU WANT ME TO FREAK OUT AND HAVE A PANIC ATTACK, Emma texted back all in capital letters.

A panic attack AND an orgasm seems like a lot for one day, Layla teased.

HAHAHA, Emma texted. *Jealous?* she added.

YES, Alex responded immediately.

It's fine, Emma texted. *I've got you and your mental picture. OH and, Layla, now I've even got your progress report: sex twice, once with an orgasm.*

OMG, Zoe texted.

Now you all need to get your shit together . . .

TRYING, Layla texted.

What happened to no pressure?! Zoe texted.

There's still no pressure, Emma teased. *You're all just missing out . . .*

Oh now who's cocky! Alex texted.

Thank you, Emma. Thank you so much, Zoe added.

You're welcome. But seriously, now what do I do?

Do it again. Do it better, Layla texted.

HA! That's basically what you said when there weren't any fireworks.

Guess that's how it works. You do it again when it's good and you do it again when it's not as good, Layla texted, feeling like there must be a metaphor in there somewhere.

I told you sex was like pizza, Zoe managed to chime in.

Layla actually laughed out loud at her phone screen. The texts paused for a moment, and Layla was pretty sure everyone else was laughing, too.

Zoe, that still makes no sense, Layla texted.

IT ACTUALLY MAKES SO MUCH SENSE.

Okay, Layla texted. *Em, start from the beginning . . . Mental picture – ready, go.*

All right. Emma obliged. *So. I was in the darkroom after school . . .*

I like this already, Alex texted.

Ohmigod.

Guys. Let Emma type.

And they did. And she did. She described all the details, especially the fireworks – and the way they *felt . . .*

Is this turning anyone else on? Layla finally had to ask, disobeying her own instructions to let Emma type. She couldn't help it. It was all too good.

YESSS, Alex texted back quickly.

Really?! Zoe texted. *Ohmigod.*

OHMIGOD YES, ZOE, Alex teased.

Layla's face hurt from smiling and her chest hurt from laughing and her heart felt full and her whole body felt warm . . .

I couldn't possibly love you more, Layla texted. *ALL OF YOU.*

SAME, Alex and Emma texted back at exactly the same time, one right after the other. It looked like Zoe had maybe also tried to text the word "same" at the exact same time, but it ended up showing up in the Chat as SMALL instead.

Small what, Zo? Layla asked, knowing she was being an asshole.

Damn autocorrect, Zoe texted. Then she tried again: *SMAEE.* And again: *SEMA.* And one more stupid time: *SMALL.*

Layla couldn't stop laughing as she thought about Zoe's adorable little fingers struggling with the touchscreen keys.

Ohmigod . . . Whatever, Zoe texted. *I told you, this keyboard sucks and autocorrect hates me. At least you all love me . . .*

THE MOST, Layla, Alex and Emma all texted at the same time.

145 Days Until Graduation . . .

Emma sat at her usual computer in the yearbook room.

She was the first one there, and the rest of the computers were still unoccupied.

It wasn't like Emma to be early – ever – but she'd woken up a full hour before her alarm clock this morning. Apparently Emma still couldn't sleep, but at least now it was from excitement and contentedness and not fear.

"Hey." Savannah suddenly appeared in the doorway.

"Hey . . ." Emma replied. Something about the look on Savannah's face told her to proceed with caution.

"Heard you had a good night last night. Or afternoon maybe."

"You *heard*?"

"Well, *over*heard. I was being nosy," Savannah said as she sat down at the computer next to Emma's and flipped open her notebook.

"Uh-oh. Why do I feel like I'm not gonna like this?"

"Sure *sounded* like you liked it," Savannah teased a little, knowing it would get under Emma's skin.

"You're the worst. Listening to gossip." Emma smiled, shaking her head. She liked Savannah's playful demeanor, but she didn't like the sinking feeling that Nick was spreading rumors about her.

"Not gossip, exactly," Savannah clarified. "His locker's near mine, so I just heard him talking to a couple of his friends."

"About *me*?"

"Well, yeah. Specifically you and him . . . in the darkroom."

"Oh god," Emma said, burying her head in her hands. "I'm gonna die . . ."

"Don't die. He said you were great . . ."

"Too late, I'm already dead."

"No. Stop. Come back. That's not a direct quote – and I swear I only listened for a minute or two—"

"A minute or two? How long was he talking about me?" Emma asked, mostly embarrassed but maybe the littlest bit proud too. "Why is he telling people?"

"Because he's excited. You told your girls, didn't you?"

"Yeah, but that's different."

"Is it?"

"I tell them everything."

"Maybe he tells his boys everything too."

"That's not exactly making me feel better."

"I'm just saying, I don't think we can blame him for bragging about you . . . You're way out of his league."

"Thank you," Emma said with a laugh. That *sounded* like a compliment, but she wasn't entirely sure.

"You're welcome." Savannah laughed back. "Whatever. Good for you."

"Yeah." Emma nodded. It *was* good. And she couldn't help but add, "It was my first time. Well, my *second* time, but the first one was with Nick too, and it was just this past Saturday, so . . ." Emma could feel the blood rushing into her cheeks. She pushed her hair behind her ears just to give herself something to do.

"Lucky guy . . ." Savannah said, with a strange sort of bite in her voice.

Emma couldn't help but think Savannah sounded a little . . . *jealous*.

Layla could feel Logan's phone buzzing in his pocket.

Layla and Logan were in the midst of a particularly heated afternoon make-out session. They'd gone off campus during their common free period to get lunch at the sushi restaurant at the bottom of the canyon near school. Off-campus privileges were one of the biggest perks of being a senior, and Logan and Layla liked to take full advantage, but today Logan's phone just would not stop buzzing – and it was killing Layla's buzz.

"Do you need to answer that?"

"Answer what?" Logan managed to ask without taking his tongue out of Layla's mouth. Layla shook her head and refocused her attention on their kisses . . .

. . . until another buzz interrupted them.

And then another.

Layla couldn't take it anymore. They were in the back seat of his car, and she was sitting on his lap. His phone was in his front pocket and the buzzing was too close for comfort.

"It's nothing," he insisted.

But before they could resume their kisses, another flurry of text messages came pouring in.

"Logan. Really. I need that to stop," she said, squirming off of him.

"You don't like the vibrations?" Logan teased.

"I can only get so excited knowing they're from Vanessa," Layla grumbled.

"How do you know it's her?" Logan asked as his phone buzzed yet again.

"*Seriously*? There'd better be a huge fire or something . . ."

"No fire, she's just—"

"Oh, so it *is* her?" Layla said, thoroughly annoyed but also vindicated.

"They're printing the posters for the food drive," Logan explained, "and they can't decide if they should be vertical or horizontal, but Vanessa wants it to be in the shape of a can. She needs approval from the school board."

"Is that your problem?"

"Not exactly, but I know what they'll be expecting. Layla, I don't know if you're aware, but I'm president of the *entire* student body . . ."

"Are you trying to tell me you're important or something?"

"*Very* important." Logan smiled, flashing that dimple of his, but Layla still shook her head, not quite ready to let the Vanessa thing go. "*Really?* Don't be mad at Vanessa. It's my fault. I offered to help."

And there it was.

Of course he had offered to help her. Logan was way too nice like that. He was always extra-offering and over-extending himself, which was all fine and good for friends and teachers or whatever, but not for Vanessa.

117

Layla knew that Vanessa didn't want his help.

She wanted *him*.

"Look. It's off." Logan held up his phone for Layla to see. "Okay?"

Layla nodded even though she honestly didn't *feel* okay.

And then they returned to making out in the back seat of Logan's car, but Layla couldn't stop thinking about Vanessa – and, even worse, she couldn't stop thinking that Logan might still be thinking about Vanessa, too.

Alex had apologized to Zoe almost a hundred times.

She didn't know what else to say.

"There's nothing *to* say," Zoe said sharply, poking her California sushi roll with a chopstick.

Alex looked over at Emma, who had just joined them and was now biting into a slice of pizza. She didn't seem to be nearly as upset as Zoe was. Alex had called both of the girls last night and told them the truth about camp and her virgin status. She'd been planning on telling them at school, but then after Emma's fireworks and all the text messages that followed, she knew she couldn't wait any longer.

Again, Alex had planned and god had laughed. Luckily, Emma had laughed a little bit too when Alex told her.

"You're telling me that *I* was actually the first one of us to lose her virginity? I totally would've lost that bet," Emma had said.

And then Alex apologized a few (dozen) more times, and Emma accepted all of her apologies, and the whole phone call was more or less painless.

Zoe, on the other hand, didn't take the news nearly as well. Not even close.

The first problem was that Zoe was hoping for a call from Dylan that still hadn't materialized, so, admittedly, she was in a bit of a mood when Alex called. The second problem was that she was confused as to why Alex was calling in the first place. Alex said it just wasn't a text-message kind of conversation. Honestly, it wasn't really for a phone conversation either – more of an in-person sort of thing – but it was already past Alex's curfew, and she didn't want to wait until morning now that Emma had already had sex twice and orgasmed once.

Zoe wasn't sure what Emma's orgasms had to do with anything.

But.

Before she could ask, Alex launched into a long apology-slash-explanation that started with: "I did not have sex at sleep-away camp."

Alex explained that it was all just a misunderstanding. She laid out the technical difficulties, said she was just trying to protect Cameron and something about a "Mona Lisa smile" or whatever, and then finished by adding that sometimes the truth feels more like a lie than an actual lie.

Zoe could tell that the whole story seemed to make sense in Alex's head.

But to Zoe, it mostly sounded more or less like bullshit.

Zoe didn't care about the other girls at camp. And she didn't really care about Cameron's feelings. Or Alex's ego. Or any of that. Zoe cared about the Crew. And their friendship. And the

119

balance that existed between the four of them. And now she knew that Alex had been lying to them for *years*.

Alex said she was sorry.

And all Zoe could say was "all right".

And then Dylan was finally actually calling, so Zoe got off the phone with Alex pretty quickly.

She had said that she didn't want to talk about it anymore, but now she and Emma were sitting at lunch with Alex, while Layla was off campus with Logan, and Alex wouldn't leave the whole thing alone.

"I just wish you weren't mad at me," Alex said, trying not to get frustrated.

"I'm not mad—"

"Or hurt. Or whatever you are—"

"I don't know what I am!" Zoe said more loudly than she expected. "You lied to all of us for two years. I think I should get more than twenty hours to process the situation."

"I swear I never meant to lie to you," Alex said after a bit of silence. "I just need you to know that."

"That's fine. And I know that. But that's still what ended up happening," Zoe said sharply. "I spent the past two years believing something that wasn't true. We all did. Whatever you actually meant to do, that feels shitty to me now."

"I'm sorry," Alex said more softly this time. "But it was . . . a year and a half."

"What?"

"Camp was only a year and a half ago. Not two years."

"Ohmigod, *really*? *That*'s what you want to fight about?"

"I don't want to fight about anything!"

"Cool. I'm glad that *now* you're worried about the accuracy of your story—"

"Jesus, Zoe, I'm sorry! I should've told you what really happened as soon as it really didn't happen, but I can't exactly go back and change it now. And I know it sucks, but honestly, what happened with Cameron sucks for me too. I have these dreams about it, over and over, and they make me feel shitty every single time . . . but I guess I just figured there'd be another boy right away, and it would happen with him for real, and then the camp thing just wouldn't matter—"

"Of course it matters!" Zoe said, raising her voice. She could see that Alex wasn't expecting such a big response from her, but she couldn't help but get emotional. "*What?* Do you want me to say I wouldn't care if I spent for ever thinking you lost your virginity to someone when you actually didn't? I care about everything that happens to you, Alex. And to Emma. And Layla. What you eat for lunch. What color your running shoes are. What kind of punctuation you use at the end of your text messages. Whatever it is, whatever you do . . . as long as it's about you, I care. You don't think I'd care about something as important as the first time you had sex?"

"No, I know you would," Alex said quietly. "Look, I've spent a lot of time since that night wondering why it didn't *actually* happen with Cameron. And maybe the truth is it didn't happen for me then so that it could happen for me now with all of you . . . Maybe we were always supposed to do this together."

"But not *together* together . . ."

"You know what I mean."

Of course Zoe knew what she meant.

And the more she thought about it, the more she thought Alex might be right. Maybe they *were* supposed to do this together.

So far that really was Zoe's favorite part.

144 Days Until Graduation . . .

Layla and Zoe stood at their lockers, filling their backpacks.

It was Thursday afternoon, and Layla was going to be late for the student council meeting, and Zoe should've been at music rehearsal five minutes ago.

The girls were rushing, but Layla still managed to notice a group of senior boys walking down the hallway. They were loud and impossible to ignore. Right in the middle was Dylan. Layla nudged Zoe and nodded in his direction. She figured Zoe would be happy to see him, but instead she got shy and dropped her eyes down to her shoelaces. Layla looked back at Dylan and then back to Zoe again, feeling like she was watching the moment unfold in some sort of slow motion, and she couldn't help but wonder if he was even going to say hi to Zoe, let alone stop and actually have a conversation with her.

Dylan managed a sideways "hey" as he walked past, but didn't even break his stride. It was lame, as if he'd hurled the stupid little word across the hallway.

Zoe nodded back, along with a nervous little half wave, which was similarly lame.

"What was *that*?" Layla could feel the frown forming on her face.

"Hmm?" Zoe asked, playing dumb. She was still looking down at her feet, seemingly consumed by the ugly tile pattern on the floor.

"Is Dylan always like that at school?"

"Like what?" Zoe clearly wasn't going to make this easy on Layla.

"I don't know . . . Like, you don't actually exist?"

The words came out of Layla's mouth before she fully realized how mean they must've sounded.

"No, it's . . . I think we just work best on the phone," Zoe said honestly.

Layla believed that *Zoe* believed that, and it might even be true too, but Layla didn't like it. Not one bit.

"I know you all think that I must like him or he must like me since we spend all that time talking at night, but you can see it's just . . ." Zoe gestured down the hallway. "It's just not like that."

Layla could hear a dozen little emotional cracks in Zoe's voice. It wasn't worth pushing any harder, and Layla made a mental note to tell Alex and Emma to back off about the Zoe and Dylan stuff, too. They all gave her a hard time about their phonefalls, but as long as Zoe was being honest about what they wanted, Layla was going to support her in that.

Layla and Zoe closed their lockers and walked down the hall together. As they rounded a corner, Layla was thrilled to see that Austin was waiting for Zoe at the entrance to the theater. Layla caught a glimpse of Zoe's face lighting up. It was absolutely adorable. The only thing even more adorable was that Layla could see the very same glow on Austin's face, too.

141 Days Until Graduation . . .

Alex decided that the blotchy bruise on Zoe's neck was fifty shades of purple.

"I just do not understand the point of a hickey," she insisted.

Zoe and Austin had gone on their second date last night, and apparently there had been a lot of sucking involved.

"Oh, me neither," Emma agreed, "but then I also kind of like that there is no point . . ."

"You would . . ." Alex laughed. "But, like, seriously, *kiss* my neck if you want to, sure, but why the sucking? Or if a boy really wants to suck on something I can think of at least twenty other body parts that would appreciate it so much more . . ."

"*Twenty?*" Zoe squeaked, clearly trying to wrap her head around that number.

Layla pressed Zoe for more details about her date with Austin. They had gone to dinner and a movie at the Grove. He paid. *And* held her hand all night.

But Zoe said that the best part happened on their way back to Austin's car. (The girls were all relieved to hear that they had ditched the dad chaperone this time around.) Zoe and Austin had ridden all the way up to the top floor of the parking garage, which had an absolutely magnificent view of the city. Austin wanted to be a lighting designer, so he appreciated a view like that more than most people. And as they stood up there together with his hands wrapped around her waist, he leaned down and asked if she wanted to be his girlfriend.

"Aw," Layla said in her very Layla way.

"Look at that . . . Zoe has a boyfriend!" Alex smiled.

Zoe also had a happy glow on her face.

The girls were all thrilled to see it.

"How about you, Layla?" Emma asked. "Where's *your* progress report?"

Layla was hoping someone might ask.

She didn't exactly have any *progress*, but there was a bit of a report.

"Well, I actually . . . I attempted to, um . . ." Layla swirled her spoon in her froyo and then realized that the visual might actually be a better way to communicate this.

Zoe and Emma didn't seem to understand, but Alex got the message loud and clear.

"You *masturbated*?" Alex asked way, way too loudly.

"Aaaaand we're totally in public right now . . ." Zoe whispered.

"Whatever. She didn't *masturbate* in public."

Emma and Layla laughed.

Zoe turned chartreuse.

"How was it?" Alex continued, pressing Layla for details.

"I don't know," Layla admitted, "and, honestly, I feel like a loser saying this, but it's almost confusing. Like, what am I even supposed to really do?"

"You . . . well, you touch yourself," Alex said matter-of-factly.

"Yeah. *That* I understand, but . . . where? I mean where *exactly*?"

"That's *exactly* what you have to figure out," Alex explained.

"It's just sort of wherever feels good," Emma offered more helpfully.

"Okay, but that doesn't really help me," Zoe piped up. "Like, rubbing my *shoulder* feels good."

"You're not gonna get off from touching your shoulder," Alex snickered.

"*Clearly*, but that's why I agree that it's confusing." Zoe returned her attention to her frozen yogurt, but then felt the need to add, "Not that I've tried . . ."

"Just keep it simple," Alex said. "Touch your boobs, vagina, butt."

"Butt? What? Do you touch your butt?" Zoe squeaked, looking to Emma.

"No," Emma laughed.

"For the record, me neither," Alex said. "I'm just saying: erogenous zones."

"I don't even know what that means," Zoe admitted.

"An area of the body that has heightened sensitivity," Layla said, explaining she read an article about it in the Sex Doc. "It said to mostly focus on the clitoris." Layla realized that might've been the first time she'd ever said "clitoris" out loud, and officially decided it was the most awkward-sounding word in her vocabulary.

"Sounds awkward . . . but feels *amazing*," Emma whispered.

"Yeah . . ." Layla grinned. "Apparently there are all these different techniques, like, for rubbing or stroking or tapping or whatever . . ."

"Tapping?" Zoe asked.

"Yeah, I dunno . . ." Basically, Layla had concluded that the masturbation options were endless and all of it was nearly intimidating enough to stop her from trying before she'd even gotten started . . . But she finally managed to get over her fear of embarrassing herself *in front of herself* and attempted to masturbate.

But . . .

No fireworks.

"Well, A for effort," Emma laughed.

"Honestly, probably more like a C for effort," Layla laughed back. Another article Layla read said it might take *weeks* of experimentation before even getting close to fireworks, and that it was practical to allow about thirty to forty minutes per session so as not to feel rushed.

"Ohmigod." Zoe squirmed.

Layla laughed. She was impressed at how long Zoe had managed to last without squirming.

"Zoe, I'm sure you'd figure it out if you tried," Alex said sincerely.

"It's really just like pizza," Emma said, causing everyone to laugh.

"No, pizza is way less confusing." Zoe giggled.

"Yes – there are so many toppings!"

"And it can be thick crust or thin crust," Alex added.

"Guys, Zoe is gluten-free," Layla managed to tease.

"I love/hate this so much right now," Zoe said, as the Crew got lost in another epic fit of giggles.

Zoe wasn't expecting to get a text message from Dylan at 5.30 p.m. It was way too early.

You home? it said.

Yeah . . . she replied. She'd just gotten home from froyo.

Okay, he texted back quickly.

Zoe hated the waiting game with text messages.

Finally, Dylan managed to text: *I'm coming over*.

It wasn't a question. It was a statement. And he texted it as if it was totally normal behavior. Like that kind of thing happened all the time.

It did not.

This would be the first time Dylan had ever come over.

About an hour later, Dylan rang the Reeds' front doorbell, and the chimes rattled throughout the whole house. Zoe scampered down the stairs, hoping to be the first one to the door.

Unfortunately, her dad beat her to it.

"Hi, Mr. Reed," she heard Dylan say. "Is Zoe home?"

"Yes! Hi . . ." Zoe said loudly, sliding up behind her dad. "I got it," she added, mustering up as much "chill" as she possibly could. She was hoping her dad would just nod and walk away, but she knew that was wishful thinking.

"Who's this?" he asked as if Dylan weren't standing right in front of her.

"I'm Dylan," he said, extending his arm for a handshake.

Good move, Zoe thought. Her dad always appreciated a good handshake. Still, he felt the need to look Dylan up and down. Zoe couldn't quite tell if he was trying to be intimidating or was just genuinely confused by the handsome water polo player standing in front of him.

After a moment, Dylan added a "nice to meet you" and Zoe's dad finally shook his hand.

"Come in," Zoe said, shooting her dad a "be cool" kind of look. But that wasn't her dad's style. "It's a school night," he said.

"Yessir." Dylan nodded.

"We just have some homework to finish," Zoe offered lamely.

The fact that Dylan wasn't holding a backpack or any books wasn't lost on Zoe's dad, but thankfully he didn't feel the need to push the issue. Instead, he simply told them to be quick about it and went back into the den to watch the rest of the Lakers game.

Zoe closed her bedroom door after Dylan walked in and then immediately felt weird about it. They weren't going to do anything that required a closed door, and now that it was closed, all she wanted to do was open it, but that just felt like it would be even weirder, so she let it be.

Dylan didn't even seem to notice the location of the door. He was too busy getting a good look at Zoe's bedroom. It felt strange that he had never actually been there before.

"Wow, Z," he said, taking in all her decorations.

Zoe's entire wall, the one above her bed, was covered in pictures and postcards and magazine clippings and things she'd printed out and collected over the years. There were quotes and song lyrics. Doodles and tickets. Awards. Blue ribbons. The whole wall was bright and extremely well curated. Zoe was very proud of it. She was always adding to it and changing it.

She felt like it was a pretty accurate reflection of who she was at any given moment in time. She noticed that Dylan took an especially long look at the Other Team ticket stub, from her concert date with Austin, which was prominently displayed on the wall.

"I feel like I'm inside of your head right now," he said.

Zoe hoped *that* wasn't true. Her head felt like a giant jumble.

There may have been a lot happening on her wall too, but at least the layout was meticulous and the composition was balanced and everything was more or less color-coordinated and, finally, and probably most importantly, everything was stuck in place and couldn't move. In real life, the thoughts in Zoe's head would not stop moving. They were jumping from Dylan and his wandering eyes and the fact that he was currently sitting on the edge of her bed, to Austin and his kissable lips and the fact that he put a hickey on her neck last night, to her hair and its constant frizz and the fact that she couldn't stop herself from thinking every thought she'd ever had over and over again . . .

"Nice scarf," Dylan said, noticing Zoe's accessory.

"Yeah . . ." Zoe said, pulling it off.

"Oh, shit," Dylan smirked, staring at the hickey.

Zoe had texted him all about it, but the visual was pretty important. "Too bad it's purple and not red," she said. "It would blend right in with my face."

"Surprisingly, your redness is mostly in check right now," Dylan admitted.

"Good," Zoe said as she sat down in her desk chair, attempting to get comfortable.

Dylan certainly was. He sat on her bed, leaning against her pillows.

"Is it strange that I feel like you've been here so many times before?" Zoe asked, knowing that it wasn't actually all that strange but trying to find a way to make more conversation. Their silences felt far more natural on the phone.

"It's not weird at all. I probably should've been here already, but it's nice to see where the magic happens. Now I don't have to imagine."

If they'd been on the phone, Zoe would've pressed him about the details of his imagination, forcing him to let her inside his head. She could say almost anything to Dylan on the phone, but now, in person, it just seemed like too much. It was almost as if it were too real. It wasn't as if what happened on the phone *wasn't* real, but the distance and the lack of visuals made it all seem safer.

After another mostly awkward silence, Dylan finally stopped stalling and pulled a CD out of his jacket pocket.

"I made this to commemorate your big date night. It's a mix CD," he added as if he were worried Zoe wouldn't know what it was. "It's a little old school, but there's this whole stack of CDs in my brother's room from when he used to DJ, and I figured it was a more substantial thing than just sending you a playlist. Also, I had to see the hickey for myself."

Dylan handed Zoe the CD. On the front, in blue Sharpie, he had written: *Zoe got some*. He'd also drawn a little awkward smiley face with squiggles around it. "That's your hair," he explained.

"Thanks," Zoe managed to say. She was touched and also a little bit overwhelmed by the sweetness of the gesture.

"I, um . . ." Dylan started. Zoe waited for him to find the right words. "I just want you to know that I'm really happy for you and, you know, Austin."

Zoe looked up, catching Dylan's eyes. He looked genuinely happy for Zoe – as he should be. Still, Zoe felt like there was something more he wasn't saying. It felt like there was a "but" missing from the "I'm happy" part of his statement . . . *But* Zoe couldn't prove that, and Dylan certainly wasn't going to just come out and say it, so that seemed like the end of the conversation right there.

"Well," Dylan said after a few moments, "I should probably get going before your dad notices we didn't have any homework to do."

"He's harmless, but yeah, that's probably a good idea . . ."

"I'm sure he's on high alert with all the boys who've been hanging around these days."

Zoe rolled her eyes.

"You know what I mean," Dylan insisted.

Zoe did know.

In the past couple of weeks, both Austin and Dylan had shown up on her doorstep. Both of them had nervously rung the doorbell. Both had given her dad an awkward handshake. Only Dylan had gotten an invitation upstairs. And only Dylan had gotten to sit on her bed. Partly because he didn't ask for permission, but mostly it was because Zoe knew there was no chance of anything happening with Dylan on her bed. But with Austin . . . *Ohmigod*. Last night they'd been sitting in the middle of a crowded movie theater, and Zoe still ended up with the world's largest, purple-est hickey. She couldn't even fully imagine what might've happened if she and Austin had been on a bed instead . . .

"What?" Dylan asked, seeing Zoe's smile. "Thinking about your boyfriend?"

If they'd been on the phone, Zoe would've been able to ask Dylan if he was jealous. Dylan probably would've laughed and said no, and then made some stupid comment about how many more boyfriends she would need to have – four, five? – in order to even the score between them.

But they weren't on the phone.

They were still in real life. In Zoe's bedroom. Sitting eight feet apart. And Zoe could see Dylan's face. And the look in his eyes. And she could see that even though he was her best guy friend, and even though he had shown up with a thoughtful present to celebrate her first hickey with her first boyfriend, and even though he was clearly doing everything he could *not* to be jealous . . .

. . . Zoe had a pretty strong feeling that he most certainly was.

She could see it all over his face – and she couldn't help but like it.

136 Days Until Graduation . . .

Alex didn't know exactly how many boys she had made out with.

She suspected it might be approaching triple digits, but she wasn't sure.

But she did know she could count on one hand the number of boys she'd been on a real, he-makes-a-plan-and-picks-you-up kind of date with.

Alex tried not to make too big a deal about too many things, but tonight's date with Oliver was certainly a bigger deal than her normal Friday night.

In the past hour and a half, she had pretty much tried on every piece of clothing in her entire closet. Now, every inch of her boring, beige carpet was covered with all of the bright or black or flirty clothes she owned. She was annoyed at herself for spending so much time and energy trying to pick out an outfit, but she wanted to get this right. She wanted to send the right signals, and she knew her outfit was an important place to start. She wanted to wear something not too serious or dressy. Something with the perfect amount of cleavage right in that sweet spot where her shirt was low enough to see more-boobs-than-not, but still high enough that the view of said boobs might just be a happy accident. The point was to try as hard as possible to look as good as possible while also looking like you didn't try at all. But all of that was way easier said than done, which was why all her clothes were sitting on the floor.

"Way to make a mess," Max said as he walked in without knocking.

"Hello to you too . . ."

"Where are you going?"

"Mini-golfing."

"Cool." Max pushed the last of Alex's skirts onto the floor, making enough room for him to sit down in Alex's rolling desk chair.

"Excuse me," she laughed.

"It's too much," he said simply.

Alex knew that Max was literally talking about all the clothes on her floor, because he always talked literally like that, but it also seemed like he was talking about how much time and energy she had been wasting trying them all on and obsessing and overanalyzing. She agreed that it was too much, but she still needed to make a decision about what to wear. Showing up to the date naked definitely wasn't the right signal.

"Final decision then: this one or this one?" Alex held up two options.

"I dunno." Max shrugged.

"Can you please pretend to care?"

"No," Max said sincerely.

"Okay, fine. Thanks for nothing." Alex laughed.

"You're welcome." Max laughed back.

Alex wasn't sure if Max understood why she was laughing, but she loved when they laughed together. It made her feel a strong connection to him. And she appreciated the brotherly reminder that Oliver probably wouldn't really care what she was wearing, either. He would be able to pretend that he did care better than Max could, but still.

Alex finally settled on a white crop top and a blue flannel shirt with skinny jeans because it made her feel cute but it was also comfortable. She wore her hair up in a casual, high ponytail and wore extra lip gloss. Alex felt really good about her outfit and the way she felt in it – and the purposely mixed signals it might be sending. She snapped a picture of herself in her full-length mirror and sent it to the Chat.

Please tell me that's a sexie, Emma texted back quickly.

Ha, Alex texted back. *Not even close*.

About an hour later, Alex and Oliver found themselves on a mini-golf course in Sherman Oaks, in the midst of a heated battle. Alex was impressed with Oliver's choice of date location. The golfing provided enough activity to fill the quiet spaces in their conversation, but also plenty of room for talking and flirting – and competing. Unsurprisingly – but true to form – Alex and Oliver were both taking the game far too seriously, doing everything they could to win.

They were tied going into the second-to-last hole.

Alex took a few practice swings before hitting her ball under a bridge and watching it land about two feet from the hole. She tapped the ball into the hole for an impressive score of two.

"Nicely done . . ." Oliver said. Alex got the feeling there was something he wasn't telling her. She wanted to ask what it was, but she held her tongue. Oliver also took a couple of practice swings, but then, instead of hitting his ball under the bridge like Alex had, he sent it rolling through a seemingly hidden passageway at the bottom of a stone-covered wall. This secret shortcut allowed his golf ball to roll *directly* into the hole for an automatic hole in one.

"Wow," Alex said, feeling dumb. "Way to make me look bad."

"Only on the scorecard," he flirted.

"Only on the . . . Did you really just say *only on the scorecard*?"

"I did."

"Okay, cool. Just checking. I think I also just heard you say it to every other girl you've ever brought to this golf course, but I wanted to be sure."

Oliver kept looking at her. He had a Mona Lisa smile of his own.

And then, even though Oliver ended up winning the mini-golf match by two strokes, he didn't gloat.

"Gotta act like you've been there before," he said.

"You mean like you've been on this date? 'Cause, *clearly*," Alex teased.

"I mean in the *winner's circle*," Oliver said as they dug into burgers and fries and chocolate shakes. They shared a booth at the diner, which was connected to the golf course and nearby arcade. "I promise I don't get around any more than you," he insisted.

"Ouch . . . And here I was, thinking things were going so well . . ."

"Oh, like you haven't kissed half the guys on my team?"

"You know I've only kissed *two* of the guys on your team . . ."

"And Trevor Morgan," Oliver added, somehow knowing Alex had forgotten him.

"Right. Okay. *Three* of your boys, but that doesn't mean—"

"I know," Oliver interrupted. "I'm trying to say you don't have to explain it to me. I know what it's like . . ."

To be mislabeled. To be called a slut. To have everyone jump to their own conclusions about you all the time, Alex thought, as Oliver searched for the right way to complete his sentence.

". . . To be able to kiss anyone you want," he said finally.

"You know, it's those sorts of comments that make other people think you're an ass."

"Luckily, I don't care what 'other people' think," Oliver said in a way that made Alex actually believe him. "I'm here with you, so . . ."

"Well. I also think you're an ass, so . . ." Alex said without missing a beat.

Oliver laughed. "I know you wouldn't be here with me if you didn't at least like me a little bit. And *I* wouldn't be here if I wasn't interested in kissing you."

"Right. I figured that had to be the reason."

"It's not the *only* reason."

"It's fine. We've already clarified that you can kiss anyone you want . . ."

"I can. But that doesn't mean I don't think kissing is a big deal."

"You really expect me to believe that?"

"It's true," Oliver said.

It took a lot of self-control for Alex *not* to roll her eyes.

"If there's something you're not going to believe, it's that I think that kissing is actually a bigger deal than having sex," Oliver continued.

Alex couldn't stop herself from letting out a quick, loud, snort-filled laugh.

"I'm serious," Oliver insisted.

"So then you've slept with more people than you've kissed?"

"Hell, no. But I swear I haven't slept with as many people as you think. Whatever number you're thinking, I promise my real one is less. *Way* less, probably. Everyone assumes about me, too . . ."

Alex shook her head slowly.

"What? You don't believe me?"

"It just sounds like another line."

"It's not a line," Oliver insisted. "I mean, of course, yeah, I've kissed more girls than I've slept with, but I still think kissing is bigger than that . . ." He trailed off, finally sounding unrehearsed. "I'm not saying sex isn't big. But it's . . . like, at some point, all the attraction takes over, and it's . . . *biological* . . . But kissing? That feels like something I can control, like it's a choice I have to make. It's more intimate maybe? Whatever it is exactly, I just know I have to feel it."

"So basically you feel like your tongue is more precious than your penis?"

"Oh, hell no. My penis is way more precious."

Alex laughed. She didn't really want to, but she couldn't help it.

"Maybe what I'm really trying to say is that I have way more control over what I do with my tongue," Oliver said as he leaned across the table. His face was only a few inches away from hers, but he was already all the way inside her head.

At this moment, the only thing Alex could think about was Oliver's tongue and all the things he was saying with it and then all the things he might be able to *do* with it . . .

After dinner, Alex and Oliver spent the next couple of hours running around the arcade, playing as many games as they could. Alex was particularly good at skee-ball and whack-a-mole. Oliver racked up tickets on the basketball shot game. It was all fun and playful, and more or less innocent. They had their flirty moments, and, as always, there was a lot of sexual tension between them, but they managed to make it all the way back to Oliver's car without even so much as a kiss on the cheek.

Oliver drove home, winding his car along Mulholland Drive. The radio played softly, filling the silence between them, as Alex replayed all the moments in her head where they had *almost* kissed. She counted seven just on the golf course alone . . . then her thoughts wandered and she noticed that Oliver's right hand was resting on top of his right leg, while his left hand steered the wheel. Alex suddenly had the urge to slide her hand over and slip it into his, but if Oliver thought *kissing* was intimate, she couldn't imagine how he'd feel about handholding. He would probably prefer a hand job, she thought.

Of course he would . . .

. . . but then she couldn't help but think that maybe she'd prefer that too.

If she held his hand that would raise all sorts of intimate questions. A hand job would raise his blood pressure, but then it would be over. And that would be it. It felt like that might just be simpler. Not that she was actually trying to do either one. She didn't want to hold Oliver's hand *or* give him a hand job . . .

Without warning, Oliver veered off of Mulholland and pulled to a stop at one of the lookout points with a glistening view of the San Fernando Valley down below. He turned off the car.

"What are we doing?" Alex asked.

"I have something for you," Oliver said.

"And you want to give it to me here? Now?"

"What's wrong with here and now?"

"I thought the whole point was to hang out somewhere *besides* your car . . ."

"We did that already."

"Oh, okay. I get it."

"You get what, Campbell?"

"You spent the whole night putting all of your charm points into my kindness machine, and now you're done and you're expecting sex to fall out."

"I don't know what a kindness machine is," Oliver smirked, "but I think it's fair to say that I'm hoping more than expecting."

"I think it's fair to say that's not how it works."

"I know, I know. I swear that's not what I'm doing. You brought it up, not me. I just . . . I know you're nervous about breaking the state record," he said, as if they'd talked about it before.

They hadn't.

They'd barely even talked about the record itself, let alone all the pressure that came with trying to break it.

143

"But I want to say I believe in you. I think you're going to do it." Oliver pulled a small box out of his glove compartment. He handed it over.

"I almost don't want to open it," Alex said, trying not to sound emotional. She couldn't help but feel like the thoughtfulness of the box would be better than whatever was actually inside. She took a moment to breathe before pulling the lid off the box. Inside was a small, silver star charm.

"It's for your shoes," Oliver explained. "You're always lacing them up in here in the morning and sometimes you even remember to bring two of the same shoe . . ." He trailed off for a moment. "I don't know. I just figured you could put it on your shoelaces, and we'll both know it's there when you break the record . . . like the star that you are." Oliver waved his hand towards the windshield as he said the word "star", gesturing to the view as if to say: *see, this is why we're up here in my car. It's so we can see all the stars.*

"Are you gonna say something?" Oliver asked after another quiet moment. For the first time all night, he seemed a little unsure of her answer.

"I love it. Thank you. I just . . . I had no idea that you were an absolute cheeseball."

"Campbell. No. Take that back now."

"It's cool. No one will believe me anyway . . ." Alex said, finding Oliver's gaze.

His eyes actually looked sincere. Alex could only hold his eye contact for so long before she had to look away. She knew if they looked at each other any longer they would start kissing.

"Is that your way of saying you don't want to kiss me?" Oliver asked, totally inside Alex's head again.

"I didn't say that . . ." She could feel his gaze practically burning a hole in the side of her head. "You were right," she said. "Kissing is more special."

"Too special?" Oliver asked. It sounded like he was hoping for a no.

"I'm not sure yet," Alex said truthfully.

"So . . . just sex then?" Oliver teased.

"Ah, yes. That *is* what you were hoping for after all . . ." Alex teased back.

"Can you blame me?"

Alex shook her head. Then . . . "How many?"

"What?"

"How many girls have you slept with?"

"Oh, okay . . ." Oliver said as if he expected they'd get here sooner or later.

"You don't *have* to tell me—"

"Two."

"Really?" Alex asked, trying to hide her surprise. That was about ten fewer girls than Alex was expecting.

"I told you not to believe everything you hear," he smirked. "Your turn . . ."

"Well, speaking of not believing everything you hear . . . I actually *haven't*."

"At all? What are you waiting for?"

Alex was surprised Oliver didn't make a joke. He waited patiently as she considered her answer. *The right person* sounded corny. *The right place and time* sounded lame. Anything else she could think of felt like it would be a lie . . . until the truth snuck up on her.

"I have to feel it," she said, taking Oliver's words about the intimacy of kissing and using them as her own.

It was a simple thought but entirely true: Alex was waiting to feel it.

135 Days Until Graduation . . .

Layla did not understand why Alex hadn't just kissed Oliver.

I can feel the sexual tension in the car all the way from here, she texted the Chat the next morning.

That would've ruined everything, Alex texted back. She attempted to explain that there was a delicate power balance between her and Oliver. She texted that she couldn't let him get the upper hand or everything would be ruined. Layla wanted to text and ask what *exactly* it was that would be ruined (since it wasn't clear what was going on between Alex and Oliver anyway) but that seemed like too practical a question.

How blue were his balls? Layla asked instead.

I dunno. I didn't look, Alex texted back. After a few seconds she added, *Do you guys want to go to Trevor's party with me tonight?*

Layla didn't really know Trevor except that he was the starting center on the basketball team. The party would probably be a lot of athletes and those sorts of kids. Layla still might have gone, but she already had plans to see a movie with Logan. Emma texted that she had a family dinner but would try to meet up when she was finished. But Zoe said she was in.

Actually, she texted, *We're in*, the "we" being her and Austin, of course. They were now apparently a package deal.

Layla had never seen Zoe so happy about a boy before. Not even close.

Alex's mom dropped her off at Zoe's house around 8 o'clock that night.

"Be home by midnight," Alex's mom said, as always, as if she were going to turn into a pumpkin or something if she didn't make curfew.

She wasn't worried about that. She was just glad to have someone to go to the party with. Oliver had invited her to come, but that didn't mean he wanted to go *with* her. He wanted to see her there, which meant she had to show up with someone else. Someone who wouldn't mind being ditched almost immediately. Zoe and Austin were the perfect wingmen. And Zoe even found them a ride to the party – Joey, her older brother, was home from college for the weekend. A bunch of his friends from the track team were going to be at the party, so he offered to be the designated driver. Alex walked up the front lawn toward the Reeds' front door, but she only made it as far as the forest-green Ford Explorer sitting in the driveway because Joey was already in the front seat, fiddling with the rear-view mirror.

"Well, look who it is," Alex said at the sight of him.

"Hi, Lexi," he said, breaking into a grin.

Alex rolled her eyes. "No one calls me that anymore." Back in Joey's junior year, when Alex was a freshman on the track team, some of the older guys had taken to calling her Lexi – as in *sexy* Lexi – because that rhymed and teenage boys can be clever like that sometimes.

"That's a shame," Joey teased.

"All the boys who thought I was sexy must've graduated . . ."

"Oh, I'm sure *that*'s not true . . ."

"How's the Bay?" Alex asked, changing the subject.

"The best. I'm sorry to hear you're going to school on the wrong side of it, but I imagine you'll manage." Joey ran his fingers through his reddish-brown hair, launching into a whole love letter to college. Alex watched him closely as he spoke: the way his lips moved and his deep brown eyes sparkled, the sweet way he pushed his thick plastic glasses back up onto his nose whenever they slipped down. Joey's glasses were round and teal, and Alex couldn't help but think that he was the only person on the planet who would look good wearing them.

The truth was that Joey didn't just look good, he looked *effortlessly* good. Back in high school, his features had been softer. His face was rounder and his cheeks were fuller. His chubbiness had been adorable, but now all of his baby fat had given way to a more angular jawline and a longer, thinner face. It was as if he'd grown into his own appearance, like he'd gotten rid of the parts of his body he didn't need. Now, Joey managed to look hot and also completely comfortable in his skin and his clothes and even his glasses, without being cocky about any of it. And as a bonus, Joey's good looks matched his dazzling personality.

"What's happening, guys?" Zoe asked as she walked out of the house.

Alex realized that Zoe meant the question rhetorically, but if she were being honest, she didn't quite know what was happening – but something was. She was leaning up against the car just listening to Joey, and she felt like she could stay in this moment for a very long time.

If Zoe hadn't walked outside, and they didn't have a party to get to, Alex realized that there might not have been a reason to do anything else.

Zoe wasn't oblivious.

And she certainly wasn't an idiot.

She saw the matching grins on Alex and Joey's faces.

But, rather uncharacteristically, they didn't concern her.

In the past she might've been insecure about her brother flirting with one of her best friends, but she wasn't now. She couldn't blame him for looking at Alex that way – boys always did. And she couldn't blame Alex either. Zoe imagined that's what she probably looked like whenever she looked at Austin. She felt funny admitting it, even only to herself, but the whole boy/girl attraction thing made so much more sense these days.

She jumped in the back seat of the car and let Alex sit up front next to Joey. They were going to stop at Austin's house in a couple of minutes to pick him up anyway.

"Zo, you have the shortest little legs," Joey said, adjusting the settings on the driver's seat, still attempting to put it all back the way he liked it.

"Oh, yeah. Thanks for the wheels."

"I'm just glad the car's still in one piece."

Zoe was a decidedly bad driver and avoided getting behind the wheel as much as possible. Normally, she rode the bus to school, but every day this week – ever since Sunday night, when Dylan showed up on her doorstep and sat on her bed and handed her a mix CD – she'd been driving Joey's car instead. Her laptop didn't have a CD drive, and she didn't want to listen to Dylan's mix on her parents' desktop computer in the living room.

The CD started playing as soon as Joey turned the car on.

"We don't have to listen to that . . ." Zoe started to say.

But Joey was already turning the volume up louder. "We don't, but we will. I want to hear what this famous 'best friend' mix CD sounds like. It's got to be good, if this is the reason you've been stealing my car all week. 'Bootylicious'," he laughed as the first song filled the car. "Dylan's a Destiny's Child fan?"

"It's actually a genius first song choice," Zoe laughed back. "The musical intro is perfection; the song builds and crescendos in all the right places."

"You've obviously thought about this quite a bit," Joey said.

Yes, Zoe had.

And she knew Dylan had too.

And that combination was probably why Zoe loved the mix so much: it was just so thoughtful – and it was just so perfectly *her*.

As far as Zoe was concerned, the mix was absolutely perfect. Even though Zoe mostly listened to pop songs and show tunes and Dylan liked rock and rap and EDM, he managed to pick twenty songs that she knew they both loved. And he put them in exactly the right order from start to finish. It had only been a week since Dylan gave it to her, but already Zoe couldn't even count how many times she'd listened to the whole thing on repeat.

She liked to think about someone's musical choices as a window to their soul. As different as she and Dylan were, he seemed to understand her in a way that tapped into something inside of her. Zoe knew that she wasn't going to stop Joey from shuffling through all the songs, but she couldn't help but feel like he and Alex were sitting inside her head – and heart and soul and all that – as they listened to the music: Marc Cohn's "Walking in Memphis", Adele's "I'll Be Waiting", Andy Grammer's "Kiss You Slow", Echosmith's "Cool Kids", "Wonderwall" by Oasis.

Joey seemed rather impressed by the selection.

Then he came across a track he hadn't heard before.

"That's this band Arkells. The song's called '11:11'," Zoe said, knowing Dylan put it on the mix as a shout-out to her strange habit of kissing the clock and making a wish whenever she saw that time on her cell phone. She didn't explain that part to Joey and Alex. That was just for her and Dylan.

"If you skip ahead a couple of songs, there's an amazing acoustic cover of Mariah Carey's 'Dreamlover' I've been geeking out about," she said.

"No one geeks out better than my little sister."

"Hey, you can turn it off at any time," Zoe said, hoping he'd take the hint, but he kept shuffling. He didn't let any of them play for more than a few seconds, but he paused for a while longer on "I Know Things Now", the one from *Into the*

Woods about being excited and scared that she'd had stuck in her head for months. It meant a lot to her that Dylan had included this song because she knew he'd never heard it before she mentioned it to him.

Finally Joey got restless and turned on the radio instead.

Then, Zoe and Alex's phones vibrated at the same time.

Try actually kissing Oliver this time, Layla texted the Chat.

No promises, Alex texted back.

Zoe giggled.

"You guys talking about me?"

"Oh, no. Alex's boy . . ."

Alex caught Joey's eyes in the rear-view mirror.

"That's not really an accurate description," she said.

"Only 'cause he's an idiot," Zoe exclaimed. "I still don't understand why you didn't make out all over his car last night."

"I would've kissed him back if he'd kissed me first. But I'm sure he knows that, which is probably why he didn't make a move in the first place."

"Wait, so he didn't kiss you because he knew you'd kiss him back?"

"No, he didn't kiss me because he wanted *me* to need to kiss *him* more than he *actually* wanted to kiss me," Alex explained.

"Your flirting ability is so far above my skill level. I don't even really know what that means."

"I don't either," Joey chuckled.

Alex appreciated Joey's sincerity. And his ability not to take himself too seriously. Oliver was so calculated about everything, always playing games.

Once they got to the party, Zoe and Austin took off pretty quickly, joining some of Austin's friends at the beer-pong table. Joey and Alex walked into the kitchen together, looking for something to drink. She spotted Oliver across the room, setting up a boat race drinking game with Trevor and some of the other guys from the basketball team. He waved her over.

"Thanks for the ride," Alex said to Joey.

"Have fun with your boy," he smirked.

"He's not actually my boy . . ."

"Then Zoe's right. He is an idiot."

Zoe might've been the worst flip cup player in the history of flip cup.

The game was simple enough: drink all your beer, flip your cup over.

But Zoe simply could not do it.

The first problem was the fact that she didn't like beer. The second problem was that Zoe couldn't drink quickly, no matter what the liquid happened to be. The third problem was the flipping, which was the entire point of the game. If the objective had been to flip the cup over and *not* have it land upside down, Zoe would've won every single time. As it was, she was a complete and total failure.

"You are so far away from doing this right, I think you might be close," Austin teased before pulling Zoe in for a big kiss.

Zoe's heart skipped a beat every time Austin kissed her, but it skipped twice whenever he did it in public. Austin would kiss her anywhere: in the hallway at school, in the senior parking lot, or right now, in the middle of Trevor Morgan's party. *As he should*, Zoe could hear all her girls saying, but this was new for her.

"Wanna go upstairs?" Austin whispered in her ear.

That kind of question was new for Zoe, too.

Zoe nodded and Austin grabbed her hand, interlacing their fingers, and together they made their way up the staircase. Halfway up, Zoe turned back, glancing down at the party below. She caught the gaze of a girl she didn't know, but the girl darted her eyes away quickly, not wanting to make it look like she had been staring. Zoe had never seen this girl before, but Zoe had definitely *been* her before. So many times. The girl watching another couple walk up the stairs and not wanting to be caught. The girl longing to trade places but not wanting to admit it. At least for now, Zoe didn't have to long for anything. She was with Austin, holding his hand, heading towards an empty bedroom.

The first door Austin pushed on at the top of the stairs was locked, no doubt already occupied by another happy or drunken couple. After trying a few more locked doors, they found the last one at the end of the hallway unlocked and unoccupied. Austin pulled Zoe into the room, kissing her as soon as he shut the door behind him. It occurred to Zoe, as they moved towards the twin bed, that maybe he had more on his mind than just kissing. They could've made out downstairs or outside in the backyard. Here, now, they had a bed and a dark, quiet room.

Here, now, they could get naked if they wanted to.

Austin pulled off his shirt. Clearly, *he* wanted to . . . and she wanted him, too. He pulled her in for another kiss. She could taste the beer on his tongue, which made her wonder if *she* tasted like beer. And she was drunk enough to ask him.

"Do you taste like beer?" Austin repeated back to her as if he was seriously considering the question. "I don't know, but I know how to find out . . ." He leaned in for another kiss. And then another one after that. He never answered the question, but it just didn't seem to matter anymore.

After a few more minutes of kissing, Austin reached for Zoe's shirt, pulling it off. Honestly, Zoe had wanted to do that herself, but she hadn't been able to get up the nerve to take it off. Austin was more than happy to help. Zoe noticed that the sheets on the bed were pink and ruffled. There was a white floral pattern around the edge. It looked like the sheets she had on her bed when she was in elementary school, which made her feel small and also more drunk than she'd been even just a few moments before. She pushed her attention back to Austin and his kisses. He moved his lips down to her breasts and then even further down onto her stomach. She moved her hands along his chest and up onto his shoulders. She couldn't help but giggle as she thought about how good it felt to have your shoulders rubbed, but how it was *obviously* not the same kind of good that caused orgasms . . . They kissed for a while longer, hovering right around second base, and just when it started to feel like it might be time to make a move to third, the door swung open and a bright light flooded into the room.

At first, Zoe couldn't see who had opened the door, but she heard the drunken giggles . . . And she could recognize that laugh anywhere – at least, the male half of it. Once Zoe's eyes readjusted, she saw Dylan standing in the doorframe.

And he saw her, too.

This was not how Zoe imagined Dylan would see her in her bra for the first time. Not that she had ever really imagined that sort of thing. Or maybe she had? It was hard to tell what was just the beer in her brain talking and what she was really feeling. The truth was, right now, it didn't matter either way.

She was with Austin. And Dylan was holding another girl's hand.

Zoe didn't recognize her. She was probably a sophomore or maybe even a freshman. She was thin and blonde. Her hair was too long and her skirt was too short. Zoe didn't necessarily *care* about any of those details, but they were impossible not to notice.

"You mind?" Austin finally managed to ask.

"No, sorry, buddy . . ." Dylan stammered before stepping back out into the hallway and closing the door behind him. It was only after he was gone and Austin's tongue was back inside her mouth that Zoe realized Dylan had been stuck staring at her all that time.

Now she was stuck thinking about *him*.

His eyes had been glassy and his cheeks were flushed, probably because he was drunk, but maybe from embarrassment too. Either way, it didn't *really* matter. Zoe was with Austin. And Austin's hand was under her skirt. And then anything she might've been thinking – about Dylan or the awkwardness or his new girl of the moment – *all of it*, was overshadowed by the way Austin's fingers felt inside of her. It was exciting . . . and also scary.

But mostly she just *liked* it.

And she liked that, too.

133 Days Until Graduation . . .

Emma was still the reigning champion of mixed emotions.

She'd liked hooking up with Nick, especially that second time in the darkroom, but she wasn't particularly excited about the idea of doing it again. Of course, Emma being Emma, she wasn't entirely sure *why* she wasn't excited, but she knew Nick was very excited and for some reason that contrast wasn't exactly helping things. She wasn't cocky enough to think Nick was falling in love with her, but it was clear that his feelings for her were stronger than just a "friends with benefits" situation. His initial friendly offer to "lend her his penis" had already been more than accomplished, but Nick still seemed to want more.

He was waiting for her at her locker when she got to school.

"Hey, hey," he said, pulling her in for a hug and a quick kiss on the cheek.

A public kiss, even just on the cheek, was a pretty bold move at any time of day, but *especially* at 7.55 a.m. on a Monday morning.

It took a lot of self-control for Emma not to wipe her cheek. She turned down the hall, heading towards the yearbook room. Nick followed closely behind, which wasn't really evidence of anything as much a byproduct of the fact that they had their first period class together.

"What are you up to this weekend?" he asked eagerly. "'Cause it's . . . you know, Valentine's Day . . ."

"Oh, yeah, I don't know," Emma said, trying to stop him from asking anything else. "I don't usually make a big deal about that."

"Me neither," Nick said. "But I guess it's also, just, you know, *Saturday*, so if you want to hang out or whatever . . ." He said "hang out" as if he were putting quotation marks around the words. He might as well have just said, "If you want to have sex on Saturday, let me know." Emma couldn't help but think that if he had actually just said that, she probably would've been down.

Emma made her way to her computer station in the back of the room. Savannah was already seated at the computer next to hers. Nick stayed right on her heels.

"All right, well, just let me know what you're thinking," he said.

"Sure, yeah." Emma nodded. And then she made sure to smile. She knew Nick well enough to know that he needed a little more positive reassurance from her before he would feel like he could walk away.

Once he did, Savannah leaned in close. "He looooves you . . ."

"He doesn't. Not even close. He just . . . has a lot of expectations about the whole thing."

"Yeah. You're super weird about expectations."

"To be fair, I'm super weird about a lot of things, but, in particular, *yes*, they freak me out." Emma got lost for a moment in all the thoughts swirling around her head. She didn't know why expectations freaked her out so much, or whether Nick was actually having any expectations, or if she was just projecting her own feelings onto him, or whether it was normal for high-school kids to think about "projecting their feelings" or if that was only something Emma thought about because her father was a therapist . . . And all her thoughts started to blend together until Emma couldn't tell where one stopped and the next one began.

Finally, Savannah's smile caught her eye. ·

"What?" Emma asked uncertainly.

"Just trying to figure out how many thoughts you're having at the same time. I can practically see all the gears moving in that pretty little head of yours."

"Then you must know that the inside of my head is anything but pretty . . ."

"Well, aesthetically speaking, the brains and blood are rather gross, but they're also incredibly complex and beautiful, so I think 'pretty' is a totally accurate description."

"Twelve," Emma answered. "I think it's safe to say that I'm always having twelve distinct thoughts at any one time, give or take."

"I'll take it," Savannah said, still smiling.

Good, Emma thought.

She'd take it too.

Whatever *it* was.

132 Days Until Graduation . . .

Layla had never been particularly good at falling asleep.

Once she fell asleep, she had no problem staying there, but turning her brain off in the first place was nearly impossible. This past week had been even more problematic than usual. She simply could not keep her head in the moment. Her thoughts would get so far ahead of her actual life that she would have to remind herself to return to reality . . .

Then, her phone buzzed. There was a new text from Logan. *4 DAYS!!!!*

Four was Layla's lucky number, and their V-card/V-Day date was only four days away. Under normal circumstances, she would've loved everything about the text message: the number, the symbolism, the appropriate amount of exclamation points. But tonight her mind was racing . . . all her thoughts and fears and hopes and dreams were running on overdrive.

She didn't know what to text back exactly, but she wanted to say *something*, so she responded with a red heart emoji. Normally, Layla didn't like emojis because she thought they were easily misinterpreted, but in this moment she could see the upside to ambiguity, to allowing the other person to interpret the communication in their own way.

Can't. Wait, he texted back. *Can't stop thinking about it . . .*

Layla couldn't stop thinking about it either, but she was pretty sure that her thoughts and Logan's were remarkably different.

She was thinking about emotions and logistics and ramifications.

Last time I fingered you, you got so wet . . .

Logan was thinking about that.

Layla couldn't exactly blame him. She realized it might've been stranger if he *wasn't* thinking about that sort of thing, but it made her realize that all the sex stuff was just different for boys.

Logan imagined it would feel good.

Layla was worried it would hurt.

Logan assumed there would be fireworks.

Layla had already lowered her expectations accordingly.

Logan knew his friends would be impressed about him doing it.

Luckily, Layla knew that her friends would be supportive of her too, but if other kids at school heard about it, they'd probably look at them both differently even though they were doing the same thing together at the same time.

You're the hottest and the best and I love you!! Logan texted when Layla didn't respond to his sext message.

Same and same and I love you too!!! Layla texted back, adding a bunch of exclamation points – but not so many as to look like it was overcompensating. She'd spent a ton of time thinking about everything, but she laughed at herself as she tried to calculate what percentage of that thinking time was dedicated to typing and/or analyzing text messages. Far too much . . .

Then Logan texted that he was going to sleep.

Layla wished she could say and do the same, but her brain still wasn't tired yet. Actually, her brain was *exhausted*, but it wasn't ready to turn off and go to sleep. Layla couldn't stop thinking about the importance of the number four and the V-card/V-Day event and sex and fireworks and how those last two were very much not the same thing. And then all she could think about was how her first time was going to be anticlimactic and firework-less, which was an extremely unhelpful and unsexy thought to be having before it even happened.

It was literally the opposite of orgasmic.

Layla knew that the odds of setting off fireworks the very first time she had sex were about as likely as spotting a unicorn in the wild, but she still hated the unwavering feeling that the outcome had already been decided. Like, no matter what happened, no matter what she did or what Logan did or what they managed to do together, it wouldn't be as good as she wanted it to be. Not even close.

Maybe the truth was that *nothing* would ever be as good as she wanted it to be, but that couldn't possibly mean she shouldn't try.

And she wasn't just thinking about sex, of course.

Life was full of expectations and failures.

Layla knew she still had to try. But she also had to be prepared to fail and try again and fail again . . . And then just like that, as always, her thoughts were racing off into the future. She couldn't seem to stop them.

She couldn't even keep up with them.

131 Days Until Graduation . . .

Zoe hadn't spoken to Dylan since he saw her bra that night at the party.

He'd been sick, apparently, and she'd been distracted by Austin, but that didn't mean she didn't want to talk to Dylan. She couldn't remember the last time they'd had a real phonefall.

"Why aren't we talking?" Zoe asked on Wednesday night once she finally managed to get him on the phone.

"What? We're talking. We're literally talking right now."

"I mean, for real. The phonefalls . . ."

"Oh. I don't know . . ." Dylan said as if he hadn't even noticed.

Zoe was pretty sure he had noticed. The last time she saw him, she had only been wearing a bra, and she was very sure he'd noticed *that* as well.

"I don't want to get in Austin's way."

"You're not. He goes to sleep early. And I really don't think he would care anyway."

Dylan didn't respond.

"What am I missing?" Zoe pushed again. "How many girlfriends have you had since chem? Six? Seven?"

"Five."

"Five, right, and I – *we* – outlasted all of them."

Dylan didn't respond to that either.

"You had no problem making me talk to you then—"

"I'm so sorry I *made* you talk to me—"

"Stop it. You know that's not what I'm saying—"

"I don't, actually . . ."

Zoe took a breath, forcing herself to pause for a second. "Look, all I'm saying is that I like falling asleep on the phone with you. And maybe *that*'s weird, but it's how we've always been. Ever since we became friends. And that doesn't have to do with Austin. Or it shouldn't, anyway. But if you don't want to do this anymore . . . I mean, obviously you're *allowed* to say that—"

"Am I? Thank you for the permission," Dylan said, sounding like an asshole.

"Whatever, Dylan. I'm just saying be honest with me—"

"I am being honest—"

"No, you're not. You're blaming Austin. You're blaming me. If *you* don't want to talk to me in bed anymore, then you need to just say that."

"I don't want to talk to you in bed."

Dylan's words were quick and sharp. She let them hang on the phone line, engulfing the conversation in silence. But it wasn't their normal, comfortable silence. This felt decidedly different, and Zoe didn't like it at all.

"Why not?" she asked, even though she could sense that Dylan wasn't ready to answer that. "Is it just because I have a boyfriend?"

"I don't know."

Zoe could hear the honesty in Dylan's voice.

It hurt.

"But I know I don't want to do this right now," he added.

And that hurt more.

"Okay" was all Zoe could manage to say before she hung up the phone. She didn't give him a chance to backtrack or say sorry or even just soften the blow. She knew him well enough to know he wasn't going to, and she didn't want to waste any more time waiting for Dylan to say something she wanted to hear.

She'd spent too many years doing that already.

129 Days Until Graduation . . .

Layla was in charge of the senior class's red carnation table.

Every year, the student council sold red carnations on Valentine's Day in order to raise money for a local food bank. Each flower cost a dollar. Students could buy as many flowers as they wanted, and the student council would deliver them to the lucky recipients. The whole thing was a giant undertaking requiring lots of organization and careful planning. Basically, it was Layla's dream come true. She was in her element manning the table, selling the flowers. Later she'd have to make sure they all got delivered to the right student in the right classroom at the right time.

Layla spotted Zoe as she got off the school bus. Zoe waved but seemed hesitant to come over and say hi, and Layla knew why. Zoe wasn't a big fan of Valentine's Day. She was scared from too many years of adolescent disappointment. Too many years of not having a valentine.

But Layla already knew that this year was going to be different.

"What's up, Zo?" she asked loudly, giving Zoe no choice but to head over. As Zoe approached, Layla held up one red carnation. "For you . . ."

"Aw," Zoe said, mimicking Layla's standard response to anything even mildly cute or sentimental. "You shouldn't have."

"I didn't. There's no slip, but it's not from me, I swear." Whenever someone bought a flower, they had the option of filling out a pink slip of paper to go along with it. They could write a note, simply sign their name, or they could choose to remain anonymous. Most people went the anonymous route. Layla wasn't going to break protocol, not even for Zoe, but she hoped Zoe would suddenly be able to read her mind and figure it out.

Zoe's entire face lit up as she realized that, for the very first time, a boy had sent her a Valentine's Day carnation.

"Thanks, Lay!" Zoe cradled the flower and ran off.

"Don't thank me . . ." Layla called after her, knowing Zoe would think it was from Austin but somehow hoping she would realize it wasn't.

Layla glanced over at the crew of water polo players sitting at a nearby table. She wanted to make sure Dylan saw Zoe get the flower.

His flower.

A few minutes later, as Dylan walked by on his way to his first period class, he nodded at Layla as if to acknowledge what had happened. Layla could tell that he wanted to keep walking, but she couldn't keep quiet.

"You should've written her a card," she told him.

"I'm not really a writer . . ."

"Just a late-night phone talker?"

That made Dylan stop in front of her table. This was already the longest conversation she'd ever had with Dylan, but she felt like she knew him because she'd been hearing about him for years.

"I just remember how bummed she was last year when she didn't get a flower. It's been bothering me, so . . ." Dylan trailed off.

"But you don't want her to know?" Layla wasn't just talking about the flower.

"As long as she's happy, mission accomplished . . ."

Layla hadn't realized he cared quite so much.

Alex jogged down the hallway carrying two dozen red carnations.

She appreciated all the Valentine's Day love, but having all these flowers just felt excessive, especially since they were slowing her down as she hustled through the crowd on her way to class. She turned a corner and ran smack into Oliver, who had been racing in the other direction with his gym bag on his shoulder. The impact caused Alex to drop all of her flowers. It looked like a small garden had sprouted on the floor.

"Sorry," he said with a grin.

"No, *I'm* sorry. It's not like you have a big game tonight or anything . . ."

The boys' varsity team was playing in the first round of state-wide play offs that night in Santa Barbara. It was a big win-or-go kind of game.

"Yeah, no pressure." Oliver bent down to help Alex pick up her flowers. "Wow, you must be breaking records with all of these . . ."

"How many are from you?"

"I can't take any credit."

Alex raised an eyebrow. She could've sworn at least *one* flower would be from him.

"Don't take it personally. I didn't give any to anybody," he added, clocking her facial expression. "Besides, Campbell, you can't just put charm points, or, you know, *flowers*, into a girl's kindness machine and expect sex to fall out."

"Yeah? Who told you about the kindness machine?" Alex asked.

"Oh . . . just this girl."

"*Just*, huh?"

"I drive her to school."

"Lucky you." Alex liked the playful banter between them, but she was finally noticing just how calculated it all was, as if they were putting on a show.

"Are you actually mad?" Oliver asked, breaking their rhythm.

"About the flowers?" Alex asked impulsively.

If she'd thought about it, maybe she would've realized that he was asking about Trevor's party last weekend. They'd spent most of the night playing drinking games and hanging out with guys on the basketball team, which was *fun* and all, but they didn't even come *close* to kissing this time.

"I don't care about the flowers," Alex said, hoping it sounded believable.

"Good. I know you think Valentine's Day is bullshit – and so do I."

"Is that your way of saying you don't have any plans tomorrow?"

"I'll text you," Oliver said with a smirk before he took off down the hallway.

"That's not what I meant," Alex yelled after him.

"But it's what you wanted," Oliver shouted over his shoulder without breaking his stride.

Alex shook her head, mostly annoyed that he was right.

Layla helped carry the crate of leftover carnations to Logan's car after school.

Logan had the brilliant idea to donate the extra flowers to a nearby retirement center. Logan was always having ideas like that, ideas that were so thoughtful that you couldn't help but be impressed by his kindness. Layla *was* genuinely impressed but, at the moment, she couldn't help being annoyed with him too.

"I got every person on the student council a carnation," he tried to explain. "Even the boys."

Layla didn't care about *that*.

But he'd gotten one for Vanessa, too.

"Was I supposed to get one for everyone *except* her?"

"I don't know," Layla exhaled. Now she was annoyed at herself for even starting the conversation. "I'm sorry I brought it up, but I saw the carnation hanging in her locker, and now she has it for ever, this romantic thing from you—"

"Layla, it's not *romantic*—"

"Okay, but *she* doesn't know that. She thinks it's special."

"Lay, come on. Can we please just forget about Vanessa?"

"I'm trying."

"All I can think about is you," Logan said, which made Layla smile but also made her feel more petty and stupid too. Of course Layla *wanted* to forget about Vanessa and her shameless advances toward Logan – she really did – but that wasn't Layla's nature. She couldn't just pretend to be something she wasn't. But she *could* stop complaining to Logan about it. And she would. Starting now.

"Thank you," she said sweetly. "I'm sorry."

"Love means never having to say you're sorry." Logan smiled.

"So, I'm *not* sorry?" Layla asked, laughing a little.

"No, I don't know . . . That's from a movie. My dad says it sometimes."

"What movie?"

"I don't know, but it's older, and black and white maybe. He's always trying to rewatch the movie with my mom, but she says she doesn't actually like the movie, and whenever he says the 'you don't have to say sorry' thing, my mom says it's the stupidest thing she's ever heard about love, so . . ." Logan always talked just a *little* bit faster than normal when he got nervous.

"Love also means never having to ask 'did you get my text?'" Layla offered, hoping to ease Logan's nerves.

"Oh. Did you text me?"

"No. That's a quote I found online. Makes more sense now that I realize it's probably making fun of your movie."

Logan smiled as he pulled a small red envelope out of his pocket and handed it to Layla.

It was the first clue.

My Layla, the letter started. The words were written in blue pen in Logan's boyishly sloppy handwriting, and just those first two words were enough to make Layla's heart melt. She almost didn't want to read the rest. Right now, everything was perfect: the card, the handwriting, the blue ink. She didn't want to ruin it. But, practically speaking, she also didn't want to stand in the parking lot for ever. She kept reading: *I want to start by saying that you are the absolute best. Pack an overnight bag – and I'll take care of the rest. Be ready tomorrow for a bright and early start. I love you with all of my big, silly heart. To the moon and back, always, Logan.*

"I wish I were better at writing or rhyming," Logan said.

"Nope. You're perfect. The card is perfect."

"If you think *that* was perfect . . ." Logan said as his lips curled into a smile.

His dimple was on full display, popping out of his cheek as he laid out the plan for Valentine's Day. He explained that there would be thirteen more clues (for a grand total of fourteen, obviously). The clues would take them all over the city. He'd made plans and reservations and had mapped out a whole schedule.

"It's going to be the most 'Layla day' that's ever existed," Logan said, pulling her in for a big kiss. "Get excited."

Zoe had stopped making excuses to sneak into the tech booth during rehearsal.

When she and Austin first started hooking up, she would pretend that she needed some more spike tape, or she needed to ask him a question about the spotlight. And then she'd make her way back to the booth, and they'd make out for a few minutes, or many minutes, or as long as they could without getting paranoid that anyone was getting suspicious. Or sometimes Austin would be the one making up excuses, finding reasons to come visit Zoe backstage. He'd say he needed to adjust the focus on one of the lights, for example, and then walk back to the utility closet where the ladder was, and Zoe would meet him, and they'd make out for a few more minutes, or as many minutes as they could.

But now, they were both getting far bolder and much cockier about their make-out sessions. They didn't even bother making anything up anymore. They'd meet in the tech booth or backstage and make out for longer and longer each and every time. And they didn't even really care if anybody noticed because it was simply too much fun.

Today, Austin had pulled her behind the curtain, which was all bunched up on stage right and provided the perfect hiding spot. Zoe wasn't sure how long they'd been kissing in this particular make-out session, but she was pretty sure that in the past couple of weeks, she'd spent more time kissing Austin than she had spent kissing anyone else *combined* in the entire rest of her life.

To be fair, Zoe hadn't kissed all that many people before, but still, this seemed like an achievement worth celebrating. She'd read somewhere that in order to be a master at something you had to do it for 10,000 hours. She wondered if it was possible to be a master of kissing (whether you kissed for that many hours or not). She wondered how many make-out sessions she and Austin would have to have before they'd even get close to that number.

Then, her thoughts returned to another familiar question.

"Am I sexy?" she asked between kisses.

"Do you really even have to ask?" Austin asked, pulling back. "I guess you do since you actually just did, but *yes*. You are *so* sexy. *Beyond* sexy."

He looked into Zoe's eyes, and she could see her image reflected in them, and she felt strangely and wonderfully beautiful. It was almost as if she could feel his attraction to her pouring out of his eyes and directly onto her. And his feelings were strong, and real, and . . . *hard*.

Or he was hard.

Zoe was almost embarrassed to admit, even just to herself, that she liked turning him on like that. She liked the fact that her kisses made him hard, and that she could feel him between her legs as they kept kissing . . . But it made her nervous, too – and also excited and scared and all that – but mostly it just made her want to kiss him more and touch him more, so that's exactly what she did.

Layla's version of "getting excited" also meant being prepared.

As soon as Layla got home from school, she climbed onto her bed, opened her laptop and read her entire Sex Doc from start to finish. Ultimately, all of the "Oh my god, I'm having sex tomorrow! What do I need to know?" advice more or less boiled down to three key points: make sure you're ready, pick the right person, use protection.

Layla knew they were using a condom. *And* she was on the pill.

She knew she'd picked the right person.

And she knew she was ready . . .

But.

If she was being perfectly honest, the thought of a "but" kept creeping into her mind. She wasn't nervous about having sex with *Logan*, but, if she was being entirely honest – with herself or the universe or whatever – the truth was that she *was* nervous about having sex in general.

Layla decided that maybe a little nervousness was actually a good thing.

It meant that it mattered.

Yes, tomorrow with Logan would be a big deal, a *very* big deal even, but it would only be one time. It would only be the first time. The whole point was that there would be many more times to come. Layla giggled at her thoughts and the thematically appropriate use of the word come – or cum.

There'd be more time for that too.

She clicked on another article in the Sex Doc called "How to Have Better Sex", which provided tips like "talk dirty" and "undress slowly" and "use the reverse cowgirl position". Layla didn't know what the regular cowgirl position was, let alone the reverse version. A Google search revealed some pictures that quickly cleared up any confusion, but now all the preparedness was just stressing her out. Even though Layla had endless amounts of information, literally at her fingertips, there was still so much more that she wanted to know.

Like, about her actual fingertips, for example.

Where was she supposed to put them during sex? And where was she supposed to put her *hands*? On Logan? On the bed? How would she know? How would she know what to do with *any* part of her body? Like, her eyes, even. Should she look at Logan? At the ceiling? Would he be on top of her? She read in the Sex Doc that it generally felt more pleasurable for the woman to be on top, but that seemed rather ambitious for her first time. Emma had said there probably wouldn't be time for more than one position, but Layla wanted to know: how long would it last? Or how long should it last? She realized that the answers to those last two questions may or may not be the same. And then what about everything afterwards? Would she feel different? Or look different? Would there be any sort of aftertaste? Or whatever . . .

Layla felt silly for wanting to ask these questions, as she realized that they were all basically things you could only know by having sex, which made the little hairs stick up on the back of her neck. She could feel her blood pressure rising and some sweat pooling on her forehead, and she recognized this feeling. It was basically the same one she'd get before a big test at school. She was as ready as she possibly could be, and now the only thing left to do was to take it already.

Or in this case, "do it" already.

Luckily, she didn't have to wait much longer.

Twenty-four hours and counting . . .

Emma watched the minutes slip into seconds as the game clock wound down.

Fifty-nine seconds, fifty-eight seconds . . . Emma could feel nervous excitement growing in her stomach. She really wasn't a sports fan, but she'd spent the last forty-seven minutes and forty-six seconds . . . forty-five seconds . . . watching the boys' varsity basketball game from the stands and getting swept up in the intensity of it all. The entire season was on the line: win and advance to the semifinals, or lose and go home. The tension was real and palpable, and Emma could feel it all pulsing through her entire body as she sat in the stands next to Savannah, who was covering the game for the school newspaper. Emma was supposed to be snapping pictures for the yearbook, but she kept forgetting to watch through the viewfinder – a rarity for Emma.

There'd already been more than a dozen lead changes in the game, and now, as the seconds fell off the clock, the Wolverines were still losing by one. Oliver controlled the ball, dribbling down the court. Beyond Alex's carpool stories, and the general rumors that existed around him and all the whispers about him in the hallway, Emma didn't actually know Oliver very well. Regardless of what was true about him, he was, without a doubt, the most impressive thing Emma had ever seen on a basketball court. To be fair, Emma hadn't actually seen all that many things on basketball courts, but still . . . she knew he was special.

With twenty-two seconds . . . twenty-one seconds . . . left on the clock, Oliver threw the ball off of his defender's foot, causing the ball to go out of bounds to stop the clock.

After the inbound play there would only be time for one more shot. Oliver would take it. He knew it. His teammates knew it. The other team knew it. Every fan in the stands knew it. And yet, when Oliver dribbled right and faked left and finally pulled up for a fade-away jumper with no time left on the close there was absolutely nothing anyone else could do . . .

Emma held her breath . . .

And Savannah squeezed her hand . . .

And then the entire sold-out, maximum-capacity crowd watched . . .

. . . as Oliver launched the winning shot into the air and through the rim, swishing perfectly – nothing but net!

Oliver did it! He won! Technically the whole team won, but every other guy on the court knew it was almost entirely Oliver, which was why they wasted no time mobbing him at center court. Left to her own devices, Emma could be incredibly jaded, but she couldn't remember another moment when she'd seen something so exciting and intense in person.

"We woonnnnnnnn!" Savannah yelled, twirling around on the stands.

"THIS IS SO COOL!" Emma yelled back, joining in with Savannah and her joyful, unbridled twirling. Emma's shoes squeaked on the sweaty hardwood floor. Her heart pounded against her chest, and her brain took a picture, and she realized that she had managed to turn the moment into a memory even while it was still happening.

Luckily she had also managed to remember to grab her real camera too, and she snapped a few dozen winning pictures of the celebration. She'd taken more than a hundred shots during the actual game, but these victory shots were by far the best. Especially when Trevor Morgan hoisted Oliver up into the air, and carried him on a giant victory lap all the way around the court.

After what felt like for ever, the cheering and twirling and screaming finally died down, and everyone, including the team and the cheerleaders and Emma and Savannah, made their way back to the school bus. The girls shared a seat up front near the coaches and trainers and members of the staff, who had all clearly given up on trying to keep any sort of order on the ride home.

Savannah pulled out her green notebook and scribbled down a few notes for her article, while Emma pulled out her camera again, hoping to snap a few candid shots. Mostly, she focused her lens on Oliver. And his blue eyes. And his cheekbones. And perfect jawline. He made her job easy.

"He's like a joke," she said, looking at his face in the viewfinder.

"What?" Savannah asked, looking at his picture.

"His face . . . I mean, the eyes alone . . ." Emma couldn't help but smile.

"Yeah," Savannah said playfully, "if you're into that sort of thing."

Emma turned around to snap more pictures and saw that Oliver had moved up a few rows. Now he was sharing a seat with Caroline. She was still wearing her cheerleading uniform, her midriff and thighs and cleavage all showing. Oliver was wearing a mesh practice tank top, his arms and abs and jawline all perfectly visible. Even from twelve rows away, Emma could see the attraction simmering between them.

"Uh-oh," Emma said. "That's Caroline. Dylan's ex-girlfriend."

"The cheerleader?"

"Yeah."

"And?"

"*And*. Alex and Oliver have been . . ." Emma stopped, realizing that they hadn't actually *been* anything, and they hadn't actually *done* anything either. "Well, I don't know exactly *what* they're doing, but they're neighbors and they carpool, and they went on a date and played flip cup at a party. I don't know . . . There's a lot of mind games going on."

"And Alex is Dylan's best friend?"

"No. That's Zoe."

"Okay," Savannah said, putting the pieces together. "So. The girl Dylan *doesn't* date anymore is sharing a seat with the guy Alex *isn't* really dating at all."

"Well. Yes."

"Is it possible I'm missing the point?"

"There's no point," Emma admitted, "but I have a feeling Alex won't be very happy if they hook up right now."

"Because she likes Oliver?"

"Technically she's not *sure* yet, but I think she does."

"And does Zoe like Dylan?"

"No. Well, I don't know. Zoe's dating Austin."

"I give up." Savannah laughed. "Your friends are complicated."

"It's one of the many things I love about them." Emma laughed too.

And then she and Savannah spent the next hour of the ride home talking about everything and anything . . . and also listening to each other, too. After a while, Emma turned around, stealing another glance at Oliver and Caroline.

"Are they kissing yet?" Savannah asked.

"No. Just sitting all close, but it looks like any minute now . . ."

Savannah turned backwards to steal a look too. Oliver and Caroline were both sitting with their heads pressed against the bus seat, their foreheads only a few inches apart.

Savannah turned her attention back to Emma, pressing her forehead against the seat only a few inches from Emma's forehead, just like Oliver was doing to Caroline. "Looks like they're having a bad case of basorexia."

"Basorexia? What even *is* that?"

"It's *your* thing. I've been meaning to tell you I looked it up. Basorexia is the feeling of having the overwhelming urge to kiss someone. Urban Dictionary said it could also be defined as a strong craving for kissing, or a hunger for it."

"Oh, well, if Urban Dictionary says so . . ."

"It's real, I swear."

"Awesome. My weirdness has a word and a definition," Emma said.

"I feel pretty good about all your weirdness," Savannah replied.

Honestly, at this moment . . .

128 Days Until Graduation . . .

Emma actually felt pretty good about all her weirdness, too.

"Happy Valentine's Day," Emma said as she realized that the time on her cell phone had just switched to midnight.

They'd been on the bus back from Santa Barbara for almost two hours.

"Hey, yeah, you too," Savannah said, realizing it was now officially tomorrow. And then she asked, as if she just remembered, "Did you get my carnation?"

"Your what?"

"I sent you a carnation today – yesterday."

"You did? Just one?"

"Ha, yeah, *just one*. Sorry, I'll make it a dozen next time."

"No, no, one is great. Like, so nice. I got it. I got two, actually. But I thought they were both from Nick since the carnation he sent me had a card."

And then Emma got strangely quiet. She didn't know what else to say, but she got the feeling Savannah was waiting for something more. "Thank you," she said.

"You. Are. Welcome," Savannah replied. "Sorry about the

lack-o-card. I'm pretty good with words usually, but I didn't quite know what to say."

Emma totally knew the feeling.

"Actually, that's a lie."

Emma caught Savannah's eyes. *What was a lie?*

"I think I knew what to say," Savannah explained, "but it was, like . . . it was like there was just too much."

Emma nodded. She totally knew that feeling, too.

Then suddenly, Emma felt like there was a reason to turn around.

And she was right.

Oliver and Caroline had finally given in to their basorexia – all the urges and cravings and hunger or whatever it was – and were now in the midst of an inevitably epic make-out session. Their lips and hands and hormones were more or less everywhere.

Emma snapped a quick picture on her cell phone.

"Is it just me or does it look like he's trying to swallow her entire head?" Savannah whispered, so as not to disturb the horny couple.

"I guess this is unequivocal proof that two sexy people kissing is not an automatically sexy situation," Emma whispered back.

Savannah had to bite down on her bottom lip to keep from laughing. Emma was more certain than ever before that the pink shade of Savannah's lips was actually the same color as her own. It was all she could think about for the rest of the ride home . . .

. . . And she woke up the next morning still thinking about Savannah's lips. But she wasn't thinking about their color so much anymore. Instead, she was thinking about the words that had come out of Savannah's mouth. Mostly the words that had to do with that one carnation.

And all Emma could really think was: *why?*

Why did Savannah send her a flower?

Was it a *friendly* flower?

It didn't *feel* particularly friendly.

As Emma wiped the sleep out of her eyes, she remembered that she hadn't sent Oliver and Caroline's make-out picture to the Chat yet.

She wasn't sure who would hate it more, Alex or Zoe.

Layla texted back almost immediately: *Oh. Damn.*

She was sitting by her cell phone waiting for Logan to text her. His first clue had said to be ready "bright and early" but she knew that Logan wasn't actually a morning person, so that was a joke. Still, it was almost 10.45 a.m. now, and she was getting antsy.

Thankfully, her phone buzzed again almost immediately. And this time it was Logan: *Your chariot awaits.*

Layla grabbed her bag and flew down the stairs, yelling a quick goodbye to her mom on the way out the door.

"Call me from Alex's!" her mom yelled back.

Layla didn't like lying to her parents, and she wasn't very good at it, but she had no choice. Even if Logan's parents had somehow been okay with some sort of sleepover situation – which they weren't – there was no way Layla's parents would ever have approved. She told her parents she was spending Valentine's Day with him, but she'd had to lie and say she was sleeping at Alex's house. Alex's parents were distracted enough not to notice, and Alex was happy to cover for her. Layla wasn't sure what Logan's actual plan was for sleeping arrangements, which made her anxious and itchy, but she trusted he had figured something out.

Layla opened the front door, and there he was . . .

Logan.

He was standing at the end of her front walkway, leaning against his car, holding a small bouquet of handpicked roses.

Some people tried so hard to do so much and none of it seemed to matter. All Logan had to do was shift his weight slightly and *lean*, and something inside of Layla completely melted. Layla had felt this feeling before. This Logan-induced, full-body-meltage kind of feeling . . . but this time was different.

This time, she could almost literally feel her heart drop out of her chest and all the way down into her feet, as if it was just too heavy, too full, to stay suspended inside of her. It felt like she needed to surrender her feelings, her heart, and maybe even a bit of herself, to gravity.

"What are you waiting for?" Logan asked, all happy and playful.

Nothing. And also everything, Layla thought as she walked to greet him.

Alex wasn't sure how long she'd been staring at the Oliver/Caroline picture.

But she felt powerless to stop.

She wanted to respond to the Chat and text something to the girls, but she couldn't seem to do that either. She'd started typing a few different times: *screw him* and then *ouch* and then *loserrrrr* with too many exclamation points, but none of those responses seemed quite right. She wasn't mad, exactly. She definitely wasn't surprised. "Disappointed" sort of – *kind of* – felt like the right word, but not entirely. Technically, Oliver was allowed to make out with whoever he wanted. He wasn't her boyfriend. He wasn't even a friend with benefits or anything like that. All things considered, he might not even be a friend at all. He was her carpool driver. They'd *almost* – almost but not actually – kissed in his car.

But they didn't.

And that was it.

He didn't owe her anything.

. . ., she finally managed to text the Chat. She wasn't exactly sure what the ellipsis was supposed to mean, but something about it felt right.

Alex finally managed to put down her phone. She decided she wasn't going to think about the picture anymore, which was easier said than done, especially as her phone buzzed again. A new text. This one was from Oliver. It felt like he knew she was thinking about him – or trying *not* to think about him. She closed her phone without looking at his text. She didn't care what he had to say. But that defiant feeling only lasted for about two and a half seconds, and then her curiosity won out. She picked up her phone and opened Oliver's text.

Wanna hang out

UGH.

No.

She did not want to hang out.

And she didn't want to respond, either.

She put her phone down again, but once again, almost immediately, it vibrated, signaling another text from Oliver. She didn't want to look but again – dammit, *again* – she couldn't help herself. She had to check.

That wasn't a question

Alex hated herself for ever thinking that Oliver's lameness had been cute. She also hated that he didn't use any punctuation. There were no question marks. No periods. He was the worst.

She started to type *no thanks*, but decided to delete it.

Then she wrote: *Why don't you call your favorite cheerleader?*

She thought for a moment before sending it . . .

Too mean? Too much?

Nope. She decided it was just right and hit send.

Ha, Oliver texted back almost immediately.

Alex waited for something more.

You spying on me now? he added after a minute.

Don't flatter yourself.

Don't try and tell me you don't want to hang out tonight

UGHHHHH, Alex thought to herself. She wasn't sure what she hated more: the fact that she did, in fact, still want to hang out with him even though he was making out with someone else last night, or the fact that he – and all his stupid cockiness – somehow seemed to know that already.

Everything she could think of to text back sounded stupid or lame or just plain petty. Instead, she turned off her phone without responding.

The only thing she wanted to give to Oliver right now was silence.

Zoe attempted to remember all the tips the girls had ever told her.

Watch your teeth.

Don't forget to use your hands.

Make eye contact.

She remembered Alex had said something about sucking on an ice cube first in order to make the whole thing feel cold or something, but Zoe didn't have an ice cube, so that piece of advice wasn't really all that helpful.

Mostly, Zoe just followed her instincts. That seemed to be working well enough. Austin *seemed* to be having a good time, but Zoe wasn't sure whether or not she was doing it right.

"You're doing it *so* right," he assured her.

Austin was sitting on the edge of his bed with his feet on the floor and his pants and boxers down around his ankles. Zoe was kneeling down in front of him.

"It feels amazing," he insisted. "Like, really, the only thing that could even possibly be better would be if we were having sex."

Woah.

Zoe stopped what she was doing again and sat back on her heels.

"You want to have sex?"

"Um. Yeah," Austin said as if that was the only possible answer. "But I know you haven't yet, so I didn't think . . . I wasn't sure if you wanted to."

"I do want to," Zoe said all at once. She was almost surprised how quickly and confidently the words came out of her mouth. Her voice wasn't shaking. Her body wasn't squirming. Her face was red, but not more than usual, and that was mostly because Austin's penis had been in her mouth until just, like, thirty seconds earlier.

She hadn't told Austin about the sex pact, but this felt like so much more than that now. Zoe wanted to have sex *with Austin*. And she told him that.

He could not possibly have been more excited to hear it.

"Now?" he asked.

Layla opened Logan's sixth red Valentine's Day envelope very carefully.

She didn't want to mess up her freshly painted nails.

So far, the first few envelopes had led Layla to the Coffee Bean on Pico for an iced vanilla latte, to the small park near her house for a quick ride on the swing set, to her favorite nail place for a mani-pedi, and now they were just finishing lunch at the Apple Pan, an old-fashioned burger spot they both loved.

Layla read Logan's sixth clue: *You wore a headband in your hair. I won a giant teddy bear. This was the site of our first real date. There are still quite a few hours until sunset, but I'm so excited I cannot wait . . .*

Of course Layla knew that their first date was at Santa Monica Pier. The teddy bear was still sitting on top of the bookshelf in her bedroom.

"Don't worry," Logan chuckled, "the rhymes are only gonna get worse . . ."

"Not worried," Layla said, but even as the words came out of her mouth, she could feel a hardening in the back of her throat. Again, she could feel her heart drop down into her feet, overcome by gravity. This moment, this day, this scavenger hunt, this whole first time, was everything Layla could've hoped for.

Logan was surpassing all of her wildest dreams.

And yet.

Layla could feel the tears welling up in her eyes as she and Logan walked back to his car. She glanced over at him. He was being so cute and so natural, so effortless . . . and Layla felt so exactly the opposite, all calculated and forced.

Logan could see it all over her face.

They climbed back into Logan's car and sat together for a minute. No music. No talking. Just their own quiet thoughts. And then a few tears rolled down Layla's face. Layla had never felt smaller.

"Talk to me," Logan said finally.

"This was my idea . . ."

"What was?"

"The . . . the scavenger hunt. The date. *Tonight*."

"Yeah," Logan said, already reading between the lines.

He knew Layla well enough to know what was coming next.

"I'm sorry." She tried to find more words to add to those first two, to find some sort of explanation for what she was feeling, for why she wasn't ready to have sex, but Logan stopped her. He didn't seem to need that.

"Hey. It's okay. And it's still Valentine's Day. Let's go to the pier?"

"Please," Layla said, already feeling lighter.

Logan started the car. He pulled out of the parking lot, and turned onto Pico Boulevard, heading west. "We have awesome dinner reservations."

"Please tell me it's sushi . . ."

"Layla, *come on*, can you please not ruin everything?" Logan teased.

"Oh god . . ."

"Too soon?"

"*Way* too soon," Layla teased back. "And I didn't ruin *everything*. There are still eight more clues, right? Seven, I guess, since I know about the sushi."

"Right," Logan said with some heaviness in his voice.

Now it was Layla's turn to read between the lines . . .

She knew him well enough to know he wasn't going to give her any more clues.

"It's not that I don't *want* you to have any more clues. But they start to get, like . . . sexy," he explained with a little smile, trying to make light of it.

Layla nodded, letting that sink in. She tried to keep her face from looking disappointed, but she couldn't help it.

"*Lay*," Logan said in a tone of voice that managed to be playful and honest and sincere all at the same time, "if it's okay for you to tell me you don't want to have sex tonight, then I think you might have to be okay with me not giving you any more clues."

Layla nodded again. "I wish the physical and the emotional weren't so tangled for you," she said as plainly as possible, but she could still hear a sharpness in her voice.

"Of course they are. I think that's how it works. But that doesn't mean whatever's *not* connected isn't . . . great."

In Layla's head the word "great" basically sounded the same as the word "awful".

193

"Layla, you know I love you, right? To the moon and back." Logan waited for Layla to nod before saying anything else. "And you gotta know I'm gonna love you even if . . . I mean, no matter what happens or doesn't happen, but I wrote the clues when I thought we were gonna have sex, so . . ." Logan paused for a moment before asking, "We're . . . we're *not*, right?"

"I feel like you're holding out on me," Layla said, avoiding the question.

"Can I say the same thing? Or does that make me an asshole?"

"You're not an asshole, but you should tell me if you're mad—"

"I'm not *mad*, Layla, but I think I'm allowed to be, like, *disappointed* if we don't end up having sex."

Layla could feel her face fall.

"I know you think I'm all perfect all the time, like this perfect boyfriend, but I'm really not . . ."

"No, stop that, you *are* perfect—"

"Then why don't you want to have sex with me?!" Logan asked, finally letting himself get heated.

"I don't know!" Layla said loudly, filling all the space inside the car with her voice and her breath and her emotions. "It just feels like . . . *pressure*. All the clues and everything—"

"I only did that stupid shit because you asked for it! I don't need any of it. You know I was ready to just do it in my car a month ago—"

"Jesus Christ, Logan! Yes, I know, your *stupid* car," Layla yelled, annoyed they were even having this *conversation* in

194

Logan's car let alone somehow still entertaining the possibility of having sex in it.

"Layla. Come on, I'm sorry—"

"Don't be. I don't want to *just* do it, but if that's what you want then maybe we should pull over. We know you have a condom in your glove compartment—"

"I actually have *two* condoms in my glove compartment!" Logan said, trying to calm Layla down, but the words came out of his mouth loudly – very, *very* loudly – which caused him to break into an unexpectedly big belly laugh.

Layla joined in on the laughing, too. And before they knew it, their laughter had taken over completely, wrapping them up in an uncontrollable fit, and giving them a much-needed break in the conversation.

"What are we doing?" Logan finally managed to ask softly.

"Driving to the pier?"

"Okay, good."

"I'm sorry," Layla said after a bit of a pause.

"It's called *Love Story*," Logan said after a bit more silence.

"What?"

"The movie with that quote, 'love means never having to say you're sorry'? It's called *Love Story*."

Layla couldn't help but think that maybe Logan had written that in one of the envelopes she wasn't going to get to read. She agreed with Logan's mom: it *was* one of the stupidest things she'd ever heard. She was in love with Logan, but she was also sorry. Very sorry. And she had to say it.

Then, the red light they'd been sitting at for a small eternity turned green.

Logan continued to drive west towards Santa Monica Pier as if absolutely nothing had changed between them.

Even though, clearly, everything had.

127 Days Until Graduation . . .

Emma glanced at the stack of phones in the center of the table.

So far it was just hers and Alex's and Zoe's . . . no sign of Layla.

Normally Layla was the first one to arrive and claim a spot in the Bigg Chill line that was usually so long it went all the way out the door. The rest of the Crew would arrive before Layla reached the front of the line, and then they'd all order together, but today, Emma, Zoe and Alex made it all the way to the front of the line without any sign of Layla. Alex had already tried every flavor. Bigg Chill Aaron had already filled their orders. And the girls had already claimed their usual table in the back corner. Now, the three of them sat more or less in silence picking at their yogurt, stalling as they waited for Layla.

Just as Emma was about to ask if maybe they should try texting or even calling Layla, she came bounding through the door of the Bigg Chill, causing the welcome mat to make its familiar, happy, ding-dong noise.

"There she is!" Alex said, using an outside voice. "Layla Baxter, ladies and gentleman . . ."

Emma applauded along with Alex, making a bit of a scene in the Sunday afternoon froyo parlor. Emma noticed that Zoe hadn't really joined in on the merriment, but she didn't want to make a big deal about it.

Layla bee-lined for the counter.

She humored the girls with a bit of a wave. She knew she was late, but she needed some froyo before she'd be able to talk to them. Luckily, Bigg Chill Aaron was waiting to take her order.

"Good timing," he said, remarking on the rare absence of the long queue. "You want the Layla?" He didn't seem to realize that he'd called her order "The Layla" until he'd already set it. "I mean, uh, *the usual*," he corrected as quickly as he could. "Half peanut butter, half chocolate, snow caps on the side?"

"Yes, please. And, for the record, I love that you just called it 'the Layla'."

"Cool, yeah. Don't worry. I'm only, you know, *marginally* embarrassed you heard me call it that." Bigg Chill Aaron flashed his sideways smile.

Layla smiled back, holding his eyes for an extra moment before joining the rest of the Crew at their table in the corner of the room.

She dropped her overnight bag on the floor.

She put her cell phone on top of the phone stack.

She pushed her bangs out of her eyes.

She stuck her spoon in her froyo and took a big bite.

And then, when she couldn't think of any more ways to stall, she took a little inhale and then just came out with it: "Still a virgin."

"Woah," Zoe said softly, almost reflexively.

"Yeah." It was still sinking in for Layla, too.

"I kind of figured . . . 'cause you didn't send a sexie," Alex admitted.

"Are you okay?" Zoe managed to ask.

Layla *was* okay. More or less . . . "You know I don't like it when the plan changes, even if I'm the one who changes it."

"Did, um, did you guys break up?" Emma asked carefully.

"What? No – *no!*" They hadn't broken up and to be honest they hadn't even discussed that as a possibility, but Layla could feel the rhythm of her voice and the weight of her body language . . . overcompensating. And the fact that Layla had to try so hard with her face and her smile and all that . . . it just made her sick to her stomach. Or maybe to her heart, which was sitting all the way down on top of her feet again. Layla had hoped some of her heaviness might disappear now that they'd hit the snooze button on their V-card swap.

Turned out emotions didn't work like that.

Layla looked over at Zoe, who looked like she was about to burst into tears, so Layla managed to put on an even braver and happier face. "I promise we're good. We still had a fun Valentine's Day – and night. We went to the pier and watched the sunset and slept at Logan's uncle's beach house in the marina, which was pretty cool. We'd never actually, like, *slept* in the same bed before."

"But he wasn't . . . mad?" Emma asked.

"Well. He wasn't *thrilled*. But I just wasn't ready . . . he understood that."

"And you gave him the best head of his entire life last night?" Alex asked, but it was more of a statement than a question.

"Duh. Twice," Layla admitted, which made her and Emma and Alex laugh.

Zoe wanted to laugh along with the other girls, but she couldn't.

A single tear dropped down her cheek.

"Oh, Zo, it's okay. Logan and I are gonna be okay. I promise."

Zoe nodded. She knew that. Or at least she believed Layla when she said it. But that's not why another tear rolled down her cheek.

"What's wrong, Zo?" Emma asked.

"I, um . . ." Zoe started to say, but a few more tears fell down her face before she could push any more words out through her lips. "I don't even know why I'm crying. I mean, *I know* . . . but . . ." The girls waited lovingly as Zoe took a deep breath and then finally explained herself: "Austin and I had sex."

"Whoa."

"What?"

"Zoe . . ."

"Yep. Yesterday."

Zoe could feel even more tears bubbling up and then pouring down her cheeks. She hated that she was crying.

"Sorry. I'm such a girl . . ."

"Hey. No. Do *not* apologize for being a girl," Alex said sternly. "Or for crying. You don't get any bonus points for pretending not to have emotions. Tears are so important. And totally underrated." It wasn't the sort of thing Zoe would expect Alex to say. Normally, Alex protected her thoughts and feelings more closely, which made it seem even more true and important.

"Why didn't you tell us when it happened?" Layla asked.

The simple answer was that Zoe hadn't wanted to step on Layla's big day. She and Logan had been planning to do it for so long . . . and it all just happened so fast with her and Austin. She figured she would text the Chat after Layla did, but then Layla never did . . .

"I'm sorry," Zoe said again. "Not for crying," she clarified, almost laughing through her tears.

She still didn't know exactly what was making her cry. She wasn't sad, exactly, but it felt like she was having a lot of emotions all at once. All of the feels, apparently. And they were showing up in her eyes and then falling down her cheeks, and she simply couldn't stop them.

"If you don't want to talk about it . . ." Layla said.

"No, I do," Zoe said.

She knew that *not* talking about it had actually been making her feel worse. As if having sex with Austin was a secret, which it wasn't. Or as if she'd done something wrong, which she hadn't. Zoe told the story as completely as she could, giving Layla and the girls the "full mental picture". She started from the beginning, explaining how she had been giving Austin head and how he'd mentioned wanting to have sex . . . and how she said she did, too. And how, even though they hadn't talked about it before, they couldn't think of a reason not to do it right then and there, except that Austin wasn't sure whether or not he had a condom. Zoe said she didn't want to have sex if he didn't have one, so he literally ripped his entire room apart until he managed to find one tucked in the back of a drawer on his nightstand.

Zoe went to the bathroom to freshen up, and when she came out, Austin had cleaned up his room the best he could and lit

201

a bunch of candles to try and set some sort of mood. It was afternoon, so it was still light outside and the candles weren't all that effective, but it was a nice, sort of romantic gesture – except that one of the candles smelled like a pumpkin spice latte, and Zoe had to blow it out because it just kept making her think of Thanksgiving dinner, which was a decidedly unsexy thought. After they figured out the candle situation, Austin turned on some music on his phone. It was a song Zoe had heard before but couldn't quite remember. It wasn't a song that Zoe would have picked, but she'd been so particular about the pumpkin candle she decided to let it slide.

After that, everything felt like it happened at the same time.

They were kissing and then they were naked and then Austin put on a condom. Austin seemed to know what he was doing, or at least what he was *trying* to do. He'd had sex a few times before, but it took a minute for him to line everything up just right . . . Once Austin found the proper angle and body position and all that, he managed to successfully push inside of her, but it wasn't very graceful. Zoe decided it was probably whatever the exact *opposite* of graceful is . . . Clumsy? Ugly? Awkward? Probably all of the above combined.

"Yeah, it's definitively not pretty." Emma laughed.

"Ohmigod, I can't even imagine what we actually must've *looked* like . . ."

"But did you like it?" Layla asked after a little bit more laughing.

Zoe had to think about that. The truth was that it felt . . . well, it felt better once Austin found a rhythm. After a little bit of time had passed, he had stopped to ask if she was okay. She was – and she said she was. And then he asked if it felt good. She knew he wanted her to tell him that it felt amazing or something all big and perfect like that, but the truth was that it actually kind of hurt. But she still told him it felt okay, which was more or less true – or at least true enough – and so Austin kept going. And then, after a few more minutes – or maybe just one more minute, Zoe wasn't sure exactly – it really did start to feel more painful than pleasureful and Zoe felt like maybe Austin was just too big for her, which, under normal circumstances, might've made her giggle except that then it *actually* started to hurt – *a lot* more than it had even just a moment before. She was about to ask him to stop or at least take a break, but before she could do any of that, he said he was gonna cum – and he did.

Afterwards Zoe felt a whole rush of emotions, including predominately pride that she had just made Austin look like that and feel that way, all primal and euphoric, but then she had two more thoughts at the very same time. One was that she didn't feel that same way (even though she maybe wanted to) and the other was that she hadn't *actually* done much of anything at all.

Austin had done most of it. He was the one moving or thrusting or whatever it was exactly. Zoe had just been on her back on the bed, trying to figure out whether it hurt or not . . . and then they'd cleaned up and Zoe had snapped a sexie that she never ended up sending.

And that was it.

And it was only then, once Zoe got to the end of the whole story, that she realized she hadn't answered Layla's original question: did she like it?

"Honestly, did I like it? I'm not sure."

"That's okay," Emma reaffirmed. "It's a lot."

Yeah. It *was* a lot. Zoe certainly didn't *regret* what had happened, but the reality of it was more than she had expected.

"Do you want to do it again?" Layla asked carefully.

"Not today," Zoe said with a little laugh. "But, yeah. I do."

A few hours later, Zoe found herself standing in front of her bathroom mirror. She was wrapped in a towel, freshly showered, staring at her reflection. She'd seen this same reflection a million times before, but tonight, she wondered if she looked any different. Would anyone be able to tell that she wasn't a virgin anymore? *Probably not*, she thought. She looked the same to herself. Same pale. Same red. Same frizz and freckles and all that.

Hi sexy.

A new text message from Austin had just appeared on her phone.

She looked back at her reflection. Apparently Austin thought all this was sexy, but she didn't *feel* particularly sexy.

It was ironic, she thought, to feel like she knew less now than she did before she had sex – or maybe she just understood that there was still so much more to know. And it made her think about "I Know Things Now", the song from *Into the Woods* that had been echoing in her head. The very last lyric of the song said that it was: "nice to know a lot . . . and a little bit not."

Now *that* is how Zoe felt: nice and also not.

Both, simultaneously.

Hi, she texted back.

Thinking about you, Austin responded quickly.

Aw, that's sweet, she thought. But *then* she thought about what exactly he might be thinking about . . . and laughed as she realized that, yes, Austin was a sweet guy, and, yes, she was sure his intentions were good, but mostly, *yes*, his thoughts were most likely dirty too. And she liked that.

But she also did not.

It was nice and it was not at the very same time.

118 Days Until Graduation . . .

Alex was running out of time.

Literally.

Lately she'd been spending as much time as she could on the track, but it still felt like there would never be enough runway to run as fast as she needed to in order to break the state record.

"You gotta believe!" Coach K said, or almost *scolded*, as Alex pulled off her track shoes after practice.

"I do believe . . ." Alex grumbled.

"Then why don't I believe *you*?"

"I don't know!" Alex said.

At least that sounded like an honest answer.

More than anything, Alex wanted to clear her mind and just focus on her feet, but it didn't work like that. She had a whole body of parts in between that needed attention. And she still had to show up at school every day. And Oliver was still her carpool driver, and they were still riding to school together, even though they hadn't actually *spoken* since Valentine's Day. And it was fine. They were both so stubborn Alex was starting to think they might just never speak to each other ever again.

But. As with so many of her thoughts, Alex was wrong.

As she approached the parking lot, Alex saw Oliver sitting on the hood of his car, his hair still wet from a recent shower.

"Hi," he said far too casually.

"Hello," she replied with enough emphasis to let him know she was surprised to be *hearing* from him let alone seeing him waiting for her.

"You need a ride?"

"I'm okay," Alex said, trying to give him a nice-but-firm brush-off.

"Are you, though? Really?" Oliver pressed. "Are *we*?"

"We?"

"Obviously you're mad—"

"Why would I be mad? Oh. Right. You said you wanted to hang out on Valentine's Day, and spent the whole night before making out with some other girl—"

"It was mostly *adrenaline*."

"I know about adrenaline, but that doesn't . . ." Alex trailed off.

"I wished it was you the whole time," Oliver insisted, as Alex rolled her eyes. "I don't care if you think that sounds like a line. It's the truth."

"Yeah, well, the problem with you is that it's too hard to tell the difference."

Oliver nodded, absorbing that.

"You sure you don't need a ride home?" he asked finally.

"I'm sure," Alex said as convincingly as she possibly could.

The good news was that she actually *felt* sure. She didn't need a ride – and she honestly didn't need Oliver either. Right now she didn't *need* much of anything and that was a phenomenal feeling. As she watched him drive away, she couldn't help but think that maybe this would be the first day of the rest of the year. Maybe now she was ready to wholeheartedly believe in herself and get over her fears and have enough faith and break the track record and all of that.

Or maybe not. Maybe Alex should just get used to feeling more wrong than right. Her phone buzzed. Oliver had sent her a text.

Two text messages, actually.

The first said: *It is bigger, I swear*

The second was a picture of his penis.

Alex understood dick pics even less than she understood hickeys. She didn't see the point. It seemed to turn boys on way more to send them than it did for her – or any girls she knew – to receive them . . .

Ugh.

Now Alex couldn't help but wonder how many other girls had gotten this very same picture from Oliver.

She deleted it without even really looking at it.

Well.

No.

That was a lie.

She looked at it for about ten seconds first. Maybe twenty.

But the whole time she was looking, a jumble of thoughts raced through her head. She wondered why exactly he had sent it to her and what he was thinking about when he took it and what he thought *she* would think when she saw it . . . And also what she *actually* thought, which was a two-part answer mixed together: the first part was that his penis was larger than she had expected – not that she was expecting anything in the first place, but still, it was – and the second was that she didn't think penises were particularly sexy-looking. At least not in pictures. As far as pictures were concerned, she was more impressed by a fierce set of abs or lips or maybe even just a piercing pair of eyes. Alex could imagine that some girls might *like* getting this kind of picture. Maybe some girls even *actually* got turned on by it, and that was fine or good or whatever, but Alex knew she wasn't one of them.

After what could not have been more then thirty seconds – *tops* – she deleted Oliver's picture.

She didn't text him back.

Of course, that didn't stop him from texting her.

Again and again.

He wanted a picture in return.

Of course he did.

117 Days Until Graduation . . .

Layla never got anything important in the mail.

Her parents got bills and junk and the occasional party invitation, but no one ever sent Layla anything important.

Until today.

The University of Southern California wasn't just Layla's first-choice school, it was basically her *only* choice. Layla's parents had gone to school there. It's where they met and fell in love, and it's the only school Layla had ever wanted to go to. Now Layla sat on her bed looking at the envelope. It was big and thick and proudly stamped with an emblem from USC. Layla knew it was good news. You didn't get a thick envelope unless it was an acceptance.

She knew her parents would be thrilled. And her siblings, too. And all her teachers. And the Crew, of course – duh. The only person she wasn't entirely sure about was Logan. Things had been decidedly different between them since Valentine's Day.

"Obviously I'm ready – whenever you are," Logan said a few days later after one of their usual off-campus make-out sessions.

They decided it would happen whenever it was supposed to happen.

"We're letting the plan go," Layla told the girls at lunch a few days later.

They all nodded and laughed, and she knew they only sort of believed her.

And then, as luck or the universe or whoever would have it, Layla ended up with an empty house that very same night. All she had to do was text Logan, and he could've come over, and they could've closed any of the doors – or all of the doors – and done whatever they wanted in any room or bedroom or anywhere.

But she didn't text Logan.

And she felt guilty about it.

But not as guilty as she would've if he'd driven all the way over, with the two condoms in his glove compartment, and then not been able to follow through. It seemed simpler to just avoid the situation altogether.

Today, she texted Logan to come over as soon as she got home from school and saw the big envelope waiting for her. Logan had to stay late. Something about a student council project.

Layla wasn't really listening. She had been too consumed by the envelope, which now sat between them on her trampoline.

"This is it," she said solemnly.

"You might want to actually open it before you start making too many big, emotional plans."

"Whatever it says, you're still gonna be in Philadelphia next year," Layla said after a bit of a quiet moment.

"Please just open it," Logan pushed, not wanting to have that conversation again.

Layla took a breath. She knew it was finally time to stop stalling. As she went to open the envelope, Layla noticed that

211

the very last remnants of her Valentine's Day manicure were still clinging to her nails. The red polish that had looked perfect just a couple weeks ago was now all chipped and fading. Now it was a mess. Layla couldn't help but think that was thematically appropriate.

"'Congratulations, Layla Baxter'," she read out loud from the letter.

"Yay!" Logan cheered, interrupting her. "Victory!" he yelled, holding up his fingers in the shape of a V. "Is this what they do? That Victory thing?"

"I don't know . . ."

"Oh, come on, Layla. Since I've known you, all you've talked about is going to school at USC. You realize that 'congratulations' means you did it, right? You're going to school at USC, and you look miserable. Are you going to tell me what's wrong or do I have to guess?"

"Nothing is wrong," she tried to lie.

It didn't work.

"We've known we're gonna be on opposite sides of the country from next year for *months*," Logan said. "What did you think was going to happen?"

Layla shook her head. She didn't know. She had tried to mentally prepare for this moment. She knew it was coming, but the reality of it still hurt. Now it was official: Logan was going to spend the next four years in Philadelphia and Layla was not. She could feel all of her emotions creeping up on her, washing over her. She felt powerless to stop them. She felt disconnected from Logan and all the things she thought she'd wanted, even just a few weeks ago.

And so.

When Logan said he wanted to take a break, Layla had no choice but to agree with him. The words had blindsided her, knocking the breath out of her chest and the blood out of her brain, dislodging the tears from behind her eyes, but, deep down, Layla had to admit she'd seen it coming.

"Okay," she said.

"You agree?"

"No. But I understand why you're saying it." Actually, she didn't. She didn't understand. That was a lie, and Layla was an absolutely horrible liar.

"I love you to the moon and back," Logan said, the way he always did. Layla knew that he meant it, he really did love her, but maybe that just wasn't enough anymore. "It's just . . ." he tried to explain, trailing off.

"I just won't sleep with you," Layla said, completing his sentence.

"Stop," Logan said sharply.

"Yeah? If I said, 'let's have sex right now', you wouldn't be walking out the door."

"Layla, *obviously* I want to have sex with you! I've made that really clear. Right now? Tomorrow? Since the first day I laid eyes on you? Yes, *please*, let's have sex. But clearly I can't do it *without* you and you won't do it *with* me, so . . ."

Layla didn't know quite what to say. She wiped a tear from her eye before it could fall down her cheek, but Logan saw it. And he heard it loud and clear.

He took a break.

He took a breath.

He ran his fingers through his hair.

And then he softened his voice and started again as sweetly as he possibly could. "I'm not trying to make you feel worse than you already do."

"I know," Layla said. She really did know that part.

"But don't you think it says something that you *didn't* want to sleep with me? Something important. This isn't me trying to pressure you, I swear. This is just me. And I'm just saying I think there's a reason you weren't feeling it."

Now all the tears were streaming down Layla's cheeks. She couldn't wipe them away fast enough. Logan watched her cry, giving her the time and space and silence that she needed. Layla appreciated him more in this moment than she had in a very long time.

"I'm sorry," she finally managed to say.

"I hate seeing you cry, but you're pretty damn adorable while you do it, so it's confusing." Logan smiled a sad, little smile. Even his dimple looked sad. And his face, too. It was full of appreciation. And love. And a little bit of loss, too.

Layla felt the same way.

"It's all the feels . . ." she said, almost laughing through the tears.

She loved *and* hated this feeling so much.

"It is . . ." Logan agreed, quickly trailing off before any more words could come out of his mouth.

It was the first time Layla thought *he* might actually cry too. And then that made her eyes burst into a fresh, new set of tears. Full, explosive waterworks. And it wasn't *just* because of Logan. It was because of everything. The end. The pact. The plan. It was all of it, and now it was all streaming down her face and staining her cheeks and causing a giant snot bubble to slip out from her nose. It was an ugly cry at its ugliest. And Layla needed it.

"I love you, Layla," Logan said again after enough time had passed. This time, his words sounded like the goodbye that they were. "And I always want to have love for you. But I'm worried if we don't break now . . ."

"Break? Or break up?" Layla asked.

"I don't want to let it get so bad that I feel like I'm going to really lose you."

"You don't have to lose me at all," Layla said after some silence.

But Logan had already made up his mind.

This was it.

After he left, it took Layla two hours and fourteen minutes to text the Chat. Layla didn't want to, but she knew that she had to. She knew that was the part that would make it feel real. That was the part that would hurt the most. And it did.

She didn't text Logan back, though.

She couldn't.

She also couldn't eat dinner.

Or talk to anyone.

She couldn't do much of anything except watch the minutes tick off the clock. And listen to her sobs. And feel all her tears. And then the phantom tears, too. The ones that didn't actually fall after all of the real tears had already rolled down her cheeks. Layla felt like there should still be more tears, but there just literally wasn't any more saltwater left in her entire body. Layla didn't know there was a limit to that sort of thing. But apparently there was.

Apparently, maybe, there was a limit to *every* sort of thing.

Even love, she thought.

Maybe, she hated to think, *especially love*.

114 Days Until Graduation . . .

Emma understood the importance of a good distraction.

"Savannah is having a birthday party tonight," Emma said, as they sat down at their lunch table. "It's gonna be a big house party at her dad's. Her friend is gonna DJ."

Emma hadn't really told the girls all that much about Savannah. They knew she worked on the yearbook and the newspaper, but besides the facts, Emma hadn't really shared a ton. Mostly it was because, Emma being Emma, she didn't know what to say *exactly*, but she knew that she wanted them to come with her to Savannah's birthday party that night.

Alex already had a *Star Wars* movie date with her brother Max, and Zoe had an actual date with Austin. Layla tried to say she was going to stay in and watch a movie, but Emma shot that down real quick.

"Nope," Emma insisted.

"Nope?"

"Friends don't let friends throw themselves pity parties."

"I'm not throwing anything . . ."

"Exactly. You're coming with me to Savannah's. You need to."

It had only been about seventy-two hours since she and Logan had broken up, but Layla was barely functioning. She was still referring to the whole thing as a "break" even though it was very clearly and definitively a break-up. It wasn't like any of the girls expected Layla to be totally "okay" all of a sudden or anything, but this was worse than Emma had ever seen her. She knew Layla needed a push in the right direction.

"The truth is, I'm really not asking you to come with me. I'm telling you," said Emma. "It's time to get up, dress up, show up."

"Oh, look at you using some of my favorite words on me . . ."

Yep. Emma knew exactly what she was doing. She rattled off a few more of Layla's favorite sayings for good measure: "Fake it till you make it. No one can make you feel inferior without your consent. Be gentle to your precious little soul."

"O-*kay*. Serenity now. I hear you," Layla said, finally cracking a smile.

Layla did not want to go to the party.

At all.

But once she and Emma got there, and drank some beer, and Layla stopped feeling so sorry for herself . . . she had to admit she was having a marginally good time. At least a much better time than she had expected.

To be fair, most of the goodness was probably because of Wyatt, the cute boy she'd been talking to for the past ten minutes. Wyatt went to Venice High School. He owned a skateboard and a surfboard and a guitar. And he had longish blond hair that kept falling in front of his eyes. When Emma first saw him approaching, she made a joke that he could be the Ken to Layla's Barbie. Layla wasn't looking for a Ken – she wasn't looking for *anything*, honestly, and couldn't stop thinking about Logan – but Wyatt's grin had managed to occupy at least a little space in her brain. Emma forced an introduction and then had somehow managed to slip away, saying she needed a beer refill, and just never came back.

So far it was all working out fine. Wyatt was easy to talk to and even easier to look at and just as Layla began to think that this enjoyable moment might be a sign from the universe, a reminder that she needed to trust the timing of her life and accept that Logan was right about needing to take a break/break-up . . .

. . . it happened.

It started simply enough.

Wyatt called her a cutie, which wasn't even all that remarkable as far as compliments go, but she couldn't remember the last time she got a compliment from a boy who *wasn't* Logan. She could feel the heat in her cheeks. And her heartbeat. It all made her look down at her feet and the floor and the ping-pong ball that just happened to be rolling down the hallway. It rolled under the kitchen table until it came to an abrupt stop next to Logan's sneaker. And she wondered why he wasn't bending down to pick it up until her eyes drifted up *his* leg and Vanessa Martin's legs and also her skirt, which was on top of Logan's hips, and then her hands, which might as well have been under his shirt, and she couldn't tell whose tongue was in whose mouth exactly, but it looked like it was both at the same time and it was the worst thing she had ever seen.

"You okay?" Wyatt asked, mostly oblivious to the situation.

Layla managed a little nod. She managed to put her number in Wyatt's phone. But then, before she could make her way out of the living room, Logan pulled away from Vanessa and looked up just long enough to catch Layla's eyes across the room.

He held her gaze for a moment. Long enough for him to see her cheeks turn red, and her lip quiver. And long enough for her to see the stunned look on his face, and Vanessa's lipstick still fresh and red on his lips.

Emma walked through the party looking for Savannah.

She didn't really know anybody else here, but she recognized everyone's faces and knew most of their names. She'd seen all of their yearbook pictures. She knew which clubs they were in and what they wore to school dances and which Superlatives they'd been awarded, but she didn't actually *know* them. Before Emma could get lost in a drunken thought pattern about how hard it was to actually know anyone in this big, crazy world, her phone started buzzing.

The Chat was blowing up.

Layla just saw Logan with his tongue in Vanessa's mouth. It was very possible she was going to puke.

Zoe and Austin just had sex for the second time. The whole thing was an upgrade from the first time even though Zoe still didn't feel any fireworks.

And the *Millennium Falcon* had just been captured by the Death Star's tractor beam, and Alex felt like it was all going to end badly. Alex had been live-texting the entire *Star*

Wars movie. None of the girls had the heart to tell her that they didn't really care about Han Solo and his new hope or whatever.

Emma tried to contribute to the conversation, but the texts were pouring in too fast and furious: Logan's hips, Austin's eyes, Princess Leia's hair . . .

"Let's dance like no one's watching," Savannah said as she slid up behind Emma, "'cause, you know, they're actually *not* since everyone's just on their phones all the time."

Emma looked up, catching Savannah's eyes. Her face had, in fact, been buried entirely in her phone screen.

"How's the Chat?" Savannah asked knowingly.

"It's, um . . . *drama*," Emma said as she texted Layla, asking where she was.

"Dance with me," Savannah said.

She grabbed Emma's hand and pulled her out into the backyard and onto the makeshift dance floor.

"I like this song!" Savannah yelled over the music.

"Me too. What is it?"

"No clue."

"I can Shazam it." Emma started to reach for her phone so she could use the music-recognition app, but Savannah stopped her, reaching out to touch her hand.

"Or . . . how 'bout let's just appreciate the song without knowing?"

Emma smiled.

And then Emma and Savannah lost track of time and space, and got lost in the music and the moment, until everything else just seemed to slip away . . .

. . . And even though Emma was very tipsy, and literally slipping and sliding across the damp grass, she felt grounded in this moment.

Suddenly her drunken thoughts felt incredibly clear. She thought about all of the times she'd thought about Savannah's lips and their particular shade of pink . . .

They're perfect, Emma thought.

There was really nothing left to do but kiss them.

113 Days Until Graduation . . .

Layla scooped a heap of snow caps with her spoon.

"I don't care about Logan and Vanessa," she said, trying as hard as she possibly could to sound like she actually didn't care, even though she knew that the girls – or Bigg Chill Aaron or any other stranger in the Bigg Chill who might be able to overhear her overcompensating – could tell that was a total lie.

Zoe, Emma and Alex had all turned their attention back to their froyo – vanilla, strawberry and salted caramel chocolate, respectively. It felt like they were all trying to come up with a new topic of conversation, but before anyone could say anything new, Layla freaked out about Logan and Vanessa again.

"Do you think they had sex in his car last night?"

"No," Alex said, with as much confidence as possible.

"How do you know? Logan has two condoms in his glove compartment . . ."

"I don't know for sure, but I really don't think they did. It's way more likely that she gave him road head on the way home."

"Alex—"

"What?"

"Not helping . . ." Zoe tried to whisper.

"No. It's okay," Layla agreed, "she's probably right. But they're going to have lots of sex, and I'm just *not* – and that's . . . that's fine . . ."

"You're not what?" Zoe asked quickly.

"I don't know . . ." Layla exhaled, not wanting to say something she'd regret. She turned her attention to Emma. "Was Savannah upset that we had to leave?"

"She wasn't *mad*," Emma said. "I don't think."

Emma hadn't really talked to Savannah since that moment on the dance floor.

That moment where she *kissed* Savannah.

By the time Layla walked over, they were done kissing and were mostly just standing and staring at each other. Emma wasn't sure what to do next, and Savannah hadn't said or done much of anything, but Layla was saying and doing more than enough for everyone involved. Logan had followed her outside, and he wanted to talk to Layla, but all she wanted to do was leave. Right away. So they did. Emma felt bad about leaving so quickly, but she had to take care of Layla.

Once she had got home, she texted Savannah to say that she was sorry and that she hoped she had a good birthday and goodnight.

Savannah had texted her back that it was "*all good*".

And that was it.

Since then, Emma estimated, rather conservatively, that she'd replayed their dance-floor kiss about a million times (give or take).

It might've been the very best first kiss she'd ever had.

Or it might've just been drunken and sloppy and confused.

One of the two.

Or possibly both.

After the girls left the Bigg Chill, Emma found herself driving over to Savannah's house. She had to. She didn't know what she was going to say but she knew she needed to be there. She pulled to a stop in front of the house and turned off her car, but she left the radio on. She needed more time to process her thoughts, which all kept returning to Savannah. She could still taste her cherry Chap Stick, and, yes, she could basically hear the girl-kissing pop song playing on repeat inside her head . . . But this wasn't just a song.

It was real.

And all of it had stayed with her as if it had just happened.

A lot of times when Emma kissed someone, she felt like she was giving something away. And not just, like, her literal spit and saliva, but something beyond that. Something intangible. Like her emotions, maybe.

But this kiss felt different.

Yes, it was only *one* kiss.

And yes, it was drunken and fast and maybe a little bit stupid . . .

But it also felt like . . . *more*.

Yes.

That was it.

Emma felt like she had pulled away from her kiss with Savannah with so much more than she had leaned in with in the first place.

But, then again, a lot of that "more" might simply be confusion.

Savannah knocked on Emma's car window, disrupting her rambling thoughts.

Emma rolled down the window.

"How was froyo?" Savannah asked.

"Good. Really good."

"Yeah? What did the girls have to say?"

Emma felt like Savannah was asking specifically what they said about the kiss or maybe just what they said about her, but the truth was that Emma really hadn't told the girls about either topic.

Savannah read Emma's face like a book. "You didn't tell them . . ."

All Emma could think to say was that she was sorry.

"For what?"

Such a good question, Emma thought. For not knowing why exactly? For feeling too many feelings at once? For being an absolute mess of a person?

"I just don't want to be weird," she said after a moment.

"I think it's a little late for that." Savannah smiled.

"Yeah, no, I mean, obviously *I'm* weird . . . I just don't want you to think that every time we're, like, sitting at the computers in the yearbook room or on the school bus or wherever, I'm suddenly gonna lean over and kiss you . . ."

"Oh . . ."

"Or that I'm even *thinking* about kissing you . . ."

Savannah let that settle for a minute. "I thought you were always thinking about kissing everyone."

226

Yes. Emma felt a strange sense of relief, as she realized that Savannah was absolutely right. She *was* always thinking about that. Always. Maybe that was it. Maybe the kiss wasn't just drunken and sloppy – and maybe it wasn't the best either. Maybe it wasn't even really a kiss after all. Maybe it was just Emma and all her inside-weirdness spilling out into the real world and onto Savannah's lips. That didn't necessarily mean that it was *about* Savannah's lips. Or at least not the fact that they were *her* lips. Whatever it was, Emma was really glad that she and Savannah had been able to talk about it and straighten everything out.

It wasn't until a few minutes later, once Emma had driven away and had a quiet moment to replay the whole conversation in her head that she realized they hadn't actually had much of a talk at all.

Zoe was tired of talking about orgasms.

She wanted to have one.

Now that she'd had sex twice, she was more than certain that having sex and having an orgasm were *not* the same thing.

Her second time with Austin had been better than the first. It lasted a little longer and hurt a little less, but it wasn't . . . well, it just still wasn't as much *fun* as she wanted it to be – or as much fun as it looked like it was for Austin. His body . . . his face . . . his eyes . . . Zoe wanted to look and feel like that too.

Apparently she was going to have to take matters into her own hands.

Literally.

And so . . .

Zoe lay in bed that night – and laughed at herself.

Zoe knew a lot about her body. She knew which foods tasted good or what gave her an upset stomach, but she honestly didn't have the first clue about what would make her orgasm. And *that*'s what was making her laugh.

Okay, she thought to herself. *How hard can this be?*

She put her right hand on her right boob and her left hand on her left boob, cupping each one. She squeezed . . . and then laughed some more.

Am I doing this right? she wanted to ask.

And she *did* ask, in her head anyway. But that made her laugh even harder because she certainly didn't know the answer! That's why she was asking the question in the first place.

Zoe realized pretty quickly that whatever she was doing wasn't actually doing much of anything for her, so she moved her fingers onto her nipples . . . which got hard quickly, *so quickly*, in fact, that it seemed strange to Zoe that they didn't get hard more often, or that they weren't somehow just, like, automatically hard all the time. After a little more touching and rubbing and attempting to listen to her body, Zoe finally – *fin-a-llyy* – felt like she was getting somewhere.

She could tell what felt good. She could tell which parts wanted more attention than others. And right now, all of that made her reach down into her pajama pants and then into her underwear and actually into her*self*, which seemed like an odd way to be thinking about what she was doing, but that was an accurate description of the situation, and it actually felt good, which was the whole point, so Zoe tried as hard as she could not to be critical of herself.

And then her phone rang.

She ignored it.

She was far too focused for phone calls.

It was just probably Austin or one of the girls. Even though . . . she couldn't help but think that none of them ever actually called her.

Then, her phone rang again.

Zoe glanced at the clock.

It was exactly 11:11.

Of course it was . . .

She touched her hand to her lips and then to the clock and then back to her lips again, and that's when she realized, thanks to a slightly salty aftertaste, that the last thing she'd touched with her hand was her vagina and all of a sudden she was overwhelmed by a bout of giggles like never before . . . And all the while, Zoe's phone was still ringing, and the clock had ticked forward to 11:12, and her hand smelled like her underwear and life was totally strange and ridiculously amazing and she was both proud of herself and also embarrassed for herself. And all the while, she couldn't seem to stop laughing . . . but then somehow she still managed to glance down at her phone and see Dylan's name on the screen and she missed him and their phonefalls and so, without overthinking it any further than she already had, she picked up the phone.

"Hello," she said, giggling.

"Hey . . ." Dylan said. "You okay?"

"Oh, yeah . . . I'm . . ." Zoe tried to control her laughter, but her breath was still pumping faster than usual.

"What are you doing?" Dylan asked, sounding as if he had *almost* managed to put the pieces together.

"Um, you know, I'm just . . ." Zoe said, focusing on slowing down her breathing. Deep breath in. Deep breath out.

Dylan heard the breaths, and suddenly it clicked. "Zoe. Reed," he said deliberately. "Sorry if I'm . . . *interrupting.*"

"What? *No*. There's nothing . . . You're not . . ."

"You sure about that?" Dylan laughed.

No.

Zoe wasn't sure about anything. She wasn't sure what she was doing or what felt good or even why she'd picked up the phone exactly, but right now she could feel Dylan's smile through the phone. "I just . . . I'd been wanting to talk to you, and I saw you were calling."

"It's all good," Dylan said without any judgment in his voice. "And . . . whatever you're doing right now, I think you should know that I, um, I like it, and I'm gonna let you get back to it."

Zoe wanted to say that she didn't want to get back to it or need to get back to it, but all that would've been a lie. A very small part of Zoe wanted to ask Dylan to stay on the phone with her, but she couldn't say *that* either. Extending that kind of invitation would mean crossing an un-crossable line.

She wasn't going to do that right now.

Not to Dylan.

Not to Austin.

And *especially* not to herself.

110 Days Until Graduation . . .

Emma had expected that things would go back to normal with Savannah . . .

. . . but they still hadn't.

She wasn't sure if it was the kiss itself or the conversation they'd had the following afternoon in front of Savannah's house that had thrown everything between them out of whack, but something just wasn't the same anymore.

It used to be easy and effortless.

Now, everything felt rather strained and calculated.

Savannah stayed after school to cover the varsity water polo match for the paper. Emma stayed too, to take pictures for the yearbook. The girls had spent most of the match standing only ten feet apart, watching the game and taking notes and snapping pictures, but the distance between them might as well have been a mile. Afterwards, Savannah headed to the yearbook room to type up her notes. Emma followed after her.

"My HD card is full," she said out loud as an explanation for why she was following her.

"You don't have to make up excuses to keep hanging out with me."

"What?" Emma said, hoping Savannah would stop and talk to her for a minute.

She didn't. She kept walking, forcing Emma to pick up the pace.

"You have an open invitation to hang out with me. If you want to stay for the track meet, if you want to come to the yearbook room, if you want to sit and do nothing, then fine, let's do it, but you don't have to make things up," Savannah said all at once. It wasn't her usual tone or the usual kind of words she used to talk to Emma, and Emma didn't like the way it all sounded coming out of her mouth.

But when Emma opened *her* mouth to try and respond, all her thoughts just came out sounding like a giant whistle.

It was the whistle that finally made Savannah stop walking. She turned back to look at Emma. "What is happening?!" she asked, clearly exasperated.

"What do you mean, what is happening?!" Emma asked just as sharply.

"I mean, what the hell are you doing right now?"

"I don't know! I don't ever know what I'm doing!" Emma shouted. "I don't even know why I was just shouting," she added, lowering her voice again.

Then.

After what felt like the longest silence in the history of silences, Savannah finally managed to say what they were both thinking.

"It wasn't weird."

"The kiss," Emma whispered back. The two little words came out of her mouth so softly she wasn't sure Savannah would even hear them.

"You don't have to pretend you didn't like it," Savannah said loudly again.

"I'm not pretending. I'm here—"

"Yeah, you're here, but only because you're making excuses—"

"Okay, okay," Emma said, stepping closer to Savannah. She reached out and touched her arm, as if to make sure she wasn't going to walk away again. "I'm . . . You know, I've been having a hard time with senior year and everything . . ." Savannah waited for Emma to find some more words, but after a few moments she could only manage two more. "It's not . . ."

"What? It's not you, it's me?" Savannah teased. "You're such a giant, boring cliché, Emma O'Malley."

"It's just . . . high school is almost over, and I feel like I know even less now than when I started even though everyone already expects me to just, like, magically be this whole person all of a sudden . . ."

"Emma. Stop. Look . . . I hate to have to be the one to break this to you, but you're already a whole person. It's not 'all of a sudden'. It's *already* happened. Like, right now, in this *actual* sudden—"

"That is not a real phrase—"

"Yeah, well, for actual and for real: you are already a fully formed human. You can still be in process. We're all still in process . . . but you're already you."

"Thank you."

"Do you hear me though?"

"I think so," Emma said even though she wasn't sure.

"You're already you – and you're already magical, so . . ."

Emma didn't just *hear* that part; she felt it, too.

"So . . ." Savannah said slowly. "Can we agree that . . . whatever this is . . . is good?"

"Yes." Emma nodded.

"Okay. So. Then. Are we . . .?"

"Savannah. If you try to 'expectation' me right now, I swear . . ."

"No, no," Savannah said quickly. "I wouldn't dare do that to you."

Good, Emma thought. Right now, for the first time in a long time, all of her thoughts were mostly clear and genuinely good.

Now *that* felt like some actual progress.

Zoe was surprised to see Dylan standing in front of her house.

He had texted her about an hour ago, saying that he needed to see her. And now, here he was, standing on the sidewalk, at 9 p.m. on a Thursday night.

"What's up?" she asked. "Another mix CD?"

"I can't stop thinking about you."

Zoe wasn't expecting that.

"And," he added, nervously biting his lip, "I can't stop thinking about the other night – and how you picked up the phone while you were—"

"Ohmigod, Dylan. I swear to god if you say it out loud—"

"Okay, I won't . . ." Dylan said, his whole face turning into a smile. "But I do want to say that . . . I think there's a reason you picked up."

"I picked up because you were calling me for the first time in *weeks*—"

"But that's not it. I know you're attracted to me—"

"Oh, okay. Thank you—"

"—and I know I'm attracted to you too! That's it. That's why I'm here. I just can't stop thinking about you."

Zoe let Dylan's words hang in the air for a moment.

She'd never heard him say anything like that before. She waited for him to say something – *anything* – more . . . but he didn't. So she filled in the silence instead: "I have a boyfriend."

"Yes." Dylan nodded. "But I . . . I don't think you should be with him."

"No." Zoe could feel her temperature rising. "I can't . . . We can't . . . I don't want to do this right now . . ."

"I feel like I'm gonna lose you."

"That's a weird thing to say."

"Why?"

"Because you never had me. You could've, maybe, at some point, but you clearly didn't want me for all these years."

"That's not true—"

"No. Dylan. It *is* true. It's painfully, absolutely true, but it's only now that I have a nice boyfriend who isn't embarrassed to be with me in public—"

"Your nice public boyfriend only started liking you once you got boobs!"

"Ohmigod."

"What?"

"That's not fair."

"Are we just supposed to pretend they don't exist?"

"I don't know! Why do you care so much?"

"That's kind of a stupid question."

"*You*'re kind of a stupid question. And, you know, I didn't really even know Austin *until* I had boobs so your argument is stupid too."

"Whatever. *I* knew you before all that—"

"And what? Do you want, like, friendship *bonus points* for being nice to the awkward, frizzy-haired charity case?"

"Being *nice*? Zoe, is that what you think I've been doing all these years?"

"Stop," Zoe said, surprised to hear the word come out of her mouth.

"Stop?"

"This isn't . . . I have a boyfriend. And I really like him."

"Do you love him?"

"I don't know! But that's not . . . I don't need you to ask that."

"I'm trying to tell you how *I* feel about you—"

"I don't care how you feel! About anything!" Zoe said, even though they both knew that wasn't true. She did care. She cared about Dylan so much. Probably too much. And she'd been wanting this moment to happen for so long. For years. But not like this . . .

"I'm with Austin, and we're having sex now, so . . ."

Dylan's face sank.

Zoe knew he wasn't expecting that.

And this was *not* how she had envisioned telling him, but it had come out of her mouth and it was hanging in the air and she couldn't take it back now. Zoe could tell by the look on Dylan's face that he didn't know what else to say, so she said what was on her mind.

"I feel like you've been lying to me this whole time!"

236

"Zoe, I never lied to you," Dylan insisted.

"I think it's time for you to go home."

"Zoe, please . . ." Dylan said as sincerely as he could. "The only lie I ever told you was that I liked you when I already knew I was completely in love with you."

"Completely?"

"Maybe not the whole time, but—"

"Of course it wasn't the entire time! You were too busy dating a parade of skinny blonde girls!" Zoe said sharply and loudly.

"And falling asleep on the phone with *you* every night," Dylan said softly.

Zoe had wanted to hear Dylan say all of these things for so long, but now that he had, now that she was listening to the words actually come out of his mouth, it just all felt forced.

"I feel like you only want to be with me now because I want to be with someone else," she said.

Zoe wasn't entirely sure she believed that herself, but it was the best she could do right now. She turned around and left Dylan standing on the sidewalk.

109 Days Until Graduation . . .

Layla couldn't remember the last time she'd had a new first kiss.

The only person she'd kissed for the past two years was Logan, and the painful truth was that he was still the person she wanted to kiss the very most, but that was no longer an option, so she made a kiss list. She wished she had a better, more brilliant idea, but it was the best she could come up with considering the circumstances – mostly that Logan was now (indefinitely) kissing Vanessa. It was the best and most "her" thing she could think of to do. She literally took out a pen and a piece of paper and wrote down a list of people she wanted to kiss.

It wasn't another to-do list, more like a wish list, and it made her feel silly and small, but she had to do *something*.

So far, she'd written down five names: Wyatt (the cute boy from Savannah's party whose last name she didn't know) followed by Jackson Clark, Miles Roth, Tyson Marks, and Channing Tatum.

Obviously that last one was more of a dream than a plan, but Layla always mushed those two things up in her mind anyway – "might as well shoot for the stars, right?" She'd said that to the girls at lunch a few days earlier. She was doing her very best to find the bright side, and trust that things happened for a reason and all of that, but right now even the stars felt like they were tainted. Logan always said he loved her to the moon and back. And they'd spent oh-so-many hours on her trampoline staring up at the moon and the stars and she hated that even as she was talking about other boys, other boys she genuinely wanted to kiss, her thoughts were still drifting back to Logan . . .

"It'd be weird if you *weren't* thinking about him," Emma said.

"But now all I can think about is that he basically ruined all the stars."

"Okay but no," Alex said, her voice sounding way too reasonable for Layla's liking. "Let's not give him that much power. Or *any* power . . ."

Easier said than done, Layla had thought.

But she trusted her girls, and also the power of step-by-step instructions, so she started at the top of her list and texted Wyatt, and that's how she ended up sitting next to him near the edge of the Venice Beach skatepark one day after school.

"You *sure* I can't get you on a board?" Wyatt asked.

"Positive. Not happening. But it's cute of you to ask."

Layla wasn't sure she remembered how to flirt. He really *was* cute. And adorable. And uncomplicated.

Right now, Layla appreciated that about him most of all.

There was so much complication with Logan, so much Layla didn't understand and couldn't quite explain. It was nice to sit with Wyatt and not be confused. He was attractive, and she was attracted to him. And that was it.

Wyatt was very playful with his kisses, and Layla liked that. *A lot.*

The only thing that Layla didn't like about Wyatt's kisses was that she couldn't stop comparing them to Logan's. She tried to cut herself some slack, considering how many thousands of kisses Logan had pressed onto her lips compared to this very first one she was sharing with Wyatt, but she didn't like that she could still somehow *feel* Logan's kisses even though it was Wyatt's tongue inside her mouth.

And then she couldn't stop thinking about Vanessa's tongue.

And what that might've felt like inside Logan's mouth.

And if Logan had thought about *her* lips when Vanessa's lips were pressed up against his.

And despite the distractions and unhelpful thoughts swirling around in her head, Layla kept kissing Wyatt . . .

But it felt far more like the end of a chapter than a beginning.

108 Days Until Graduation . . .

Zoe heard Layla's words, but she didn't understand them.

"What do you mean, you're *done?*" she asked sharply.

"Um..No. Okay, 'done' is maybe the wrong word," Layla backtracked.

She pushed some of the lettuce from her half-eaten salad back and forth with her plastic fork. The girls were all sitting around their lunch table. It was a Friday, the last day of school before spring break, and tensions seemed to be running high.

"I just . . ." Layla tried again. "I guess maybe I'm just trying to say that I don't think it's going to happen."

"Well, I didn't either at first." Zoe smiled. "I'm sure you'll figure it out." But Zoe's certainty withered as she saw a gloss wash over Layla's eyes . . .

"Maybe. But it doesn't feel like it's gonna work without Logan."

"Is it too soon to say it didn't exactly work *with* Logan either?" Alex said, which made Emma and Zoe giggle – while Layla, noticeably, did not.

Zoe got the sinking feeling that it really *was* too soon. Or maybe too late. Or both.

"Sorry, Lay," Alex added quickly when she saw that Layla was actually rather upset.

"It's okay," Layla said, sounding like she was trying as hard as she could to sound like she meant it.

"Of course it's okay," Zoe insisted. "You've still got more names on the kiss list. Your bullet points didn't just disappear or anything. There's still a due date. All of the things. It's all still happening . . . right?"

Zoe was expecting a "right" out of Layla, even if only a tepid one.

Instead, she just got a short, clipped exhale.

And Zoe did not like the sound of it one bit. It was off-putting and out of character and it made the little, red, frizzy hairs on the back of Zoe's neck stand up straight.

"Unless . . ." Zoe started again slowly, ". . . 'done' simply means *done* . . . and then that's it."

"Well, that's not *exactly* what I'm saying," Layla attempted to explain.

But Zoe already felt like an idiot. A mess. All of a sudden, Zoe remembered the feeling she got the first time Layla had smiled at her about the pact as they sat at their table at the Bigg Chill. Right now, in this moment, she felt the exact opposite. She could also feel a dark pit growing inside her stomach, as if she already knew what Layla was going to say next.

Zoe was *furious*.

Absolutely.

She went from zero to livid in no time flat.

"That sucks," Zoe spit out sharply – more sharply than she'd anticipated. Zoe realized that it might sound off-putting to

Emma and Alex, as if her fervor had come out of nowhere, but Zoe could feel Layla abandoning the pact and the Crew and maybe even her too . . . and she hated all of it.

"I'm just trying to be honest," Layla said, which pissed Zoe off even more.

"Thank you, Layla, I *really* super appreciate your honesty . . ."

"Oh, shut up, Zoe. I know you do—"

"This is different—"

"Can one of you please actually say something? Like, can someone complete a full sentence? Anytime." Alex looked from Zoe to Layla and then back to Zoe again.

Zoe didn't want to have to be the one to say it out loud, but she couldn't stand all the silence that seemed to be sitting in the middle of their table anymore. "Layla is quitting the pact. She doesn't want to do it."

"It's not that I don't *want* to—"

"Right, sorry, *Logan* doesn't want to, so Layla couldn't possibly—"

"Hey, Zoe . . ." Emma spoke up, trying to lower the temperature.

"Sorry, but this is bullshit and you know it," Zoe said to Emma, before turning back to Layla. "I'm sorry you and Logan broke up, but that doesn't mean you just have to give up on us, too."

"I am not *giving up*, but can we be real clear for a minute? Logan dumped *me*. If I had my way, we'd still be together. I still want to be with him."

"Yeah, but you probably still wouldn't have had sex with him anyway . . ."

"That's a low blow," Layla said, raising her voice for the first time.

"It's fine, Layla, whatever—"

"Obviously it's not fine if you're going to get this mad at me."

"I'm only mad because I thought this was about us, together. Or *together* together. Or whatever it was supposed to be. But now I'm realizing that it was really just about Logan this whole time. Did you ever even care about the pact?"

"Of course I did! That's lame!"

"Being done is lame!"

"I don't want to do this if I can't do it right."

"What does that even mean? *Right?*" Zoe asked, reaching a fever pitch.

"I don't know! The problem is that I don't know what it means. I'm trying to tell you how I feel – or that I don't know how I feel – and apparently none of that is allowed."

"Just do whatever you want, Layla," Zoe fumed. "Clearly I can't make you do anything you don't want to do."

"Did I make *you* do something you didn't want to do?"

"No—"

"'Cause if you didn't want to sleep with Austin—"

"I never said that!"

"—you shouldn't have slept with Austin—"

"I'm not talking about Austin! I'm talking about you, Layla. You're giving up . . ."

"I tried, Zoe! I tried with Logan, I just tried with Wyatt . . ."

"Oh, okay . . ."

"Do you think I didn't? What else am I supposed to do?"

"Try again! Try harder! Eat pizza. Whatever! Just don't be a hypocrite."

"How about you try not to be an asshole?"

"Fuck you, Layla," Zoe snapped.

"Should I maybe just *pretend* I'm still in? Will that make you feel better?"

"Don't do me any favors, Layla."

"I feel like that's exactly what you're asking for."

"It's not, I swear."

"Good, because this isn't just a favor. This is a big, huge deal."

"I know exactly what it is. I'm the one that's had sex."

It wasn't just what Zoe said, but also the way she said it – the harsh tone in her voice, and all the honesty behind it – that seemed to hurt Layla so much. And Zoe had felt how mean her words were before they even came all the way out of her mouth, but it was too late for her to take them back.

And Layla didn't say anything else.

She couldn't.

Instead, she just got up and walked away.

101 Days Until Graduation . . .

No one had texted the Chat since Layla and Zoe's fight at lunch.

It had been seven days, and still none of the girls had anything to say.

Or maybe they all just had *too much* to say.

Whatever the problem was exactly, no one seemed to know how to fix it, which had resulted in a week of complete radio silence, which was insane, considering the longest Chat silence before this one couldn't have been longer than a day or two.

The fact that it was spring break wasn't helping the situation because it meant that they weren't forced to see each other. Or maybe the break was actually just giving the girls the time and space that they needed.

Either way, the silence in the Chat was deafening.

98 Days Until Graduation . . .

Still nothing.

Three more days. Seventy-two more hours.

And still – *still* – no one had texted the Chat, which now brought the grand total of nothingness up to ten days.

Emma had spent all of those days without cell phone service.

She'd gone camping at the national parks in Utah with her parents and sisters, but the truth was that she probably wouldn't have texted anything anyway.

She didn't know what to say.

Zoe didn't know what to say either.

She spent the first week of spring break up in the Bay Area with her mom, visiting family. They went sightseeing, and she even got to hang out with Joey on campus. He took Zoe to her first frat party. Normally, she would've texted the girls all about it, but she felt like there was so much else she had to say first. She wanted to apologize to Layla for some of the words she'd said at the lunch table, but she was still mad that Layla wanted to give up on the pact, so it all amounted to more silence.

Layla hated the sound of silence so, *so* much.

Luckily she'd had a bit of a distraction, as her family had rented a house in Santa Barbara for a week. They'd caught waves at the beach and played games, and Layla had even managed to get a tan (and no tan lines) but it all felt rather like a consolation prize. Clearly, the moment had spiraled too far with Zoe, and Layla wished she could take back some of what she said, but she didn't know where to start either . . .

Now that Layla was home she couldn't help but miss Logan, and she missed the girls too, and there was still almost another week until they'd all have to be back at school again. Layla decided she needed a break from her spring break, so she drove over to Alex's house after dinner Monday night.

Alex had spent all-day-every-day of the first week of spring break on the track.

Meanwhile, Oliver had spent all-night-every-night texting her (*begging* her) for a naked picture, so she was doing her best to avoid her phone altogether and probably noticed the quiet the least. But she was happy to hear from Layla.

The girls ended up outside on the chairs in Alex's backyard, swapping stories about Layla's trip, and Alex's track practices and how the closer she got to breaking the record, the further away it actually felt.

Then their thoughts and conversation drifted to Zoe and the fight . . .

"Are you really done?" Alex asked, treading carefully.

Layla thought for a moment. Alex wanted her to say no as much as she knew Zoe did, but she could see the hesitation all over Layla's face.

"I don't know," Layla finally exhaled after a bit of time had passed. "It was my stupid idea in the first place."

"Oh no. It is *not* a stupid idea. In fact, it might be the most brilliant idea you've ever had," Alex said, quoting Layla back to herself.

"Thanks," Layla said softly.

"Hey. Don't do it if you don't want to, but don't *not* do it because of Logan."

"It's not *because* of Logan. I mean, I *want* to say that he has absolutely nothing to do with how I'm feeling . . ." But they both knew that wasn't true.

"Zoe *does* have a point," Alex said after another moment. "It was *supposed* to be together."

"Yeah, well, it was *supposed* to be a lot of things," Layla added.

"Maybe that's the problem," Alex said, thinking back to that night at sleep-away camp. "Maybe how we think it's supposed to be is what really messes us up the most. Look. If you *really* don't want to do the pact anymore, that's your call. But don't bow out now just because you're scared about what it might feel like if you don't end up crossing the sex pact off your to-do list," Alex said, sounding all Zen and wise even though she felt like a bit of an imposter. She wasn't sure if she'd be able to take her own advice to heart when it came to thinking about the track and the record and her faith being greater than her fear and all of that, but at least she believed it wholeheartedly for Layla.

"Thanks," Layla said.

Alex could tell her friend needed that, which made her feel good.

And then it got quiet for a while as the girls sat together, thinking.

"What's on your mind?" Layla asked, after who-knows-how-much-time had passed.

Honestly?

Alex's mind had returned to Oliver's dick pic.

She still hadn't told anyone about it, but Oliver had been texting, over and over, asking for a pic of Alex. She maybe should've just blocked his number or told an adult or done something (*anything*) that could be classified as responsible . . . but she didn't.

Instead, she did something stupid.

She put her knees inside a red, lacy bra, the sexiest one she had, and took a picture that made it look like they were her boobs. It was something she'd seen on the internet, but the online version looked way better than her own. Alex thought her picture looked ob-vi-ous-ly fake since there was way more cleavage involved than she had in real life, but, objectively speaking, it *did* sort-of-maybe-kind-of look like actual cleavage. Still, she was more or less certain that Oliver would know it wasn't real.

She was wrong.

Less than ten minutes later, Oliver sent back a *very* real video of himself really jacking off to her fake boob picture.

That's what Alex was thinking about.

But instead of getting into all of that, Alex simply said, "Oliver."

"Boys are stupid."

"So stupid."

"Girls too, though."

Alex laughed.

And Layla laughed, too.

The truth is funny like that, Alex thought.

92 Days Until Graduation . . .

Emma decided it was time to break the ice in the Chat.

It was far too quiet.

She knew Layla and Zoe were both equally stubborn, but the silence had lasted for far too long, more than two weeks – *sixteen* days to be exact.

Emma had spent the last few days of spring break in Minneapolis visiting her cousins and had taken a pretty stellar selfie while she was on the SpongeBob roller coaster at the Mall of America. Then yesterday, once she got back to Los Angeles, she texted it to the Chat and hashtagged it as a sexie. If anything was going to get everyone talking again, Emma thought, it might be that pic.

Layla texted her back separately, directly, to say that the pic and the hashtag made her laugh out loud. Emma could tell she wasn't responding to the Chat on purpose.

Alex and Zoe didn't respond at all.

Even before Layla and Zoe got into it, the girls had decided to take a break from the Bigg Chill for spring break, since everyone was going to be traveling at different times. They were all back in town now, but *still* no one was texting and Emma figured it wasn't going to happen.

Zoe texted her just to say hi, and they decided to meet for coffee right across the street from the Bigg Chill. It felt weird to be near that intersection and not have any rainbow sprinkles on the table, Emma thought.

But then when Zoe asked her what she was thinking about, she said Savannah instead. Emma hadn't really talked to the girls about her, but this felt like the right time to say something.

"We've been texting over break," Emma explained. And then she told Zoe how they kissed at her birthday party that one time.

"Like. Kiss *kissed*?"

"Yep. Tongue. Butterflies. Goosebumps . . . And I liked it."

That last part, the part about *liking* the kiss, as opposed to just doing it, seemed like the more substantial portion of this conversation. Sometimes girls would randomly get drunk and make out with other girls at parties just because. Because it was trendy. Or because it got them attention. Or whatever. But this wasn't like that. Emma knew this was so much more than a "just because".

"So then you like Savannah?" Zoe asked.

Emma knew she meant "*like* like" without even having to ask for clarification. And she knew that she did, too. She grinned.

"All right then." Zoe smiled. "That's cool . . ."

"What?" Emma asked, sensing that there was more to Zoe's thought.

"Are you going to . . . come out?"

"Oh . . ."

"Ha, yeah, I know how much you love labels . . ."

"It's not about the label of it all," Emma said, trying to wrap her thoughts around her feelings. "It just feels like too much attention . . . and so definitive . . . and what if I change my mind?"

"I think that's allowed," Zoe said sincerely.

Zoe didn't want to make *too* big a deal about this moment . . .

. . . but she didn't want to make it too small either. This was important. She could feel that. That was part of the whole best friend thing: you could *feel* each other. It was part of what had made her and Layla yell across the lunch table at school a couple weeks ago. Caring for a friend's emotions as if they were your own could be muddled and difficult and confusing. Sometimes, even the togetherness could be overwhelming. *Especially* since there were four friends involved in the Crew dynamic. All the emotions felt exponential.

"I'm excited to hang with her," Zoe said about Savannah. It was her way of letting Emma know that it mattered to her, without saying too much.

"You will." Emma smiled. "You all will."

"Yeah . . . if Layla ever talks to me again."

"Or you talk to her."

Of course Zoe was going to talk to her. "I'm just not even sure who owes who an apology . . ." she explained.

"Maybe it's not an 'I'm sorry' kind of thing anymore. Maybe you should just start with more of a hi," Emma suggested.

"A hi?"

"Yeah. Like a little peace offering."

Zoe was just about to tell Emma how wise she was when an incoming text message buzzed into the Chat.

Hi.

It was from Layla.

"Woah," Zoe said, overwhelmed by the serendipity of the moment. "Did you give her the same advice?"

"Nope."

"She must've felt it."

"Definitely."

And ten minutes later, the girls found themselves sharing a side of rainbow sprinkles at their usual table at the Bigg Chill.

Layla was definitely still in.

"I was just having a moment . . ." she explained once everyone had settled into their chairs, and their phones had been stacked, and rainbow sprinkles had been distributed and everything.

"I know," Zoe said, "but if it's more than that, you really don't have to just say that for me."

"I'm not," Layla insisted. She didn't want to make any promises she couldn't keep, but she wanted to be a part of the pact. It mattered to her. "So. Tell the universe: still happening."

"Totally happening," Zoe agreed.

Zoe finally felt like herself again.

It had only been two weeks, but she'd missed her girls. She filled them in on the latest Austin progress report. They'd now had sex four times. And each time was better than the last, even if there were still no fireworks to be found.

Emma told Layla and Alex about Savannah.

"Wait, wait, wait," Layla said with one of those giant smiles on her face. "You know what this means, right?"

"Do I?" Emma asked cautiously.

"You're gonna lose your *girl* V-card," Alex said, totally hopping on Layla's train of thought.

"Ohmigod, *yes* . . ."

Emma hadn't really thought about it like that, but the girls were right.

"Can't wait for *that* progress report," Layla said.

Alex still didn't have much to report . . .

. . . but she finally told all the girls about Oliver's dick pic.

"Can I see it?" Zoe asked, surprising everyone at the table and prompting another round of giggles.

"I deleted it," Alex said.

"Too bad." Zoe laughed. "Let me know if he sends you another one . . ."

Alex already deleted his jacking-off video too, but she didn't tell the girls about that. She still wasn't entirely sure how she felt about it, but she knew she didn't want to talk about it.

"Maybe you guys should just do it already," Layla suggested.

"Oh *god*, you should talk," Alex teased back.

And everybody laughed.

And it felt like everything had fallen right back into place.

Unfortunately, that feeling didn't last very long . . .

91 Days Until Graduation . . .

Emma saw it first.

Nick forwarded her the email at 11.45 p.m.

You still up??? he texted her at the same time.

At first, Emma thought it was just a horny text message, a sext-me-maybe kind of text, but something about all the question marks tipped her off and made her think that it wasn't.

Yeah . . .? she texted back.

Check your email he texted. *Sorry, but I thought you should see.*

OH, she texted back as soon as she opened it.

It's totally obviously fake. I can tell, Nick texted.

Emma could tell, too.

It was Photoshopped.

The skin tones were all wrong.

The body was two shades lighter than Alex's *actual* skin color, and it didn't match her neck or her face – at all. But maybe that mismatch was something you could only notice if you looked closely.

Emma had a feeling that everyone who looked at this picture was going to be looking closely . . . but she didn't think anyone would be looking closely at *that*.

90 Days Until Graduation . . .

Alex woke up in a panic.

Her mind was racing and her palms were sweaty.

It was as if her body knew what had happened, even before she saw a hundred missed text messages on her phone and dozens of copies of the same email forwarded to her inbox. She scrolled to the bottom of her inbox, searching for the original email. It was sent at 11.37 p.m. last night, five minutes after she'd turned off her phone and gone to sleep.

The subject of the email was "superstar". All lowercase letters.

There were no words in the email.

Only a picture.

Alex got up out of bed. She couldn't lie or sit or even just stay still anymore. Instead, she started pacing around her bedroom and her bathroom.

She finally stopped long enough to open the photograph . . .

As soon as she saw it – really, clearly saw exactly what it was – she turned around and threw up all over the tiles on her bathroom floor.

It was the most awful thing she'd ever seen. And most of

it was her. Well, *some* of it was her. The head, at least. It was still entirely awful.

Zoe could feel every pair of eyes staring at her and Layla and Emma.

"This is insane," Zoe whispered as they walked down the hallway.

It felt a little bit like a nightmare where she accidentally showed up to school naked. But it wasn't a dream. This was really happening.

And the girls weren't really naked, but everyone was staring.

And Alex wasn't really naked either, but her picture made it look like she was, and everyone was talking about it as if it were real.

Alex's real head had been Photoshopped onto a naked body.

It wasn't her real body, but it looked real enough.

And everyone in the hallway had definitely looked at it.

It was only the second day back from spring break, Tuesday, and Alex had stayed home from school. She said she couldn't face anybody.

Alex had texted the Chat, something about plans and god and a sick sense of humor, but Zoe couldn't quite keep it all straight right now.

The Crew met Alex's parents at the door to the principal's office. They had just been in a meeting, demanding swift repercussions, but the head of the IT department informed them that – long and nerdy story short – they didn't know who sent the email, and they couldn't trace the IP address associated with the account.

"Do you know who might've had a reason to send this?" asked their principal, Mrs. Bowers, as if there was going to be a simple answer to that question.

As if Alex didn't have a reputation.

As if people didn't make up stupid stories about her all the time.

The girls were thinking all of that, but they didn't say any of it.

They promised to alert the principal and Alex's parents right away if they heard anything that might be helpful.

Afterwards, they huddled up in the hallway.

"It had to be Oliver, right?" Layla asked.

All the girls wanted to say yes. They wanted to be able to prove that it was definitely Oliver. And of course that made sense. And it was probably more likely than not that it really was him . . . but they couldn't prove it.

And the hard part was, as Emma articulated, "It could've been anyone."

"At least it's not *real*," Zoe said.

She was trying to find the bright side, but it didn't seem particularly bright.

85 Days Until Graduation . . .

Alex hadn't really responded to anything or anyone all week.
  She couldn't.
  The Crew had unsuccessfully tried to come over after school
on Friday. And then on Saturday, too. And now it was Sunday.
It was a quarter to four. It was almost time for froyo. But Alex
still just couldn't get out of bed.
  So the girls got the froyo for Alex instead.
  They bought medium-sized servings of every flavor on the
flavor board at the Bigg Chill (ten flavors altogether) and
brought all of them to Alex's house along with a dozen possible
topping options.
  "Bigg Chill Aaron says he's sorry and he hopes you feel
better," Layla said as she passed out the plastic spoons.
  "Oh my god . . ." Alex said. "Bigg Chill Aaron saw the
picture?!"
  "Well. At first I was thinking, he just thought you were sick,"
Layla explained, "but then he also said to tell you to 'keep your
head up' so I think it's probably safe to say he did."
  Yep, Alex thought. *Bigg Chill Aaron had definitely seen it.*
  Everyone with an internet connection had seen it.

It . . .

Ugh.

Alex still couldn't bring herself to say "me", mostly because the picture mostly wasn't *actually* her, but also because the whole episode felt like such a mistake, such an awful, horrible joke, that she still wasn't entirely sure it was real.

"At least the body is hot," Alex said, attempting some levity.

Ugh. *The* body . . .

It's not that Alex *wanted* it to be her body – she actually very much did *not* want that – but at least if it was hers, she could claim some sort of ownership of it. She could've said, "yes, that's me, take it or leave it . . ." – but it wasn't. It was a sick, Photoshopped fantasy, which felt like a violation on top of a violation.

Everyone thought she wasn't a virgin.

She was.

Everyone thought she was naked.

She wasn't.

Alex's reality was overshadowed by everyone's thoughts and feelings.

And, really, no one knew exactly where the picture came from. "There's no proof," the girls had all said, resigned to the uncertainty.

Alex wasn't *entirely* sure, but she had one pretty strong guess.

84 Days Until Graduation . . .

Alex needed to get back on track, literally and figuratively.

Her parents had given her permission to stay home from school again, but there were only so many track meets on the calendar, and the record certainly wasn't going to break itself.

Luckily, her body seemed to agree. She found herself awake and dressed for school and leaning against Oliver's car a whole twenty minutes early. Her shoes were already on and the laces were tied and all her possessions were packed inside of her backpack. None of that had ever happened before, let alone all of that at the same time. She stood outside in the driveway, waiting. Watching. Noticing everything. Like the thin morning breeze. And the paint scratches on Oliver's car. The way her toes felt inside of her sneakers.

And then Oliver walked outside. It felt like he knew Alex would be early for the first time all year. He raised his hands up as he walked toward her as if to say he came in peace, or that he wasn't guilty, or maybe a little bit of both.

"Alex," Oliver said in a tone of voice she'd never heard before.

This wasn't "Oliver the flirt" talking or "Oliver the basketball star" or even "Oliver the asshole". This was just Oliver, the boy next door.

"I'm sorry," he said. It wasn't like the way he apologized for kissing Caroline on the bus. This was an actual, real-life "I'm sorry" for something seriously worth being sorry about.

"I didn't do it," he added.

Alex didn't know how to respond. She just stared at him for a moment. *Through* him, really. And into his piercing blue eyes. She didn't *want* to believe him, but there was something about the way he looked, his quiet face, his strong jawline, the way he held his body as it got closer to hers . . . And something about the way he said he didn't do it – his tone, his sincerity, the measured speed of his words as they slipped out of his mouth – forced a big lump in Alex's throat. She hadn't cried since it happened. Not once . . . She had puked more times than she could count, and she wasn't really sleeping or eating or combing her hair, but she hadn't cried . . .

. . . until now.

The lump in her throat turned into a fire in her eyes. And the tears – the hot, sticky, uncontrollable tears – came spilling out. It wasn't just *a* tear. It was *all* of the tears . . . tears for all of the bad jokes and the rumors. For the cat calls and the cattiness. The two minutes and thirty-five seconds that Max held his breath. The months – *years* – she'd lied to her friends about that night at sleep-away camp. All the Mona Lisa smiles and the city lights near Mulholland. The star charm on her sneakers. The superstar email with all-lowercase letters.

The way it never happens the way you want it to.

All of it.

Oliver respected Alex's space, staying near, but not too close, until her sobs finally reached a crescendo, and he had no choice but to step forward. He moved toward her slowly, but purposefully, until he stretched out his arms and wrapped them around Alex's back, pulling her into his chest, holding her.

Even after that, Alex cried for a very long time.

Oliver held her until she didn't need to be held anymore.

They were both late to school, but it didn't matter.

82 Days Until Graduation . . .

Emma got her very first college acceptance on April Fool's Day.

Of course she did.

She'd spent the past few months, basically all of senior year, feeling like the universe was playing a giant practical joke on her, so *of course* she'd get into college on a day where everything was supposed to be some sort of joke.

"Yeah," Savannah said, "you should probably check your spam folder."

Emma hadn't considered that.

But just before she started to panic some more, Savannah continued, "I'm kidding. Deep breaths. You're good. And I'm proud of you."

She put her hand on top of Emma's and squeezed it reassuringly. She held on for a moment. Emma could feel a layer of sweat coating her palm. She pulled her hand away as slickly as she could (which wasn't very) and wiped it on her corduroys. Savannah didn't seem *thrilled*, but public handholding really wasn't her style. Emma tried to carry on the conversation instead, rambling on about how her parents wanted to celebrate and have a whole big dinner. Her mom

266

wanted to use the nice china plates. Her dad wanted to make a speech.

"So, dinner . . ." Savannah said tentatively. "Do I make the cut on that?"

Honestly, Emma hadn't even considered it. Her parents had insisted that she invite "the girls", but to them that just meant Zoe and Alex and Layla of course.

"Or just forget I asked," Savannah said, before Emma had figured out how to respond.

It wasn't that Emma didn't *want* Savannah to be there, but it just felt like a lot all at once.

"We wouldn't want to make any sudden movements or anything," Savannah added rather pointedly.

"Hey," Emma said, pushing back.

"I'm not . . . it's not about *dinner*," Savannah replied.

Emma could hear the frustration in her voice, and she couldn't exactly fault Savannah for that either. They'd been hanging out at school a lot, and things were decidedly "good" between them, but their kiss count was still stuck at one. It wasn't that Emma was *avoiding* kiss number two, but she hadn't exactly put herself in a position to let it happen either.

"It just feels like . . . what's that expression? 'If a tree falls in the woods when no one's around, can anyone hear it?'"

"Oh, you mean: does it make a sound?" Emma asked.

"Do I?"

"I think so. 'Cause obviously if no one's around then no one can hear it, but the point is about sound. Like, did it really happen at all?"

"Right." Savannah nodded.

"Ha. Yeah," Emma said, still trying to understand what she was getting at.

"It's sort of like: 'if you fall for a cute girl but she's too embarrassed to tell anyone about it, are you really falling?'"

There it was.

That's what Savannah was actually mad about.

"No?" Savannah asked, forcing the issue. "Does that one not work?" She got up and walked out of the classroom.

Emma followed right after her. "Hey. Stop. I'm not embarrassed."

"You sure about that?"

"Yes! Jeez. Come to dinner if it's that big a deal—"

"I already said it's not about *dinner*—"

"Then why are you making such a big deal about it?"

"You make a big deal about everything!"

"And you don't! That's why this is so weird!"

"I know you don't want me to have, like, expectations or whatever, but I don't think that's realistic anymore . . . And I know you're confused, but the thing is: I'm not. I know who I am. And I know how I feel. And I'm not trying to push you . . . but if you weren't so scared, I'd kiss you right here in the hallway."

"I'm not scared," Emma said as forcefully as she could, but it still came out sounding mostly shaky.

Savannah stepped even closer to Emma. Now their noses were practically touching. Emma could feel Savannah's breath on her lips. She was basically daring Emma to kiss her. Right here. Right now. *In public.*

Emma wanted to . . . but she didn't.

And before she could do much of anything else, Savannah spun around and took off down the hallway. Emma wanted to yell out "wait". She wanted to stop her. But she couldn't. So she didn't, *again*.

And Savannah didn't come to dinner.

Alex felt like she was late for carpool even though it was 7.30 p.m.

She'd stayed late at athletics and lost track of time and now she was running late to dinner at Emma's house. Alex hustled toward Emma's front door. Zoe's forest-green Ford Explorer was parked right out front. The engine was still running.

"Hi, Zoe," Alex said as she approached the driver's window.

"Well, it *rhymes* with Zoe," Joey corrected.

Alex's heart skipped a beat. Actually, it felt like her heart stopped for an entire moment as she laid her eyes on Joey Reed.

"Spring break," he explained as he fiddled with the radio.

"Nice to see you."

"Nice to see you too," Joey said. Something about the way he said it made Alex wonder if he'd seen the picture. Her picture. "I'm sorry," he added. And she didn't have to wonder anymore.

"Yeah . . ." was all she could think to say.

"Did you hear about that time I got pants-ed in the middle of the track?" Joey asked, seemingly out of nowhere.

No. Alex hadn't heard about that. And Joey launched into a whole story about his sophomore year, and how his asshole friends had pulled his pants down around his ankles. In front of *everybody*. And how he was absolutely mortified. Joey explained the whole thing in a way that Alex had *felt* but hadn't been able to articulate.

Joey just got it.

And truth was, his story was way worse than Alex's because it really was his penis everyone saw. Joey explained that the pants-ing episode was the final straw that helped him lose all the "baby fat" he'd been holding onto for so long.

"This is way more of a conversation than I was expecting to have with you," Joey admitted once he'd reached the end of it.

"Thank you," she said.

"You're welcome." He ran his fingers through his hair. It felt like they were both trying to figure out what to say next. It felt like there was so much more they *wanted* to say, but it all just came out sounding like silence instead.

Then Zoe burst out through the front door. She'd forgotten her cell phone in the car. Joey unplugged it from his charger and handed it over. "Nice work, goober. You're lucky I didn't drive off yet."

"We were just catching up," Alex offered. She felt lame for thinking the situation needed any sort of explanation at all.

"Cool, cool," Zoe said, mocking the way Joey would say it. "But, like, get your own friends? Thanks, bro."

Zoe seemed mostly oblivious to the sexual tension simmering between them. She slipped her arm through Alex's and pulled her towards Emma's front door. Alex looked back over her shoulder one more time before they went inside, stealing another glance at Joey.

Obviously he'd been waiting for her to look back.

He winked at her.

Oh wow.

That wink, Alex thought.

She could feel it in her entire body.

And a few hours later, as she stood in her bathroom, getting ready for bed, she could still feel that wink as if it had just happened. She'd thought about it all through dinner, while Emma's dad had made a speech. And she'd thought about it after dinner too, while the girls had smoked a joint on Emma's roof.

"Wyatt's dad has a medical card," Layla had explained as she pulled the tightly rolled joint out of her pocket. The Crew didn't get high together very often, but everyone decided they could use a break from the insides of their heads and all their rambling thoughts and feelings for a minute or two. They passed the joint around for a while, and then they sat on Emma's roof, laughing about how big the universe was and how small they all were – and they officially decided they needed some more quality time together.

Zoe had suggested that they have a sleepover. Her parents were going to be out of town Friday night. She said Joey might be home, but he could probably score them some alcohol. All the girls were down, but Alex was especially glad she wasn't going to have to come up with an excuse to see Joey again.

That wink.

Alex was still feeling it.

And she was feeling a new sense of contentment pouring over her even an hour later as she stood in the bathroom, washing her face and brushing her teeth and getting ready for bed. She wasn't sure exactly where this feeling was coming

271

from, but she knew that she liked it. Maybe it was because she was high. Or maybe it was because this was one of the best nights she'd had with her girls in a really long time. Or maybe it was because of the story Joey had told her outside of Emma's house, and how she'd connected to it . . .

Whatever it was, she couldn't stop thinking about that wink.

It was totally possible that she was reading too far into it, the same way her friends at camp had read too far into her Mona Lisa smile. Maybe she was exaggerating their connection. Maybe it wasn't really as strong and seemingly instantaneous as she felt it was. Maybe she was overanalyzing the situation.

Or maybe she was just simply crazy . . .

Then she glanced down at her phone. There was a waiting text message. It was from Joey.

Heard you're sleeping over tomorrow night . . . glad I don't have to make up an excuse to see you again.

Maybe, actually, she wasn't so crazy after all.

80 Days Until Graduation . . .

Alex couldn't remember the last time they'd had an actual sleepover.

The girls crashed at each other's houses all the time, after parties or late nights or sometimes for no reason at all. But the last time the main plan of the evening was a sleepover? Alex had no clue.

"Wanna watch a movie?" Zoe asked, turning on the movie projector.

She was expecting to see the Netflix home page, but instead . . .

"Oh, shit," Layla laughed.

"Are those . . .?" Zoe asked, turning her familiar shade of red. She wondered why her cheeks didn't just stay that way permanently.

"Yup. Two girls kissing." Alex smiled.

There were, in fact, two naked girls making out on the screen.

"It's Joey's . . ." Zoe explained. His laptop was still hooked up to the screen.

"Well, it's hot," Alex said. She wasn't sure if she meant the video itself or the thought of Joey watching it. Probably a little bit of both.

"I'm down," Emma chimed in.

"Me too," Layla said.

"Ohmigod," Zoe squirmed, clearly outnumbered, "it's fine. I'll just be over here trying not to think about my brother getting turned on by this . . ."

Now that was *all* Alex could think about.

"Can we at least pick a different video?"

Alex's phone buzzed. It was a text from Joey: *Upstairs.*

Alex couldn't help but notice the period at the end of his text.

It wasn't a question.

It was a statement.

And she liked it.

"Pick something hot," Alex said. Then she added a stupid excuse about wanting to go grab a Diet Coke real quick. It was the only thing she could think of that they hadn't already brought out to the guest house. She would have to go back into the kitchen to get it.

"Anybody want anything else?" she asked, trying to appear casual. Inside, her heart was already racing.

She walked into the Reeds' living room, right past the kitchen and upstairs towards Joey's room. Her bare feet were cold against the hardwood floor. She could feel the word "magnetic" swirling around in her head, as if that explained everything: she was being drawn towards Joey.

"Hi," she said as she walked into Joey's room.

"Hi," he replied, standing up to greet her.

Before she knew it, they were only a few inches apart.

That magnetism.

A spark from Joey's deep brown eyes slid down his face and parted his smile, and in one fluid movement he pulled Alex towards him, pressing his lips – firmly, sweetly, *perfectly* – against hers. The kiss was so natural and so obvious and so necessary that it was actually the pulling apart afterwards that felt strange. All she wanted to do was kiss him again.

But before she could, her phone buzzed. It was the girls, getting anxious.

"They're waiting for me – to watch your porn collection," Alex explained.

Joey smirked and then pulled her in for another soul-melding, mind-crushing, body-bursting kind of kiss.

Alex's phone buzzed again.

"Ugh. Okay." She smiled. "To be continued . . ."

"Please stay?" Joey said as if the word had escaped through his lips without permission.

"I can't," Alex said. She wanted to, but she couldn't. Not right now. "Chicks before dicks," she added with a little laugh, knowing it would drive him crazy.

It did. And she liked that.

"All right, fine . . ." he said with an adorable shake of his head. He ran his fingers through his hair. "Me and my 'dick' are gonna go take a cold shower."

79 Days Until Graduation . . .

Emma woke up the next morning with a hangover.

It felt like a happy hangover, but still, her head was throbbing.

The girls had an incredible time last night. They drank and ate and giggled and watched porn. They spent some time in the Reeds' Jacuzzi, laughing about the warm jets and how if they positioned themselves just right on top of them, it might set off a fireworks display. It had been perfect – except for the fact that the hours they spent together might as well have been just a few minutes. Their time felt like it was flying, dripping away, and there was nothing any of them could do to hold it or stop it.

Emma's stomach was growling and her heart felt strange. All she wanted to do was be with Savannah. And talk to her. And maybe dance with her. Or maybe even kiss her again . . .

. . . but Savannah had stopped responding to her text messages ever since Emma had been stupid enough to forget to invite her to dinner.

Clearly, Emma should've handled the whole situation better, but she hadn't. She'd messed up.

Emma went home and took a nap and woke up to a flurry of new texts in the Chat. Layla had sent a whole string of new inspirational quotes, as Layla so often did, and the last one was particularly pertinent for Emma's current state of mind. It was a picture of a bike along with the words "to keep your balance you have to keep moving".

Emma felt that.

For months, basically all year, she felt like she had been out of balance, entirely unsteady. But now she realized that maybe she was going about it all backwards. Maybe her unsteadiness came from the fact that she was effectively attempting to stay in the same place. Everyone around her was moving forward. Because that's what people did. They moved. They evolved. Despite her fears, Emma wanted all that too. But first she needed to find her balance.

All Emma wanted to do was jump on her bike and pedal to Savannah's house.

So she did.

In her car, this hill leading up to Savannah's house just seemed like a little incline. Now, on her bike, it might as well have been a mountain. When Emma finally did make it to the top, she was covered in sweat. This certainly wasn't how she envisioned this moment with Savannah, but she didn't work so hard just to chicken out now.

She took a few deep breaths, attempting to steady herself, but she knew the only way she was going to find steadiness or balance or whatever she wanted to call it was to actually move forward.

So that is exactly what she did.

She walked up the steps and knocked on Savannah's front door.

"What are you doing here?" Savannah asked, stepping outside to talk to Emma and closing the door behind her.

"You said I didn't need to make up excuses to hang out with you . . ."

Emma smiled, which made Savannah smile back too. And then, Emma could feel why she was there. *This*, she thought as she looked into Savannah's eyes. This is what it was supposed to feel like. The hormones. The racing. This moment felt like everything she'd heard Layla and Alex and Zoe talk about. This was good. And it wasn't like Emma *hadn't* felt good before, because she definitely had. And it wasn't like she hadn't been aroused before . . . she had. But all of that? All of that *before?* It simply wasn't *this*.

She could feel that much for sure.

Emma could also feel her blood and her boobs and the butterflies and all of the sweat, still dripping down her back and neck and knees. She could see it all from the outside and feel it all from the inside and she knew she owed Savannah an apology and more honesty and a grand gesture too, and so she stepped forward onto Savannah's welcome mat and kissed her perfectly pink lips.

This kiss was long and hard and on purpose.

This! Emma thought.

This was balance and movement all at the same time.

"Look at Emma O'Malley, kissing in public and everything . . ." Savannah said after Emma pulled away.

Emma laughed. "Does it count as being 'public' if there's no one around to see it?"

"I don't know. What if a tree falls in the woods and there's no one around to hear it?" Savannah asked, joining in on Emma's laughter.

This, Emma thought again as she caught Savannah's eyes.

"So. We can agree this is good, right?" Emma asked, repeating Savannah's words from the water polo match.

"Emma. If you're trying to *expectation* me right now . . ."

"I'm not *expectation-ing* anything," Emma said, smiling with her entire face.

After a few more kisses on the front step, Emma found herself pedaling home even harder and faster than she had on the way there.

I kissed a girl and I liked it, she texted the Chat as soon as she got home.

OHMIGOD YES, Zoe texted back almost immediately.

I love it so much, Layla texted.

Lucky Savannah, Alex added.

Lucky me, Emma thought.

Alex's thoughts had been entirely consumed by Joey Reed.

The last time she saw him was about twelve hours earlier as she'd snuck up into Zoe and Joey's shared bathroom to say goodbye before she went home after the sleepover. She'd said hi, and then he'd said hi, and they'd been stuck staring at each other for a moment until Joey said he had to see her again before he went back to school. And then he kissed her and it rattled her soul, and it took every single ounce of self-control in Alex's body not to melt into a puddle on the floor right then and there. And then somehow she'd managed to survive the rest of the day and most of the night.

As soon as her parents went to sleep, she'd texted Joey to come over. He'd snuck out of his house and now here he was, tiptoeing into the Campbells' kitchen, through the back door, as quietly as he could.

At first sight, Alex wanted to kiss him everywhere and all-at-once and the urge was so strong and overwhelming it had the exact opposite effect: it stopped her in her tracks. Alex felt like once she started to kiss him she may never be able to stop, and the thought was absolutely terrifying and amazing all at once.

"I know . . ." Joey said, as if he could read her thoughts.

"You know?"

"You're bad news, Campbell." Joey grinned.

Alex led him up the stairs and into her bedroom, slowly closing the door behind her.

"Hi," she whispered, not wanting to wake up her parents or Max.

"Hi," Joey whispered back. Then he laughed.

"What's funny?"

"I feel like I've been with you all day because I haven't been able to stop thinking about you. And now that I'm here, literally looking at you, and I already miss you . . ." Joey laughed at himself. "So much for playing it cool, huh?"

"Cool is overrated," Alex said with another smile.

"Thanks . . ." Joey laughed.

"You know what I mean," Alex said. Besides, she felt the same way.

Alex and Joey spent the entire night kissing.

Basically *just* kissing.

There was some touching too, but mostly they were just running from first base to second base and back again, in the most enjoyable circles. They'd stop every once in a while to laugh or hold each other or share a secret or tell a story, and then they'd inevitably start kissing again.

And again and *again* . . .

And again and again it felt like things might escalate physically, and they *could've*, certainly, but Joey and Alex just didn't seem to be in that kind of a rush.

For Alex, the girl who had been known to get bored with a boy before the end of their first make-out session, the girl who felt like she was always rushing, the girl who was always trying to move faster – *to literally break speed records* – this was an incredibly important moment of stillness. Of slowness. Of general *now*-ness.

Most of the time, Alex felt like she was being pushed and pulled and prodded to be something she wasn't . . .

. . . but right now with Joey, the only thing she had to be was herself.

78 Days Until Graduation . . .

Alex and Joey managed to kiss until the sun came up . . .

. . . but it still didn't feel like nearly enough time.

"I'm gonna miss you," Joey whispered. He smiled with a little pink in his cheeks, as if he was surprised that the words had come out of his mouth.

"I'm gonna miss you too," she said, thinking it was strange, considering how little time they'd actually spent together, but knowing it wasn't strange at all considering all the feelings she was feeling through her whole body.

"I miss you already," Joey said, laughing at his own corniness.

"Same," Alex replied, full of sincerity and a little bit of sadness.

She'd known Joey for about twelve years, ever since she and Zoe had been friends, and even though they'd formed their own friendship through the track team, they'd never really spent any time alone together.

Until now.

And it felt like the most natural thing in the entire world.

Being together, with their lips and everything touching or their fingers and legs intertwined, felt right. But Joey had to leave. He had to sneak out of Alex's house and back into his before Zoe or his parents had a chance to notice he was gone.

So he kissed Alex goodbye one more time. Softly and slowly.

He said he'd text her as soon as he got back to his dorm room at Berkeley.

And he did.

Hi, he said simply.

Hi, she texted back.

I miss you, he added. And then also: *Ugh*.

Alex felt exactly the same way . . . all the way down to the *ugh*.

I miss you too, she texted back.

She really did miss him. It was actually almost physically painful. Alex wasn't sure how to explain her feelings for Joey because they came on so fast and strong, but if she knew anything, anything at all, it was that they were the most real feelings she'd ever felt. For eighteen years, she'd had this space inside her, below her heart and above her stomach – maybe it was the place where the butterflies and the fireworks live – but it hadn't really registered before now. Like, if she'd walked through an X-ray machine, even just yesterday, there would've only been blank space inside her.

But now . . . *Ugh*, she thought, which was both the best and worst feeling all at the same time . . .

Now, Joey Reed – and his spiked hair and those teal glasses and that wink – was sitting inside of her, filling an entire space that she hadn't even known existed.

Now, she didn't want to even consider feeling any other way.

74 Days Until Graduation . . .

Zoe was starting to worry that something was seriously wrong with her.

She and Austin were still dating. And they were still sleeping together semi-regularly. And it was mostly fun, and she liked it, but she still hadn't had an orgasm.

"Maybe I'm, like, physically incapable of having one," she'd proposed at froyo last week, but none of the other girls was willing to humor her.

It's totally gonna happen, they all assured her.

"Trust the process," Emma had giggled.

Zoe did trust the process – sort of.

But she decided she also wanted some professional reassurance that everything was working down there the way it should, so she'd made an appointment with her gynecologist. Also, she figured it was probably a good move to go on the pill. She and Austin had been using condoms, but still.

Zoe stood by the oak tree next to the senior parking lot, waiting for her mom to pick her up, when she saw Dylan heading towards her. Well, really he was heading towards the pool with a pack of water polo boys, but it was the closest they'd come to being in the same place at the same time in a long time.

She wasn't even expecting him to wave, let alone walk over and say hi, but he did. Zoe didn't realize how much she'd missed him until he was standing right there in front of her, but she didn't realize the words were just going to tumble out of her mouth . . .

"I've missed you too," he said before her cheeks even had time to turn red.

"I got into Michigan," Zoe blurted out, realizing she hadn't told him yet.

"Oh hell, yeah," Dylan said. He'd already had an early admission to Colorado. His older brother went there, and it was the only school he wanted to go to. And he got in. It was pretty undramatic as far as the college process goes.

Zoe's college applications had been that way too. She wanted to go to a big school where people rooted for things and wore face paint and went to frat parties, but she also wanted a theater department. Zoe thought Michigan would be the perfect fit. Luckily, Michigan thought so too.

Then, Zoe's mom pulled up and waved. It was time to go.

But before Zoe walked away, Dylan asked if she wanted to phonefall later that night.

Zoe had never said yes faster.

72 Days Until Graduation . . .

Alex and Joey had been texting constantly.

Ever since they'd spent the whole night kissing, they'd been continuously texting about anything and everything. Embarrassing stories. Childhood memories. Stupid jokes. They'd texted about their hopes and dreams and all their thoughts on god. About drugs and alcohol and rainbow sprinkles. Alex's running shoes and how they occasionally didn't match. She even texted him about the star charm on her shoelaces. The one Oliver gave her. They texted about their daydreams and nightmares . . . Alex admitted that lately *he*'d been keeping her up.

She even texted him to say that she couldn't stop thinking about him, which wasn't the kind of thing she normally wanted to admit, but it felt like Joey already knew that. He texted her back and said he felt exactly the same way.

Alex couldn't imagine having all of these text message conversations with anyone else. She'd never really cared what *any* boy thought about these topics, let alone what one particular boy thought about *all* of them. But with Joey, she wanted to know everything.

The only strange thing about all of their texting was that it accounted for all of their communication. She liked texting much better. She appreciated having the time and space to respond in exactly the right way.

But.

Considering the fact that none of these words *had* actually come out of her mouth, and also that she hadn't actually heard any of them come out of Joey's mouth either, the whole thing was starting to seem like a strange dream. And to make matters worse, she still hadn't told the rest of the Crew about Joey. She certainly didn't want to lie to Zoe, not after the Cameron stuff, but she knew how weird Zoe could get about things, especially things that involved her brother, and she didn't want to have to get all into it if things with Joey weren't going to last. Maybe that was lying by omission, but Alex wanted to figure out what was actually going on between them before she opened it up to the Crew.

Alex climbed into bed for the night and grabbed her phone.

Can I ask you a question? she texted Joey, innocently enough.

If it's "what am I wearing?", it's gonna be awkward, he texted back.

Alex smirked. That *wasn't* what she was going to ask, but now she wanted to know. She and Joey had texted for an incredibly long time without crossing into any sort of "sext message" territory, and Alex had recently started to wonder when or if Joey was going to make that sort of a move.

(The answer is nothing), he texted before she could respond. Then he added, *What about you?*

The truth? She was wearing flannel pajama bottoms and an oversized track T-shirt, but she was pretty sure that wasn't the kind of answer Joey was hoping for. She lied – well, fibbed – and texted that she was wearing *black panties*. She hated the word "panties", but underwear just didn't sound sexy enough.

UGH, he responded. *I want to take them off.*

Yes, please, she texted back quickly.

And then it was on . . .

. . . and they were turning each other on as a flurry of sext messages replaced their usual text message rhythm. Joey told her where he wanted to touch her and how he wanted to touch her, and before Alex knew it she was actually touching herself. And Joey was touching himself too . . . And pretty soon there were fireworks on both ends of the phone.

Or so Alex had to assume.

She liked texting Joey, and she liked sexting him too, but all of that was only taking place in the glow of her phone screen.

Alex was starting to worry that it wasn't real.

Part of the problem was that it felt too good to be true.

70 Days Until Graduation . . .

Layla was still spending far too much time thinking about Logan.

It wasn't that she was still mad at him anymore or hurt by him or anything like that, but she simply couldn't get him out of her head for any extended period of time – and it was driving her crazy.

And now.

Logan and Vanessa were *officially* a couple, and they were almost always making out all over campus. And Layla was pretending not to notice or care, both of which were horrible lies. She was focusing on schoolwork mostly, still trying to get her grade up to an A in AP Lit, doing some extra-credit assignments. She was also trying as hard as she could not to focus on the calendar or her to-do list and its due date.

And so, for the first time all year, Layla had actually succeeded in losing track of time, which was very un-Layla-like. But then, last night, as she was lying in bed, searching for new quotes and still feeling uninspired, she suddenly felt compelled to count the days on the calendar. And so she did. She counted down, all the way down from today, Monday, April 12th, to

Graduation Day on June 22nd, and she simply had to laugh. She certainly believed that the universe had a mind of its own, but she didn't think it was *perverted*. Then again, maybe it was.

She counted the days on the calendar again, a second time, and then, just to be safe, a *third* time too, and realized that as of tomorrow, Tuesday, there would be exactly sixty-nine days until graduation. Sixty-nine. Of course she *would* reignite her interest in the calendar and the counting and all of that right before the most overtly sexual day of the whole countdown.

If Layla had ever gotten a sign from the universe, this might be it.

She texted Wyatt right away and made a plan to see him after school.

They'd hooked up a couple times since that first make-out session at the skatepark before spring break. He was still fun, and still uncomplicated, but Layla still knew that she didn't want to sleep with him, but that didn't mean she couldn't make some sex-pact-related progress with him.

"You're gonna sixty-nine him?" Alex asked as she unwrapped a protein bar.

"I think we should say that I'm gonna sixty-nine *with* him," Layla said so seriously that it caused all the girls to laugh.

"Okay, grammar police . . ."

"No, it's just . . . it's not something I can just do to him," Layla said. "He has to do it to me too, which is kind of the whole point . . ."

69 Days Until Graduation . . .

Layla drove over to Wyatt's house right after school.

They quickly found themselves alone in his room. On his bed. With the door closed. Wyatt's parents weren't home from work yet, but Layla got the vibe that they wouldn't care about an "open-door policy" even if they were. Wyatt was pointing out all the constellations on his ceiling: the Big Dipper, Orion's belt. He'd arranged all of them with glow-in-the-dark stickers. He was very proud.

"Wyatt?" Layla said, interrupting his tour of the galaxy.

"Yeah?" he asked with a big smile on his face. A big smile crept over Layla's face, too. "Whatever you're thinking, I can already tell that I like it."

"I've never . . ." she started, and then stopped to make sure she was choosing her words carefully. "I graduate from high school in sixty-nine days."

"Woah, crazy . . ." Wyatt said.

Layla could tell that he didn't entirely understand what she was trying to say.

"And I'm realizing that's something I've never done before."

"Graduate from high school?" Wyatt asked, clearly teasing.

"The other part. And, um, the reason I've never done it is because no one's ever . . ."

". . . gone down on you?" Wyatt asked, completing her sentence. "Is it because you didn't want them to?"

"I'm not really sure what I wanted," Layla said truthfully.

"But now you do," Wyatt said, his grin still finding ways to grow.

"I, um, well . . ." Layla said, trying to qualify her statement or maybe just even lessen it in some way, so as not to seem too brash or demanding.

But Wyatt didn't seem to need any of that.

"I got you . . ." he said, before sliding down to the bottom of the bed, taking Layla's jeans and underwear down with him.

The universe might have a sick sense of humor, Layla thought as she looked back up at the constellations on Wyatt's ceiling, but in the grand scheme of things, it definitely seemed to know what it was doing.

After Wyatt spent some time between Layla's legs, he stopped what he was doing and asked if she wanted to sixty-nine, since it was numerically appropriate and all.

The answer to Wyatt's question was unequivocally yes.

Yes, she wanted to do that. And yes, it was the right day and all that, but that wasn't *why* she wanted to do it. To be totally honest: she just did. It was the same way she knew she *didn't* want to have sex with Logan. She just didn't. And that was okay. And this was okay too . . .

. . . and once they finally (awkwardly) got situated in a sixty-nine position (on their sides facing each other), it all became so much more than okay.

So. Much. More.

And then . . .

. . . after a while of tongues and lips and pressure and pleasure . . .

. . . it all exploded into *synchronized* fireworks.

Yes, Layla thought afterwards.

So. Much. Yes.

68 Days Until Graduation . . .

Alex had been successfully avoiding Layla's progress reports for a few weeks.

After Oliver and the picture and all that, the girls had given Alex some space in the boy department, but now they were starting to ask questions again.

"You sure there's nothing you want to tell us?" Layla asked.

"Oh, I'm sure." Alex grinned, trying to play coy.

She *wanted* to tell the girls about Joey, she really did, especially after how mad Zoe got about her lying about Cameron and camp and everything. But the problem was that she didn't know what to say exactly. She wanted to at least know *what* was happening before she told the girls that it *was* happening, but in order to get any clarity about the situation she was going to have to ask Joey. Her fear was that asking him about what it was exactly would ruin whatever it was actually. And it all still just seemed so strange and dreamlike. Still, no one else knew what had happened. Alex had never even said the words "I kissed Joey Reed" out loud. She had no one to say them to.

To Alex's surprise, Joey was the first one to bring up Zoe.

You can tell her if you want, he texted late one night when they were both already in bed.

I don't want to tell her if it's just gonna be a fling, Alex texted back.

After an oversized pause, Joey replied: *Yeah.*

Alex noticed that Joey had added a period to the end of his "Yeah" and she suddenly hated it so much. That period. It was so small, but also so stupid and so frustratingly definitive. What she wanted him to say was "of course it's not a fling". Or "the truth is, I'm really into you". Or "I want to be with you". Or "I might even love you. Let's make out for ever and ever".

Any of that – or all of that – would've been perfect . . . Alex waited for what felt like another for ever for him to type something else, something more, something, *anything*. But he didn't.

Unfortunately for now, that one small, stupid word was all Alex was going to get out of him.

So she texted it back exactly the same way.

Yeah.

She hoped he'd notice the period at the end. She hoped he'd hate it as much as she did. She hoped he'd be hoping for more, too . . .

. . . and maybe he was, but he still didn't text anything else. And neither did Alex.

She turned off her phone just to be sure.

64 Days Until Graduation . . .

Emma and Savannah held hands in the movie theater.

Overall, the handholding only lasted about five minutes, but that was more than four minutes longer than Emma had ever held anybody else's hand.

It was their first real date night. And Emma figured that handholding was the sort of thing you were supposed to do on a real date night.

So she obliged . . . for four-ish minutes.

But it was something.

And Emma could tell it meant a lot to Savannah.

After the movie, the girls ended up back at Savannah's house. Emma's parents were going to pick her up on their way home, but they were running late.

Emma certainly wasn't complaining about the lateness.

Especially when she and Savannah found themselves alone in Savannah's bedroom. Actually on Savannah's bed. And Emma realized it was the first time they'd ever been alone somewhere that wasn't the yearbook room.

Savannah pulled Emma in for a kiss . . . which then quickly turned into a whole *string* of kisses . . . And soon Savannah's hands were everywhere and then Emma's hands were also everywhere, and things were decidedly different (and better) than ever before because part of that "everywhere" included Savannah's boobs. Emma had touched her own boobs before and that always turned her on, but touching Savannah's boobs was even more exciting than that.

And then – *then* – when Savannah touched *her* boobs . . . Emma almost didn't have words to describe the sensation, except that it almost felt like there was a connection between her nipples and her vagina and she could feel the blood pushing between her legs as Savannah touched her chest, and Emma sincerely thought she might firework from that feeling alone . . .

. . . but then Savannah pushed forward and unzipped Emma's pants and slid her hand into Emma's underwear . . . and now Emma could feel Savannah's touch all over the rest of her body.

And it was the fastest orgasm she'd ever had in her whole life.

"Shit," Alex said in an uncharacteristic whisper as Emma finished recounting the whole date night/hook-up story at the froyo table.

"You should've taken a sexie." Zoe smiled.

"Yeah, but Savannah didn't firework, so . . ."

"Is that how it works?"

"Well, no, it's just, my parents showed up, like, two seconds later, and I had to go home, so I didn't get to . . . you know . . ."

"Is that how it works?" Zoe asked sincerely. "Is it only . . . I mean . . . is it . . . ?"

"Zoe . . ." Alex laughed.

"I'm trying to ask what it means to have sex with a girl if you're a girl, but that might just be a stupid question, so . . ."

297

"Definitely *not* stupid," Emma insisted. "I had . . . I might even still have the same question."

"But you fireworked?" Layla asked for confirmation.

"I did."

"But it wasn't sex?"

"Well. I don't know." Emma laughed. "I think we have to define what 'it' actually is."

Emma's thoughts drifted back to the day after she'd had sex with Nick. They'd had to define what "good" and also "it" meant . . . with a boy the "it" was easy: penis in vagina. Ironically, the good had been so much harder to define. With Savannah, the "good" was incredibly obvious – it was the "it" that was harder to figure out. Emma was still trying to wrap her head around the "it" part.

"I think Savannah also has to firework in order for it to really count as sex," Emma replied.

"Since when do you care about counting?" Alex asked. "I thought it was all about the process . . ."

"Well, the process is totally fun." Emma laughed. "But I want to make Savannah feel that way, too."

"Oh, you will . . ." Layla said reassuringly.

"Oh. Cool," Zoe said, newly frustrated. "According to that definition, if I was a lesbian, I'd still be a virgin."

"Or maybe then you would've orgasmed?" Emma asked, trying to make a joke, but it just came out sounding rather insensitive. "Sorry, Zo," she added.

"It's okay," Zoe said, returning to her froyo.

"Savannah said her ex-girlfriend considered 'sex' any hook-up that involved an orgasm for either girl, so maybe then technically you could say we did have sex, but I think it should go both ways before I'll feel like it's official."

The other girls realized that was the first time the G-word had come out of Emma's mouth. G-word meaning *girlfriend*, not graduation. But none of them pointed it out to Emma. They didn't want to freak her out. And, to be fair, she hadn't described Savannah as being *her* girlfriend . . . she was talking about Savannah having an *ex*-girlfriend who used to do the kind of things with Savannah that Emma was now doing, but still.

Suffice it to say, the word did not go unnoticed.

Then, the stack of phones in the middle of the table started to buzz.

Zoe thought it might be Austin. She had told him that he could come over later. She told Emma that she could check.

Emma reached for the phone stack. She checked Zoe's phone, but the new text wasn't for Zoe.

It was for Alex.

Alex had a sinking feeling about the situation.

"Who is J?" Emma asked slowly.

"Um. Why?" Alex asked, trying to sound as calm as possible.

"Well. He just asked what you're wearing, so . . ."

The girls all laughed as Alex breathed a little sigh of relief. Considering some of their past sext messages, she knew his question could've been *a lot* worse. Also, she was *so* incredibly grateful that she'd put him in her phone as "J" and not "Joey". She had no clue how she would've explained *that* to Zoe right here and now. Luckily, she didn't have to.

"It's Jordan, isn't it? From the basketball team?" Layla asked, in detective mode.

And Alex smiled that Mona Lisa smile. The one that kept getting her into trouble. This time, she thought, it might be her saving grace. She still didn't want to tell the girls about Joey. Not yet. Not until she knew if it was real or not. So she just let her smile say yes.

"I knew it!" Layla laughed, thinking she'd solved the case.

"Should we text him back?" Emma asked.

"Oh, no . . ." Alex shook her head.

But then Alex's phone buzzed again.

And it was still sitting in the middle of the table, and the girls saw the text before Alex could hide the screen.

PLEASE tell me it's the panties again

Now, Zoe, Emma and Layla all lost it, exploding into a new burst of giggles that made the heads of all the Bigg Chill customers turn towards them and their corner table.

"Again?" Layla squealed.

"Who says 'panties'?" Zoe laughed.

"At least he didn't call them *moist* – that is *literally* the worst word."

"Shhhhh," Alex said as her light-brown cheeks turned a distinct shade of red. She slid the phone towards her, trying to hide the screen, but it was too late.

"You have to text him back," Layla insisted.

"Yes," Zoe agreed.

Alex knew Zoe would die, *absolutely die*, if she knew who J really was, but she wasn't sure how to get out of it now, especially as yet another text came in.

Or just say nothing. In my head I've already taken them off. With my teeth.

"Oh. My. God," Layla said.

"Okay, see, *now* you have to say something," Emma pushed.

Alex didn't seem to have much of a choice.

Mmmhmmm, she texted back.

"And what does that mean exactly?" Layla asked, taking mental notes.

TURNED ON, Joey texted back.

"Oh okay, got it." Layla laughed.

"And now what?" Emma asked, after a few minutes. "Why isn't he saying anything else?"

"He's probably jacking off," Alex said matter-of-factly.

"Ohmigod," Zoe said, shaking her head.

She turned her attention back to her vanilla froyo as Emma and Layla brainstormed some sexy things for Alex to text next. Alex couldn't help feeling bad about how Zoe would feel if she knew who was on the other end of this phone, but she was already feeling bad about Austin, and Alex didn't want to do anything that might make the girls suspicious . . . She knew there was nothing left to do but go with it.

And so they did. Laughing and squealing and sexting . . .

"Can everyone just please remember that we're in public?" Zoe asked when it all got particularly loud at one point.

"Sorry," Alex said.

Really she was apologizing for the entire situation and not *just* the volume of their conversation . . .

Luckily, Zoe was blissfully oblivious.

Alex decided that was definitely for the best.

61 Days Until Graduation . . .

Alex sat in the front seat of Oliver's car on the way to school, texting Joey.

Lately, Alex and Oliver's carpool rides had been quiet and friendly, mostly just filled with the sound of the radio. They'd nod to say hello. And then they'd wave goodbye on the way out of the car. But that was it. They really didn't have much to say to each other. Not since the crying and everything. It was just too much. And now that Oliver was *dating* Caroline – not just hooking up – there was even less to talk about.

This morning, Alex found herself laughing out loud at one of Joey's text messages. She wasn't trying to rub it in Oliver's face, but it just sort of happened like that. She could tell that Oliver wanted to ask her about who she was talking to and what he was saying and all that, but he didn't or he wouldn't or whatever.

Then, Joey said he had to tell her something serious.

The word "serious" jumped off the screen. She certainly wasn't laughing anymore.

Ugh, Alex thought. *He's breaking up with me.*

But then she felt stupid, because they weren't even officially together. What exactly was there to break?

But quickly Alex realized that the seriousness wasn't about them at all . . . it was about her. *Her picture.* Joey was still friendly with some of the younger guys on the track team, and apparently he'd been included in a big group text, along with a bunch of athletes. And just last night, Oliver admitted to doing it.

Doing what? Alex started to type, before she realized that Joey was trying to tell her that Oliver had, in fact, Photoshopped the naked picture of her and sent it to everyone on the internet.

Apparently, Oliver had been bragging about it pretty extensively. At first, Alex wanted to argue with Joey. She wanted to say that Oliver couldn't possibly have done that; he'd told her he hadn't done that . . . but of course she knew deep down that his word didn't really mean much of anything at all.

Joey texted Alex a screenshot from the group chat, and there was absolutely no use in arguing. There it was, in black and white, right on her phone screen. *You're welcome*, Oliver had texted all the guys as he took credit for his photo-editing skills, like the cocky asshole he was.

"Stop the car," Alex said.

"Excuse me?"

"Stop. The. Car." Alex's words were calm and measured, but they were also unquestionable. "I'm getting out."

"We're, like, two miles from school."

"I'm not asking you."

Oliver pulled up to a red light and was forced to stop, which gave Alex enough time to hop out.

"What are you doing?" Oliver yelled at her through the open window.

All Alex knew for sure was that she couldn't sit next to him anymore. She hadn't really thought about anything else, but she figured she was less than two miles from school. It was a flat, easy jog along Ventura Boulevard.

And so Alex took off, running towards school.

Oliver had no choice but to drive off without her. He couldn't stop in traffic, and Alex refused to get back into the car.

About fifteen minutes later, by the time Alex got to school, a bit sweaty from the run, Oliver was standing at the entrance waiting for her.

"What is your problem?" Oliver asked.

Alex didn't have a problem.

Not anymore.

She bent down and untied her shoelace, all slowly and deliberately.

"What are you doing?" Oliver asked, getting more and more agitated and flustered with each passing moment, which made Alex want to move even slower. She knew she was driving Oliver absolutely crazy. It was an empowering feeling.

She slid the star charm off of her shoelace and held it up for Oliver to see before dropping it in a nearby trash can.

"You're actually crazy," Oliver said.

"And you're *actually* an asshole," she finally replied. "You're welcome," she added, echoing the text message he'd sent the boys. "For the Photoshop skills."

Oliver's face turned instantly pale.

He was so cocky and stupid; he thought he was actually going to get away with the whole thing. Not just the picture. Not just the embarrassment and all the ache he'd caused Alex.

But the bragging too. He thought he could get away with that. And that was the worst part, Alex decided.

"Are you going to tell on me?" Oliver asked, sounding like a small, sad, sniffling child.

"No," Alex said, making the decision as the word came out of her mouth. "What's that going to do for me? Make your life miserable? Maybe. But I already won so long ago. For the rest of my life, I get to be me, and you have to be you, and I feel incredibly good about both of those things."

Before Oliver could respond, she added, "And I'm so glad you had so much fun jacking off to my knees . . ."

Alex turned triumphantly, and walked away with her head held high.

59 Days Until Graduation . . .

Emma drove to Savannah's house without wearing any underwear.

She wasn't expecting to make that sort of bold move at 11 p.m. on a Friday night, but she wasn't expecting a lot of the things that had happened to her over the past few months.

Recently, her older sister Heather told her that the secret to being an adult and knowing what you were doing just meant Googling the answer without asking anyone else first. So, mostly as a joke, she Googled "what should I do with my life?" And it led her to a website about taking a gap year. Emma had never considered that option before. The only option that seemed to be on the table for the following year was her freshman year of college, but now, as she opened her eyes and figured out how to move forward, she realized that simply wasn't true. Emma spent some more time Googling – and exploring the real possibility of a gap year. It was an exciting prospect.

But not nearly as exciting as spending more alone time with Savannah.

Can I come over? Emma had texted.

PLEASE, Savannah texted back almost immediately.

Emma was already wearing her pajamas, so she got up and got redressed. Or undressed. Or both. Either way, she decided she only needed to be minimally dressed for what was going to happen next. She put on a pleated jeans skirt. And her favorite purple zip-up hoodie. And a pair of flip-flops.

And that was it.

No underwear whatsoever.

Emma's parents were already asleep, so she made sure to be quiet as she slipped out the front door. And she snuck into Savannah's house, making sure not to wake up her parents either. And then as soon as Emma stepped into Savannah's bedroom, the girls picked up right where they'd left off after their date night . . . and kissing and fingertips . . . and Savannah reached for Emma's zipper . . . and the moment she realized Emma wasn't wearing a bra was an instant, immediate, perfect memory.

Savannah's face and her eyes and *everything* . . . it all just lit up.

"Oh, if you think that's fun . . ."

And Savannah seemed to know exactly what she was getting at, because she wasted no time slipping her hands under Emma's skirt . . . and confirming her happy suspicion that Emma didn't have any underwear on down there either.

"You. Are. The. Coolest," Savannah said as the kisses continued.

They moved their kisses over to Savannah's bed, and pulled off the rest of their clothes, and a few minutes later Emma found herself on top of Savannah, and Savannah's fingers were in between Emma's legs, but she reached down and grabbed her hand, stopping her . . .

"You don't like?" Savannah grinned.

"Too much . . ." Emma exhaled. "This first," she said, pinning Savannah's hands up above her head.

Emma kissed her way down from Savannah's lips, passed her neck and her boobs and her stomach, until she found herself between her legs . . . and the truth was, she didn't know what she was doing – *at all* – but she knew what *she* liked. She remembered the last time she was in the darkroom with Nick and how worried she'd been about where his face had to be and now that her face was there, she realized she had wasted way too much time worrying and even though she enjoyed the process she could've been and should've been just enjoying it so much more . . .

Savannah didn't seem to have any of those same fears – or if she did, Emma certainly couldn't tell . . . Especially since Savannah was too busy telling Emma how much she liked what she was doing with her tongue and her lips and her fingers and all that . . . And just as Emma felt like she was really getting started . . .

Savannah finished.

Fireworks. Everywhere.

This, Emma thought.

And then Savannah flipped over, on top of Emma, and it only took a few quick moments before Emma set off her very own display . . .

Afterwards, Savannah curled into Emma's arms.

"This is good," Emma managed to say out loud with a bit of a laugh.

"Yeah, it is . . ." Savannah laughed back. "Ineffable," she added as if she'd been waiting for the right moment to say that.

"Ineffable?"

"That's the word for when something is too great to be described in words."

Exactly, Emma thought.

Ineffable.

That's exactly what this was.

58 Days Until Graduation . . .

Zoe knew what she had to do as soon as she saw Emma's sexie.

Emma and Savannah had "officially" had sex last night and Zoe could see the glow on Emma's face and feel the "rightness" of it all even just by looking at it through the phone screen, and it helped her confirm what she'd known was true for a few weeks now . . . Things between her and Austin had run their course.

Zoe didn't want to be Austin's girlfriend anymore, and not just because she didn't want to have sex with him anymore – even though, truthfully, she didn't – but mostly because he didn't make her feel the way Emma looked in her sexie.

She didn't have any *bad* feelings towards Austin, but she simply felt like there just wasn't a good reason to force it anymore.

Zoe knew it was time to break up with him.

But it was still easier said than done.

Finally, she called him just before dinnertime. And said she wanted to break up. And then it was done. She probably should've driven over to his house and told him in person, but she couldn't. At least she didn't text it. The phone call was short, but all of their phone calls were short, so that wasn't really much of an indication.

Even though Zoe caused the break-up, she was still upset about it. She'd never had a boyfriend before Austin, and now he was her first *ex*-boyfriend.

She texted the Chat.

And everyone told Zoe they loved her. And she knew that already. And she felt like the luckiest, but she also felt like crying.

And so she did.

And she felt worse for a while but then also better, too.

Alex was right.

Tears were *so* underrated.

50 Days Until Graduation . . .

Zoe could not bring herself to order vanilla frozen yogurt again.

Layla ordered "the Layla".

Emma ordered cake batter.

Alex ordered graham-cracker caramel.

And, for Zoe, today it was time for something different.

She ordered strawberry.

"You reached maximum vanilla capacity?" Layla teased, as the girls settled around their usual table.

"Yes, I guess. Maximum vanilla capacity. Maximum *Austin* capacity . . . I just had to get all of this out of my room." Zoe gestured to the shoebox she'd brought with her. It was full of little memories she'd collected over the past couple months. It all reminded her of Austin, and she just didn't need it anymore. Each item on its own felt small, but piled together it was more than Zoe needed. The dried carnation from Valentine's Day sat on the very top. "Is it lame that I want to keep this? Not 'cause of Austin, but just . . . it dried so perfectly."

"Well. It's not from Austin," Layla said, treading carefully.

"What?"

"Dylan bought it for you."

Zoe laughed until she realized that Layla was serious, then suddenly she got serious too. "Why didn't you tell me? Why didn't *he* tell me?"

"He said all he wanted was for you to be happy. That was his 'mission accomplished'."

Zoe had been *so* happy that she hadn't even thought to press Austin about the flower – she just assumed it was his because that's what she'd wanted at the time. Now, looking backwards, she would've been even happier to know that it was from Dylan . . .

But that's not how life worked.

Life had to be lived forward.

And it all had to happen exactly the way that it did or she may not have found herself here, in this moment, with her friends and a brand new froyo flavor.

After the girls finished, Zoe threw the Austin shoebox in the trash can in the parking lot of the Bigg Chill, but she made sure to keep the red carnation. She put it on the passenger seat next to her and drove towards Dylan's house.

She blasted his mix CD as loud as she could and turned what might've been a twenty-minute ride across the city of Los Angeles and into the valley into a two-hour drive. There was still so much that Zoe didn't know, but right now she knew she needed this time and this space, and most of all she needed this music.

She pulled up in front of Dylan's house and turned off the car's engine, but she left the key in the ignition so she could listen to the end of the last song on the mix: Jimmy Eat World's

313

"Sweetness". It was Dylan's all-time favorite song, and one of Zoe's, too. Even after the song ended, the last lyric – "with a little sweet and simple numbing me . . ." – still continued to ring in her head as she sat in the front seat, trying to build up the courage to get out and go talk to Dylan . . .

And then . . .

After two minutes of sitting in silence, after two full minutes of getting lost in her thoughts and her feelings and holding out hope that Dylan might just telepathically realize she was sitting outside and open the front door . . . another song started to play.

Zoe had been listening to Dylan's mix CD for weeks on repeat. She had heard every song on it *at least* a hundred times. But, up until this moment, she'd always started the CD over again immediately once it ended. She'd never thought to wait for something more until now. She didn't know there was a secret song, *but* then again, maybe she didn't need to know about this song until this very moment.

It was a "Bless the Broken Road" cover by Rascal Flatts. Zoe had heard the song before but never quite like this.

And, as the song ended, Zoe knew that it was finally the right time. She'd had feelings for Dylan since that first day they got paired up in chem class. But those original emotions – that first crush or attraction or whatever it was – couldn't even begin to compete with the layered and complex love she felt for him now. It was real . . . and she needed the whole entire broken road to get here.

Now all Zoe had to do was get out of the car.

And ring Dylan's doorbell.

She did.

And he answered and invited her inside. He wasn't expecting her, but he wasn't all that surprised to see her either. They made their way down the hallway into his room. It was all dark blue and plaid. Lots of trophies and sports memorabilia on the wall. She looked at Dylan's bed and tried to count how many times she might've heard his voice from it. She'd never seen it before. Until now.

"Why didn't you tell me about the carnation?" Zoe asked.

"Why did you pick up the phone that night?" Dylan smirked.

"Ohmigod . . ." Zoe rolled her eyes. "God bless the broken road, I guess," she added with a bit of a laugh, which felt like it answered both of their questions at the same time.

"You can't make a perfect mix CD without a secret song," Dylan said in agreement.

"It's not really a secret anymore," Zoe said, talking about so much more than the song.

And then finally – *finally* – after all their phonefalls, after all the *thousands* or maybe even millions of words they'd exchanged, there were only four more that Zoe wanted to say: "I love you, too."

Dylan pulled Zoe in for the kind of first kiss she'd literally been dreaming about all this time.

Soon they moved to Dylan's bed, and they kept kissing and kissing and *kissing*, until Dylan finally found the courage to move his hands from Zoe's back . . . and onto her boobs. And Zoe laughed. It wasn't a nervous giggle. It was a big, rich, full-body kind of laugh that made her boobs jiggle in Dylan's hands.

"Ohmigod," he said through kisses, mimicking Zoe and also expressing his happiness. "I've wanted to do that for ever."

"I've only had them for, like, four months," she teased.

"What. Ever. Feels like for ever," he teased back.

For the first time, their "for real" in-person conversation felt like it did when they spoke on the phone.

Zoe kissed Dylan again. Even though they'd only been doing that for about four *minutes*, it felt like for *ever* too, but in the best possible way. They spent the next couple of hours rolling around on his bed, laughing and teasing and talking and *kissing* . . . until Zoe had to leave so she wouldn't be late for curfew.

She sang along to "Sweetness" on repeat all the way home.

And then she got ready for bed as quickly as she could and called Dylan like he made her promise she would before she left his house.

And he picked up on the first ring.

And they talked for another hour or two – or tonight it might've actually been *three* – until they both managed to fall asleep . . . together.

47 Days Until Graduation . . .

Emma had taken more pictures in her lifetime than she could count.

She couldn't even count how many she'd taken in the last five months, which was proving to be a bit of a problem, as she'd gotten the idea in her head that it was time to develop all of them. She needed them. But right now, staring at the filmstrips in the darkroom, it seemed like an overwhelming task.

Thankfully, there was a knock on the door.

"Em?" Nick asked. "You in there?"

Emma's lips curled into a smile as she was transported back to the memory of the last time she had heard Nick knock on the darkroom door and all the fireworks that followed. She didn't have to explain her smile to Nick. She could tell by the look on his face that he remembered too.

"Thank you for agreeing to help me . . ."

"You. Are. Welcome." Nick laughed. "Last time you asked me for help, I offered you my penis, so I figured it couldn't be any more awkward than that."

"Hopefully not awkward at all," Emma said, as Nick walked

across the small room and slid up next to her. "But I have the strongest sense of déjà vu."

"My mom says that having a feeling of déjà vu means you're exactly where you're supposed to be," Nick explained.

"I love that," Emma said, feeling the truth in Nick's words. They were so simple yet also profound. Emma's thoughts drifted back to the very first time she met Savannah in the yearbook room, and she remembered the sense of déjà vu that had washed over her. Of course, back then things were just starting to fall into place. Now Emma was more clearly rooted in this time and place – but all of it just felt right. Weirdly right.

Emma was so present, and so in the moment, that it was all she could think about. But she did her best not to *over*think it for once.

She was just in it.

Emma had learned that moments like this one were fleeting. But she'd also learned that every once in a while, if you trusted the process, everything would fall into place . . . it just wouldn't *stay* in place.

Balance required movement.

Emma and Nick spent the rest of the day in the darkroom, developing pictures.

For the first time in the longest time, Emma felt like she was really getting somewhere.

43 Days Until Graduation . . .

Alex was in the same place she'd been many times before . . .

In a galaxy far, far away, watching *The Empire Strikes Back* with Max. Truth be told, this was Alex's favorite *Star Wars* movie, and she loved spending time with her brother, but she was ready for some movement.

Her phone buzzed.

It was Joey, unsurprisingly.

What are you doing?

Alex was relieved he didn't ask what she was wearing this time. Being with her girls was one thing, but she would not have humored him like that while she was sitting on the couch with Max.

Joey said *The Empire Strikes Back* was his favorite *Star Wars* movie too. *I love it*, he texted.

The word "love" jumped out at her. There had been *endless* texting between them, but no one had dropped an actual "love" bomb yet. Normally, Alex would've waited and played some sort of game to make sure that Joey was the one who said – or typed – it first. But Alex was tired of playing and this, whatever *this* was exactly with Joey, felt so much more real than that.

I love YOU, she typed.

She watched as the message was delivered.

She knew he had seen it.

She waited for a response.

And waited.

And waited . . .

. . . until she felt so incredibly stupid that she decided she might never send Joey Reed a text message ever again. Honestly, she might never send *anyone* a text message ever again in her entire life. In fact, just as she was about to decide to give up her cell phone altogether and become a nun and live by herself on the top of a mountain in the middle of nowhere, Joey texted back . . .

I know.

And that was it. Two words. One period.

That's his response?! she thought. *I say "I love you" and he says "I know"?*

Alex was about to lose it and throw her phone across the room . . . when, as if on cue, Max pointed to the TV screen and said, "I know."

"What?" Alex asked as she looked up from her phone.

Max's words had sounded like an echo of the thoughts in her head, but they weren't about her at all. Max's eyes were glued to the screen. To the movie. To his favorite scene.

"I love this part," he said.

And Alex watched along with Max as Princess Leia turned to Han Solo to tell him that she loved him, and then – then! – Han Solo responded with his perfectly infuriating, incredibly classic line: "I know".

Alex's heart burst inside her chest, filling her entire body with an incredible amount of warmth. It was as if she could feel Joey winking at her through the phone.

Thank you, Han Solo, she texted back as quickly as she could.

Ugh! Joey responded, including that well placed exclamation point.

You're perfect, he added, this time without any punctuation. *And I love you too.*

Alex noted the period at the end of that last text.

Joey Reed and his stupid periods, she thought.

Right now, she even loved those too.

Zoe picked up her phone on the first ring.

"What's wrong?" she asked.

"Hi to you too," Joey said.

"Are you okay?"

"Why wouldn't I be okay?"

"You never *just* call me. Only if something's wrong or you're trying to find me in a crowd."

"Okay, well, I'm not *just* calling . . . But I don't want you to be mad."

"Uh-oh . . ."

"No, no. It's fine. It's good, actually. Very good."

"Joey. You are killing me right now—"

"I kissed Alex when I was home for spring break."

"Excuse me?" Zoe asked, her voice squeaking.

"I kissed her in my bedroom the night of your sleepover, and then I kissed her all night, the next night, in her bedroom."

"I don't even understand what you're saying," Zoe said.

321

Joey explained that the point was, there had been a lot of kissing between them. And now, ever since then, there'd been a lot of texting. And Alex wanted to tell Zoe what had happened almost immediately, from the very beginning, to avoid lying to Zoe or anything like that, but they had decided it was better to wait until they made sure that it was really worth talking about first.

"We wanted to make sure it was real," Joey explained.

"Okay," Zoe said, still trying to put the pieces together. "So. Is this your way of telling me it's real?"

"Yeah," Joey said after a bit of a pause.

"Oh my god, wow," Zoe said. But not in her usual freak-out kind of way. The words were slow and deliberate. "You're in love with my best friend."

"I am . . ." he said with a happy exhale.

"And she knows?"

"Oh, she knows. And she loves me too."

Zoe didn't say anything for a moment as she began to replay memories from the last few weeks in her head.

"I feel like you're about three seconds away from freaking out on me . . ."

"No. I'm . . . *Ohmigod* . . ." Zoe's thoughts found their way back to the Bigg Chill and the group sext-message conversation, and the only thing she could do was laugh.

"I knew it . . ." Joey said, mistaking Zoe's laughter for meltdown.

Really, it was just the realization that her brother – OHMIGOD, *HER BROTHER* – was the J they had all been texting with on Alex's phone.

322

Despite the awkwardness, Zoe had a feeling they would all laugh about this together one day, but she thought she'd let Alex fill him in on the details . . .

38 Days Until Graduation . . .

Alex was actually, technically and completely about to run out of chances.

This was it.

Today, Friday, May 15th, was the last official qualifying track meet of her high-school career. It was time to "go big or go home".

Well, realistically, Alex was going to have to go home either way, but hopefully it wouldn't be empty-handed.

For so long, she'd felt as if she had been carrying the weight of the world with her. Since the first day of her life, she'd been carrying part of Max and all of her parents' hopes for him. As she grew up, she held onto the way people looked at her. With all her speed, she'd convinced herself that she was capable of outrunning her baggage and leaving it behind her in the dust. But that wasn't what she had been doing at all. She wasn't actually leaving anything behind; she was still forcing herself to carry it all with her. Now she could see the difference between what she had and what she needed.

It would've been too simple and trite to say that it was because of Joey – or because of the way she felt – or even the way he felt about her. That would've given him far too much credit and power, and she knew he never would've accepted a compliment like that anyway, but she also knew that something real had happened between them. It felt so right, and they just fitted so well, that she didn't even have to carry any of it. It was just there all on its own. And it was majestic.

Every track meet of her high-school career, Alex would stand on the same spot on the track and take a minute to visualize the race before it began. For the past few months, she'd been standing in that spot trying to convince herself that she could break the record. Today, she knew that whether she broke it or not, she was going to run the race in a way it had never been run before. She was going to do her best no matter what the outcome.

As Yoda liked to say: "Do or do not. There is no try."

Today, Alex knew she wasn't trying. She was doing. She wasn't worrying. She was being. She was entirely and completely alive. And in the moment. Yet she couldn't help but think that the only thing that could possibly make this moment better and sweeter and more complete was . . . Joey.

And then there he was.

Standing on the track in front of her as if he'd just appeared out of nowhere. But he hadn't, of course. He'd bought a plane ticket and flown from Oakland to Burbank. And Zoe had picked him up at the airport in his Ford Explorer and driven him to the track.

"You're a dream," she said as soon as he finished the explanation.

"And you're the most real."

It might've been the best compliment Alex had ever received in her entire life. And this might've been one of the best moments of her life. She loved Joey, and he loved her, and at the very same time they both just said, "I know."

"Okay, cool." Alex smiled. "Now I'm gonna go do this thing."

"You got this."

And Alex knew that she did.

But.

She didn't break the record.

She won the track meet as she had so many times before. And she was the fastest runner on the entire track. But it still wasn't enough.

Alex felt like a giant failure.

There was nothing she hated more than that feeling. It stung. And it sucked. *So much*. But the world kept spinning, and Alex didn't fall apart. Coach K insisted that all of the seniors take a victory lap around the track. Alex led the pack. A few months ago, Alex might've said this last lap was just a consolation prize, but she knew that the journey to get here – all of the hours of practice and beads of sweat – was the real victory.

She'd gone big – and now it was time to go home.

It wasn't until a couple hours later, sometime between dinner with her family and ending up on the couch in Zoe and Joey's guest house, that Alex realized what her buddy Yoda really meant when he said, "Do or do not. There is no try." He wasn't saying that it was impossible to try, or that it wasn't worth trying . . . he was saying that trying *is* doing. Of course you had to do whatever the "it" was in the right way. You had to try with every ounce of yourself, but if you *did* that then that was doing, too. Alex could not have trained harder. She simply could not have done anything more. At least for now, for this moment, this really was the absolute best she could do. And the truth was, she loved herself more in the midst of this supposed failure than she ever had before.

Alex's thoughts drifted to her sex dream and Cameron and the pact . . . All this time she thought she'd been waiting to have sex until she felt the right way about another boy. Now she knew that what she had *really* been waiting for was the opportunity to feel that way about *herself*.

Joey made her feel like herself without even trying.

There was that "try" word again. Even though she understood what Yoda meant, she also knew that trying to have sex wasn't the same as actually having sex. Not technically, not completely, not at all. And even though there was a time when *she* thought and wished that Cameron had been her first, clearly god or the universe or whatever-was-in-charge had other plans.

And those plans led her to this moment.

To this couch. With Joey and Zoe. Watching a movie.

After a little while, Zoe's phone buzzed. It was a text from Dylan.

"I'm gonna go talk to my *boyfriend*," she said. "Have fun with yours . . ."

It was only then that Alex realized that she and Joey hadn't been alone together since their all-night make-out session.

They wasted absolutely no time and picked up exactly where they left off . . . but this time all their kisses turned into so much more than just kissing.

This time would be Alex's first . . .

. . . actually, technically *and* completely.

It was sexy and fun and all sorts of magnetic.

Joey was on top, and Alex's shoes were on the floor next to the couch, and he knew to put a towel down underneath them, and she had a smile on her face the entire time (even when it got awkward and she wasn't sure where to put her hips and he wasn't sure where to put his hands), and they both just couldn't stop staring into each other's eyes . . .

"Wow," Joey said afterwards.

He was lying on his back, looking up at the ceiling. Alex was curled on her side next to him. He turned his head to look at her.

"You . . ." he started sweetly, but something about the sound of the word made Alex roll her eyes. "Oh, stop with that roll! You don't even know what the end of my sentence is going to be."

"Something about the way I look right now? The beauty of it all?"

"The beauty of it all has absolutely nothing to do with the way you look," Joey insisted. "You're gorgeous, Alex. Deal with it. But that's not . . . I think your looks pale in comparison to the way your soul feels when I look at you."

She felt Joey's words all over her body . . . and deep inside too. No one had ever talked about Alex's soul before, but she appreciated it more than any other compliment she'd ever received.

Afterwards, Alex went into the bathroom to pee and wash up . . . and then she took a long moment to look at herself in the mirror. She couldn't help but think that it may have been the first time she'd ever really seen herself in her entire life. She snapped a sexie. And sent it to the Chat.

Zoe had been expecting the picture, but it still made her groan into her phone.

"What?" Dylan asked.

Brotherfucker, Zoe texted back to Alex and the Chat.

She added a smiley face to make sure the girls knew she was joking. Well. She wasn't *joking*, but she wanted them to know she wasn't mad.

"Are you texting?" Dylan asked.

"Yes. Sorry. The girls . . ."

Zoe realized that in order to explain Alex's sexie, she would have to tell Dylan about the pact. So she did. She explained everything. "So that might explain the time you called and I was . . ." She knew he knew exactly what she was talking about. The now infamous phone call.

"Yeah . . . So. Would you now?" Dylan asked quietly.

"Would I now *what*?" Zoe was going to make him say it out loud at least.

"Would you now . . . I mean . . . do you want to touch yourself?"

"Only if you tell me where," Zoe said rather boldly.

She could feel her entire face and all of its redness. And her entire body and all of its . . . *everything* as their conversation got sexy and intimate in a way it never had before . . .

The girls had all told Zoe (and she'd also read in Layla's Sex Doc) that the key to having an orgasm was foreplay . . . and she realized as their conversation finally turned sexual, that she and Dylan had effectively been foreplay-ing on the phone for almost four years. They'd had so many conversations, and had spent so much time talking and laughing and flirting (even when they were supposedly just friends) that now, as they talked about how hard or fast or slow to touch themselves, and exactly where and how they wanted to touch each other, it wasn't much of a surprise that all of it finally . . . *finally* . . . erupted into Zoe's first orgasm. It really did feel like fireworks. And it was more than worth the wait.

36 Days Until Graduation . . .

Layla, as always, sat at their usual table in the back corner at the Bigg Chill.

But.

For the first time ever . . .

. . . Layla was the only Crew-member who showed up to froyo.

Occasionally, one of the girls would be late. More rarely, someone might decide not to come at all if they were sick or had too much homework or something like that. But this had never happened before.

There's a first time for everything, Layla thought.

She briefly considered texting the Chat to check in on everyone, but ultimately she decided against it. She knew where everybody was. It had been a big week.

First, Emma had asked Savannah to prom. She'd printed a whole photo album and presented it to her as a gift, along with a handwritten letter. Of course Savannah said yes.

Then, Dylan had asked Zoe to prom. He decided to go big with it and asked her with a sign on the Jumbotron screen at Dodger Stadium. He knew Zoe had been insecure about his feelings for her and him showing them off in public, so he decided to ask her to prom in the most public place possible. Of course Zoe said yes too.

And finally, just two days ago, Joey had flown down from college and surprised Alex at her track meet, which he knew was so much more important to her than prom.

Now, Alex was with Joey.

Zoe was with Dylan.

Emma was with Savannah.

And Layla was here.

By herself.

But she was okay. She didn't cry, even though for a moment she thought she might. And she didn't even *really* feel sad.

Layla knew this was going to happen sooner rather than later.

But she wouldn't have imagined *this* exactly. This aloneness.

She wouldn't have planned it this way either. But something about the timing and the truth of it seemed to make sense to her.

The Crew would always be friends. *Best friends*. But being together and being best friends would not always mean the same thing as it did right now.

It wasn't until later – *hours* later – that Alex, Zoe and Emma realized what had happened. Layla was right. Alex *was* with Joey. Zoe *was* with Dylan. And Emma with Savannah. Individually, they knew they weren't going to make it to froyo, but they each thought that they'd be the only one. They didn't realize that all three of them had the same no-show plan. And none of them texted the Chat even though they all probably should have . . .

. . . And so, as soon as they could, Zoe and Emma and Alex showed up at Layla's front door.

And very soon after that, all four of them ended up on Layla's trampoline. It was quiet for a while. The trampoline swayed softly beneath them.

"Layla," Alex started, trying to find the right way to apologize.

"I am so sorry," Zoe said, already looking like she might cry.

"Guys . . ." Layla said, brushing her bangs out of her eyes. "It's okay. Really."

"No it's not, *really*," Emma said.

"I know you've all been busy . . . with the boys or the girl."

"Yeah, but . . ." Emma said. "That shouldn't be more important than *this* . . ."

"It's not more important," Alex insisted.

"Not at all!" Zoe added.

"I know, I know," Layla said.

"Like, all those people," Emma explained, "they don't even compare—"

"Emma, stop—"

"No, you stop. They're important, yes, but it's not really about them. They're orbiting in an entirely different universe than we are. Or at least they should be. There's just no contest."

"We really are the luckiest . . ." Zoe said, as they always did.

Layla knew that, too. And for some reason, it was the happiness of knowing that that finally made her cry . . .

"See. I *knew* you were sad," Zoe said, a tear streaming down her face too.

"No, but I'm not . . ." Layla tried to explain. "The thing is, when I was sitting there, all by myself . . ."

"Twist the dagger . . . ." Alex teased.

"She's allowed to twist it if she wants to twist it." Emma laughed.

"I'm not *twisting*." Layla smiled. "I'm saying that I was sitting there, and I kept thinking that maybe I was *going* to cry, but I didn't. And I . . . you know, I *want* to say that I don't know what to do without you or that I don't know who I am without you guys, but the truth is that I *do*. The truth is that I know who I am even when I'm 'without you' because you're all already a part of me . . ." A few fresh tears ran down Layla's cheeks. "I just . . . I know that these tears aren't because I needed you this afternoon and you *weren't* there . . . It's because you weren't there, and I didn't need you." The feeling was absolutely gut-wrenching, but it also filled Layla with gratitude. "Sorry, I swear I'm not *actually* sad," she added, still wiping tears.

"Then why are you crying?" Alex asked, feeling tears well up in her eyes, too.

"Because this really feels like the end now," Layla said.

"No! We still have three weeks!" Emma said. "And summer! And grad night! And prom!"

"Right . . ." Layla said. She had always had lots of grand visions about prom, but they all circled back to Logan.

"We're going together, right?" Alex asked.

"Of course," Layla said.

"No, I mean we're going *together* together. 'Cause I literally can't think of anyone I'd rather pose for pictures with."

As soon as Alex said the word "picture", a single tear ran down Emma's cheek. She'd been the last non-crying hold-out.

"Not you too, with the tears," Layla said through more tears of her own.

"I can't help it," Emma said. She sincerely couldn't help it. None of them could. They were all crying now. And the tears were mostly happy. Or at least more happy than sad, but they were still a little bit sad too.

They all knew that no matter what happened from here on out, it would never be exactly the same between them. After graduation, they would simply never all be together in high school again. And soon even the memories would fade. All the late nights and the all-nights and the rainbow sprinkles. All the crushes and the soul-crushing kisses, and all the texting and the touching and sexies and sex . . . One day all of it would simply blur together.

"Kind of like an orgasm . . ." Emma laughed. "At some point, all the feelings, all the sensations just kind of blur together."

"I think that's how the memories will be too: blurred into our souls," Layla said.

"A soul of fireworks," Alex said, clearly liking the sound of that.

"Fireworks really are the perfect metaphor," Zoe agreed. "They're so bright and bold and fill up the entire sky, but then they also fade away just as quickly."

"Oh, now you get it." Alex laughed.

"I do, actually. I *finally* do."

"Zoe. Reed," Layla said, putting the pieces together. "Tell me everything . . ."

"Phone sex, late last night."

And all girls erupted into one of their epic fits of laughter.

"Finally!" Alex squealed. "I love that so much."

"Me too," Zoe agreed.

"Me three," Emma added.

"This is perfect," Layla concluded.

"The only thing that would be even more perfect is if we had . . ."

". . . frozen yogurt," Emma and Zoe chimed in, along with Alex.

"It's already in my fridge," Layla said.

"You got frozen yogurt? For all of us? Even though we were assholes and didn't show up?" Zoe asked as both a question and an apology.

"Have you met me?" Layla laughed.

She didn't know for sure that they'd all end up on her trampoline like this, but she had certainly hoped that they might. It was a dream. And in Layla's head, dreams and plans were still sort of the same thing. The girls went inside, into the kitchen, and ate all of the froyo.

Layla couldn't help but think that it was wrong when she had said that this felt like the end. It wasn't the end. Not yet anyway.

But it was, perhaps, the end of the beginning.

28 Days Until Graduation . . .

Emma invited Savannah to come over and have dinner with her parents.

"First prom, now dinner with your parents?" Savannah teased. "What happened to the Emma I know and love?"

But that's exactly it, Emma thought.

Savannah did love her.

And Emma loved her, too.

There were very few things in the universe that Emma was entirely sure about, but at least right now, and for the foreseeable future, she was sure about Savannah – and she wanted to make sure her parents were, too.

The O'Malleys both seemed to be in a good mood before dinner even began, but they were absolutely thrilled to have a teenager at the dinner table who was glad to answer all of their questions. Savannah talked to them about school and her classes and her plans for the future. Unlike Emma, she didn't cry every time anyone mentioned the word "college".

Then, the conversation finally wound its way around to prom.

"We're actually going to prom together," Emma said.

"Oh yeah?" Her mom smiled, not quite registering what that meant. "Layla and Alex are going together as well, right?"

"Yeah. They are." Emma nodded. "But they're just going as friends."

That statement seemed to get her parents' attention.

"Savannah is my girlfriend," Emma said simply.

She didn't say it to shock them or try to rile them up.

She said it because it was true, and because it mattered to her.

And she wanted her parents to know.

Emma's parents looked at each other and then glanced back at Emma and then across the table towards Savannah . . .

. . . And then her dad said, "Sounds good" and her mom asked if Emma knew what she wanted to wear to prom – and that was it. The conversation marched on.

Emma said she had no clue what she wanted to wear, but Savannah chimed in and said she was thinking about buying a new suit. Savannah felt like one of them should wear a suit – 'cause it would look better for the pictures or something – and Savannah said she wanted to be the one to do it. Emma's mother agreed that it would look better. Especially if Savannah's suit or tie was color-coordinated with Emma's dress. Turned out that's *exactly* what Savannah was thinking too.

And the rest of the dinner conversation continued like that, back and forth across the table . . .

This, Emma thought, as she listened to the pleasant chatter. Just simply: *this*.

23 Days Until Graduation . . .

Layla could not have been happier to cross it off her to-do list.

It had been 146 days since she first wrote it down, and now she finally had blonde highlights in her hair. It was additionally important for her to cross this off her list, especially since it was looking less and less likely that she was going to cross anything else off . . . but it was prom night, and Layla was determined to have the best time of her life.

Layla and Alex, Emma and Savannah, and Zoe and Dylan lined up on the staircase and took a million and one pictures. The girls were glowing – and, honestly, Dylan was too.

And Layla's highlights looked absolutely perfect.

The Crew (and company) took a limo to prom, which was at a fancy hotel in Santa Monica. And the six of them spent the entire night on the dance floor . . .

At one point, when the DJ switched songs and everybody screamed, Layla looked across the crowded dance floor and saw Logan and Vanessa dancing. And also kissing. Really, it would've been more accurate to say that Vanessa was just sucking on his tongue. But Layla didn't care. Well. It wasn't that she didn't *care* but it certainly wasn't enough to ruin her night . . . absolutely nothing could do that.

As things started to wind down, Layla and Alex realized that Emma and Savannah had disappeared and so had Zoe and Dylan . . . but Layla and Alex were still there, still dancing – and having the time of their lives.

It might as well have been just the two of them on the dance floor.

Zoe and Dylan headed upstairs at the hotel to share their very own hotel room.

As they were getting undressed, a new thought occurred to Zoe, something she hadn't considered until this very moment. Dylan had dated a whole string of girlfriends throughout high school, but he hadn't slept with any of them. Thinking back through all of their phonefalls, she couldn't even remember him ever mentioning it as a possibility.

"What were you waiting for?" she asked.

"You," Dylan said.

"Okay, but don't just say that . . ."

"I was waiting for you to get boobs," Dylan teased. "Obviously I can't say I was *actually* waiting for you," he added more seriously, "because that wouldn't be entirely true. But, looking back on it now, it kinda feels like that."

That's how it works, Zoe thought.

You couldn't fully understand things until you looked backwards.

The hard part, of course, was that you still had to live it all forwards.

But Zoe realized that it couldn't happen any other way. At the beginning of the semester, she couldn't even *say* the word "orgasm", let alone try and have one. And now . . . here they were.

Dylan and Zoe got lost in each other for a while . . . in their nakedness and paleness and laughter and oh-so-many kisses . . .

"I love that I can feel you smiling while I'm kissing you . . ." Dylan said. "And I can feel you blushing, too."

"No, D, come on . . ."

"You come on . . ."

"You cannot *feel* my blushing. You just know that I am because I *always* am – it's an unfair advantage."

"Oh, Z, don't tell me what I can and cannot feel." Dylan laughed.

And that made Zoe laugh too.

And they continued kissing. It was incredible how natural it all felt. After so many years of friendship and phonefalls and inside jokes . . . this felt *right*.

Afterwards, and after some more cuddling and more kissing, Dylan went to take a shower and Zoe found herself lying alone in bed. It seemed rather fitting considering how many nights she'd spent alone in bed, talking to Dylan on the phone.

And then she remembered her own phone, and the Chat, and the fact that the Crew were all waiting for a prom sexie. Zoe never liked the way she looked in pictures, but she wanted to take one now. She stayed in the bed with the sheets wrapped around her. She held her phone straight out in front of her, her arms fully extended, and snapped the picture. Just one.

341

She looked at it, expecting to need to take another one. Or two or three. But she didn't.

Her face was as red as her hair.

Her hair was as frizzy as it had ever been.

She'd never felt prettier.

4 Days Until Graduation . . .

Layla got an A+ on her final AP English paper of the year.

That lifted her grade from an A- up to an A for the whole year, which meant that she'd officially crossed every single bullet point off of her high-school to-do list . . .

. . . except for the one about having sex.

As glad as Layla was to cross another bullet off of her list, it was a glaring reminder of the one she wouldn't finish. It looked so lonely all by itself.

Luckily, Layla didn't have to stare at it very long, as Alex was already outside, honking.

"Usually I'm the one getting honked at," Alex said as Layla climbed into the back seat of her car, along with Emma.

Zoe road shotgun and DJ'ed as the Crew drove out to Malibu for a party at Trevor Morgan's beach house.

The party was fun in that everyone-was-wasted sort of way, but after a while it just felt like too much fun and Layla needed a breather. She walked down to the waves, pulled off her sandals, and stuck her toes in the Pacific Ocean. The water was freezing, but she liked the cold. And she liked the way the moon reflected off the waves. And just as her eyes and thoughts drifted up to the stars – or at least whatever stars she could see through the California haze – she heard a familiar voice behind her.

"There she is . . ."

It was Logan.

He said it as if he'd been looking for her, which, apparently, he had.

"What are you doing out here?" he asked. "Hiding?"

She wasn't, but all of a sudden she wanted to.

"You know I love you to the moon and back, right?" he asked as if they hadn't broken up back in February. As if he hadn't chosen Vanessa instead. As if he still really loved her.

He had *tried* to ask as if he wasn't actually drunk, but clearly he was.

He was wasted.

Layla didn't know quite what to say, so she just didn't say anything.

"A penny for your thoughts?" he asked.

It was the kind of question Layla would've found so charming back when they were dating. Now he just reeked of alcohol and a bit of desperation.

Layla held out her hand as if to ask for an actual penny. Logan didn't have one to give her and probably mistook her gesture anyway, so he grabbed her hand and held on, squeezing it tight, which felt familiar but also foreign at the same time. After a moment, Layla pulled her hand away.

"We broke up." Layla knew that Logan was talking about Vanessa, but it was also exactly what she wanted to say to him. Layla had heard about it already.

"I told you she always flirts with everyone . . ." Layla said instead. She'd been trying not to pay *too* much attention to the whole thing, but apparently something dramatic happened at prom, and Vanessa went home with someone else.

"Shoulda listened to you . . ." Logan laughed. "But then you should've listened to me too."

"O-*kay* . . ." Layla didn't quite know what that was supposed to mean.

"There were gonna be rose petals."

"What?"

"On the beach. That was going to be the last clue on Valentine's Day . . . I was gonna decorate the sand in front of my aunt and uncle's with a whole entire, like, *bed* made out of red rose petals. And we were gonna have sex on top of the petals, on top of the sand, under the stars and the moon and back—"

"Logan, I really don't . . ." The missing word at the end of Layla's sentence was "care" but she decided she didn't want to say it out loud. Or she couldn't.

Either way, she decided it was time to go back inside the party. Layla started walking back to the house.

Logan followed after her.

"Okay, I'm sorry—" he said, trying to stop her.

"You don't have to be sorry—"

Logan reached out and grabbed her hand again. And she pulled hers away again, as fast as she could, but she did stop walking.

"Are you mad at me?" he asked.

"What kind of a question is that?"

"You just don't seem to want to talk to me . . ."

"Logan, I'm not gonna make *small talk* or whatever—"

"We can make big talk if you want." Logan laughed.

"You're drunk, Logan. Go home."

"Would love to," Logan said with crassness in his voice. "Before you walk away, can we just agree that we should've lost it to each other?"

"No."

"No?"

"I didn't lose it," Layla said, feeling strangely liberated.

Clearly that was the last thing Logan expected her to say. "What about your to-do list?"

"What about it?" Layla asked.

"*O-kay*," Logan said, sounding even more drunk than he had just a moment before. "Who are you and what have you done with the Layla Baxter I dated for two years? That girl would've made sure to finish her to-do list."

"Yeah, well, maybe that girl isn't me anymore . . ." Layla said.

And she truly meant it. She didn't have to pretend. Not with her face. Not with her voice.

Not with any of it.

It was a glorious feeling.

"And that's okay," she added.

"It *is* okay," Logan smirked, "but it could be better . . ."

Before Layla could ask him what he meant exactly, Logan pulled her in for a kiss.

It was big and hard and fast and slow all at the same time.

And all of a sudden, all the old feelings came rushing back. The attraction, the hormones, the love . . . all of it. And Layla

346

kissed him back just as hard and fast and slow as he kissed her. And even though she knew it really would be okay – *way more than okay* – if she didn't complete her to-do list, she also couldn't help but think, at least for a fleeting moment, that maybe she and Logan should just . . . do it.

They could have sex on the beach – right here and now – and Layla could cross it off her to-do list and that would be it.

But then, for ever, that would just be it.

And it just simply wasn't what Layla wanted . . .

She pulled away from Logan, stopping his kisses.

"Aw, come on. Let me help you finish the to-do list. You'll be happy, I'll be happy . . ." He leaned in for another kiss, but Layla held up her finger, touching it to his lips. "What's wrong?" he asked.

"Nothing." Layla smiled. "But we're not doing this."

"Oh come on," Logan said, sounding all drunk and harsh and mean. "You're gonna miss your deadline."

"Due date," Layla corrected him with a laugh. She couldn't help herself.

And she couldn't be something she wasn't.

And she wasn't going to do something that she didn't want to do.

Layla knew, without a shadow of a doubt, that *not* doing this bullet point was actually the most important thing she'd done all year.

1 Day Until Graduation . . .

Layla laid out her graduation outfit on her bed.

It was hard to believe that it was all really happening in the morning.

HAPPENING, she texted the Chat as the doorbell rang.

"Lay-la!" her mom called from downstairs a few moments later. "Guess who's here?"

Layla had teased her mom for thinking that someone might show up at her front door without texting first, but that's exactly what Logan had done.

"I figured you might tell me not to come over," Logan explained as Layla closed the front door behind them.

They sat down outside on the front steps. He'd asked if she wanted to hang out on the trampoline one last time, but Layla had said no. This felt better.

"I just wanted to say sorry," Logan said.

"Doesn't love mean never having to say you're sorry?"

"Yeah, well, my mom thinks that's the stupidest thing she's ever heard, so . . ."

Logan smiled, popping that signature dimple into his cheek. Now that he wasn't dripping alcohol, he looked and sounded like his old charming self again. They hadn't been alone like this, really alone and just together themselves, since the day they broke up. Layla had missed him so much, but looking at him now, and smiling with him, she could feel that he wasn't the same person as before.

And neither was she.

And Layla couldn't help but think that was a good thing.

"I still love you to the moon and back," Logan said as the beginning of his goodbye.

"I love you too," Layla said.

And she meant it.

But it was a different kind of love than she'd had for him before. She knew that no matter how many times she might fall in love in the future, there'd always be a small quiet place in her heart that belonged only to Logan.

And that was okay.

More than okay.

In a way, Layla loved Logan more now than she ever had before.

The good news, though – maybe the *best* news – was that she loved herself more.

Graduation Day . . .

. . . was as bittersweet as it gets.

Layla, Zoe, Alex and Emma posed for pictures on the athletic field in their caps and gowns. At some point, as the cameras were flashing from every direction, Emma thought to whisper to the girls that the real reason she liked photographs so much was that they never changed, even when the people in them did. Everyone wanted to say that wasn't true, that they wouldn't change – or at least, if they *did*, they would still manage to grow and change in the same direction and fit this neatly together for ever.

But they couldn't say that.

They knew that wasn't the kind of thing you could promise.

Layla, Alex, Zoe and Emma spent their grad night at Disneyland. Twelve glorious hours running around the happiest place on earth. No boys or other girls. No sex. No distractions. Just four friends. And a hundred rides.

The last ride of the night (slash morning) turned out to be Splash Mountain. It was Zoe's favorite, even though the big drop at the end scared her beyond words. It had actually been their first ride of the night too, but Zoe asked to ride it

350

one more time. Layla loved the symmetry of that, and Alex and Emma were game, and so all the girls ran back through the park for one last splash. As they crept up the conveyor belt in their fake plastic log, edging towards the largest drop, Layla, Alex, Zoe and Emma all managed to have the very same thought at the very same time: the best part about this ride was that they were on it together. Honestly, that was the only thing that really mattered.

Just before the sun came up, the girls stood all together watching an *actual* fireworks display in the sky above the magic castle. Of course they couldn't help but think about their own personal fireworks, the ones they'd set off by themselves or with the lucky people they'd let step inside. And the thoughts and feelings were enough to make them want to cry . . . but it all turned into laughter instead because sometimes emotions are so close together it's impossible not to feel them all at once.

Sometimes emotions know what you need even when *you* don't.

This was it: the final, fleeting moment of high school.

All of it was bright and exploding, and then just as quickly fading, and finally disappearing into the sky. The girls felt each blast as if it was happening just for the four of them and no one else in the world. And the whole thing was already a memory – a forever-and-always kind of memory – before the fireworks display even ended. Maybe, honestly, before it had even really begun.

It was just that special.

This moment.

This magic.

This friendship.

This glorious time of their lives.

And they knew it couldn't last for ever, not really anyway, but they could feel that it was already a part of them. It had burrowed into their hearts and melted into their minds and blurred – *irrevocably* blurred – into the depths of their souls.

This was it – and this was everything.

The End of the Beginning . . .

The story started in a froyo shop, and that's effectively where it ended, too.

Even though it didn't officially, *actually* happen for Layla until the very end of the summer, it was all set in motion right at the beginning, on the first day after graduation.

After they came home from Disneyland and napped, the Crew decided the only thing they wanted was froyo. This meant breaking tradition and showing up at the Bigg Chill on a Tuesday, which would've been fine. Totally, absolutely fine. Except, for the first time all year – maybe even possibly for the first time *ever* – there was no peanut-butter option on the Bigg Chill flavor board. There was *always* peanut butter. And Layla *always* ordered it.

Layla tried very hard to act like it wasn't a big deal, but Bigg Chill Aaron could tell that it was a *very* big deal. He decided to be bold and recommend his favorite flavor instead: honey Greek yogurt.

"It's different," he cautioned, "but I'm a big fan."

Layla tried it. She liked it. And she ordered it without too much of a fuss.

Then the girls sat in their usual table, in their usual corner, and laughed and ate too many rainbow sprinkles and were just happy to be together.

And that was it.

Alex had a week until she had to leave for Stanford and summer track practices.

Emma's one-way ticket to South East Asia was scheduled to leave two weeks after that. She'd officially decided to defer her freshman year of college and take a gap year. Emma was going to travel around the world, volunteering and working and taking pictures as she went.

Zoe had to move into her dorm at the University of Michigan the second week of August.

And Layla would start her freshman year at USC a week or so after that.

It was *all* happening.

That first day after graduation, Layla had left the Bigg Chill feeling strangely alive. She felt invigorated, like the world was an open door, a book with only blank pages.

Layla climbed into her car, put the key in the ignition . . .

. . . and simply got stuck.

She couldn't drive. She could barely even move. She was petrified. She desperately wanted to be the kind of person who could drive off into the sunset and not look back, but that wasn't Layla's style.

Yes, plans could change and she would survive. There was no peanut butter froyo, and she had lived to tell it. But she liked her lists and her systems and all of her due dates.

Layla was unapologetically *Layla*, and she wasn't going to

stop that now, but, apparently and unfortunately, it felt like she wasn't going to go anywhere either.

And then . . . just when she thought she might get stuck sitting in the parking lot of the Bigg Chill for ever, her phone buzzed.

It was a phone number she didn't recognize, with an unfamiliar area code.

Too soon to make a plan?

It was Bigg Chill Aaron.

Layla looked up from her phone and saw him smiling at her through the wall of glass windows. His grin filled his entire face. Layla had given him her number just a few minutes earlier. She said she would love to hear from him sometime. And she meant it. The fact that he almost immediately texted her *and* used the word "plan" in his very first text was an absolute dream.

Almost instantly, Layla and Bigg Chill Aaron fell hard and fast, as text messages and timid smiles turned into fully fledged butterflies and endless make-out sessions. He insisted he wasn't normally like this, all head over heels and "all in" and everything, but their connection was infectious and palpable and there was no reason to fight it.

Bigg Chill Aaron's name was soon shortened to "Aaron" because there was far too much discussion about him in the Chat to keep typing all three words over and over again.

A few weeks later, Aaron asked to be Layla's official boyfriend.

A few weeks after that, they said "I love you".

And then, about two months after that very first text . . .

. . . it happened.

It wasn't even an official date night. It was just an end-of-summer Saturday, a few nights before Layla was scheduled to move into her USC dorm. Aaron texted Layla when he got off work at the Bigg Chill earlier than usual. They decided, last minute, to grab a quick dinner and see a movie. They shared fries. They held hands. They laughed at the big screen. And then, what began as just another seemingly endless make-out session turned into the first time Layla never realized she always wanted.

It was passionate.

It was spontaneous.

It was sexy.

And loving.

And a little bit silly, too.

And it all went down exactly sixty-nine days after high-school graduation. The sexy numerological wink from the universe seemed almost too good to be true.

But it wasn't too good.

It was real.

Layla Baxter lost her virginity . . .

. . . in the back seat of her car.

To be honest, the sex pact wasn't always part of the plan.

Even Layla could not have planned it better if she tried.

It was perfect.

All of it.

Mostly, because the girls did it together.

Together together.

And that really was, without a doubt, the very best part.

Acknowledgements

You never forget your first time.

Trust me, I know.

And I'm already certain that I will never forget this first time either. The process of writing my first novel — spanning from the first blush of an idea, to this final, finished product — has been exhilarating, terrifying, humbling and immensely rewarding. I am sincerely grateful — for all of it. And I know it would not have happened without the unwavering support of my family and friends who have held my hand — both literally and figuratively — every step of the way.

Thank you to everyone at Simon Pulse for championing the story of these four friends and their fireworks. Thank you Mara Anastas, Liesa Abrams, Mary Marotta, Lucille Rettino, Carolyn Swerdloff, Tara Greico, Jennifer Romanello, Jodie Hockensmith, Christina Pecorale, Mandy Veloso, Regina Flath. An extra special thank you to my editors, Jennifer Ung and Sarah McCabe, whose enthusiasm knows no bounds. Thank you for your fearlessness and your patience. Thank you for helping me find the rhythm and pace of the book. You are the best.

Thank you to my wonderful literary agent Jess Regel for

helping me navigate this process and for being excited about Cherry from day one. Thank you to my manager, Josh Turner McGuire, for helping me keep my head on straight. I don't know what I'd do without you. And thank you to the rest of my team: Melissa Orton, Bryan Diperstein and Tara Kole.

Thank you to my crew of early readers, fellow writers, 'technical' consultants and very best friends: Elyssa Caplan, Caroline Rothstein, Emma Sugerman, Aaron Karo, Jordan Ross, Harper Dill, Marissa Freeman, Melanie Mason, Sasha Salinger, Samantha Billet, Sara Sargent, Jessie Rosen, Emma Goidel, Ilana Caplan, Lindsay Katona, Jamie Epstein, John Krause and Molly McCook. Thank you all for your notes and wisdom and insight. Thank you for your pep talks and the 'you got this' text messages. Thank you for humoring me. And loving me. And reminding me to laugh and sleep and breathe. Cherry wouldn't be what it is without you — and neither would I. An additional and endless thank you to Elyssa, Caroline and Emma — my girls and founding members of my tribe and executive committee — who went above and beyond the call of friendship and read every single draft of Cherry along the way. We really are the luckiest.

Thank you to my friends from high school. The ones whose pictures were taped to the walls of my bedroom. The ones I made mix CDs for. The ones I hung out with in Rugby Theater, or in my parents' backyard, or the back seat of my car. And especially the ones I've eaten frozen yogurt with at The Bigg Chill. Thanks for being a formative part of the story of my life.

Thank you to my extended Rosin and Passman families — my relatives by blood and the ones we've adopted by choice. The regular days and the holidays and all the moments in between wouldn't mean nearly as much if I couldn't share them with all of you. I want to especially thank my 99-year-old grandmother, Helen Rosin, who I've had the privilege of updating about the Cherry writing process every step of the way. The first time I told her about the plot of the book I chose my words rather carefully, saying that it was a story about four friends during their senior year of high school. Then I added that it was 'a little bit sexy'. Without missing a beat she replied, 'That's okay, people like that.' I'm so very glad she said that. Hopefully, she was right.

Thank you to my Andy Grammer and 'Aint It Fun' Pandora stations and all the songs that played on repeat. Thank you to all the baristas at my favorite Coffee Bean and Tea Leaf (10897 Pico Blvd) for making the best vanilla lattes around. Thank you Santigo Huckleberry scented Voluspa Candles. Thank you to Converse sneakers. And thank you Pilot G2 ball point pens, size 10, which I used as I wrote the entire first draft of Cherry by hand.

Thank you to my dog, Dodger, who sat by my side or at my feet or on the purple shag carpet on my office floor as I wrote almost every word of this book.

Thank you Mom, Dad, Maxine and Avery — for everything. I'm not sure what life would be like without the 'lovies' group chat, but I wouldn't want to live it any other way. I love you all to the moon and back — and so far beyond that too.

Thank you to my husband, Josh. I love you forever. Long story short: there were two ducks.

And finally, thank YOU for reading.

Lindsey Rosin

Lindsey Rosin is a fourth generation Los Angeles native, who lives in close proximity to her favorite froyo spot, The Bigg Chill, along with her husband, Josh, and their poodle-mix, Dodger. She drinks iced vanilla lattes and almost exclusively wears Converse tennis shoes. For more information, please visit www.lindseyrosin.com and follow her on Twitter @lindseyrosin. *Cherry* is her debut novel.

HOT KEY BOOKS

Thank you for choosing a Hot Key book.

If you want to know more about our authors and what we publish, you can find us online.

You can start at our website

www.hotkeybooks.com

And you can also find us on:

We hope to see you soon!